***"It's different being . . .
you know . . ."***

"Dead? We've got to talk," I said. "You're buried at Garden View. We can meet there. Tonight after work. Let's say seven. Your grave."

"But—"

"Do you want me to take your case?"

"Yes, but—"

"Seven tonight," I said.

I can't say for sure, but I think right before he disappeared in a puff of smoke that smelled a whole lot like pot, Damon nodded.

And a new thought struck.

For the first time in as long as I could remember, I had a date. A date with a hot, sexy guy.

Too bad he was dead.

By Casey Daniels

TOMBS OF ENDEARMENT
THE CHICK AND THE DEAD
DON OF THE DEAD

CASEY DANIELS

TOMBS OF ENDEARMENT

AVON
An Imprint of Harper Collins*Publishers*

This is a work of fiction. Names, characters, places, and incidents are drawn from the author's imagination or are used fictitiously and are not to be construed as real. Any resemblance to actual events, locales, organizations, or persons, living or dead, is entirely coincidental.

AVON BOOKS
An Imprint of Harper Collins*Publishers*
10 East 53rd Street
New York, New York 10022-5299

ISBN: 978-0-06-082150-0
ISBN-10: 0-06-082150-7
www.avonmystery.com

First Avon Books paperback printing: October 2007

Printed in the U.S.A.

10 9 8 7 6 5 4

For Anne and David

TOMBS OF ENDEARMENT

Chapter 1

"*That's one of the really wonderful things about* working in a cemetery. You get to do things that are not only interesting and educational, but fun. Imagine, spending an entire day researching the immigration records at the County Archives! Could anything be more exciting than that?"

Needless to say, I am not the one who spoke these words. They came from Ella Silverman, the community relations manager at Garden View Cemetery and—not incidentally—my boss. Nobody but Ella could possibly get so hopped up about the prospect of spending the day poking through dusty old books full of equally dry information.

When I didn't respond with the enthusiasm Ella expected, she tried to manufacture some. She beamed a smile at me across my desk and patted the notepad she'd brought with her into my office. It contained a list—a long list—of the Garden View residents (Ella's word for the folks buried there) whose files she wanted to beef up with a little more information. "Well, Pepper, really! You should be excited. Think of all you'll learn!"

I was thinking about it. And it practically put me to sleep. But hey, if the months I'd worked as Garden View's only tour guide had taught me anything, it was to prevaricate like a pro.

Then again, in addition to my gig at the cemetery, I was also the world's one and only private investigator to the dead, and—at least as far as I knew—the only person around unlucky enough to not only see dead people, but talk to them, too. They always wanted something from me, those dead folks, and whatever it was (and take my word for it when I say it usually involved getting threatened, beaten up, and/or shot at), it always conflicted with what I was supposed to be doing in my real life. Was it any wonder I could tell a lie with a smile on my lips and a song in my heart?

"Of course I'm excited." To prove my statement to Ella and maybe convince myself, too, I sat up straight in an eager-beaver sort of way. "But are you sure you can spare me for the whole day? I mean, you said it yourself in the staff meeting yesterday. With the holidays right around the corner—"

Ella nodded sagely. "You mean because of the ghost hunters. The ones who show up every year at this time, right before Halloween."

Halloween wasn't the holiday I'd been referring to. It wasn't even something I wanted to think about. Believe me, when it came to things that went bump in the night, I'd had my fill. As far as I was concerned, the dearly departed could stay right where they belonged. Which was, in case there's any question, as far away from me as it was possible to get.

I'd done my part. Hand in hand (figuratively

speaking, of course) with the dead but regretfully not departed, I'd solved two murders with a paranormal twist, one the past spring and another right after. So far—knock on wood—I'd managed to get through the balance of the summer and most of the fall without another close encounter of the woo-woo kind.

It was my goal in life to keep it that way.

"Actually, I meant the Christmas choral concert you mentioned yesterday," I told Ella. Better to show her I'd been paying attention at the meeting than to entertain even a smidgen of a thought about how working for the dead had a way of always putting me in danger of becoming one of them. "And the tree-trimming ceremony, the Hanukkah festivities, and the community Kwanzaa celebration the cemetery hosts. That's going to take a lot of planning."

"It does. But we do it every year. Honestly, I could do the groundwork in my sleep. The ghost hunters . . . well, of course, that's another story."

As the saying goes, any port in a storm. Right about then, the impending storm was research, and if talking about ghosts (in a purely theoretical way, of course) was going to change the direction of the conversation and keep me away from the County Archives, I was game. Reluctant, but game.

In a gesture designed to assure her we were two bodies but one mind, my nod mirrored Ella's. "Ghost hunters. Exactly. Obviously, I should stick around. In case you need any help. They're practically overrunning the place."

"Happens every year." She didn't look happy about it.

"And we can't keep them out?"

Ella's shrug said it all. "It's a public place. There's nothing we can do to make people stay away. As long as they're not doing any damage or causing any disruption and they're not getting in anyone's way doing what they do."

"And they do . . . what?"

"Look for ghosts, of course." Her smile was sympathetic.

It didn't fool me. "You think they're wasting their time."

"I think if there were really such things as ghosts, one of us would have seen them by now, don't you?"

Little white lies were one thing. Whoppers were another. I sidestepped the question and got back to the matter at hand. Which was, as far as I could remember, how to keep myself from being condemned to a day in research hell.

"No way you can keep those ghostbusters in line by yourself," I told Ella. "You'll need me to stay here and help."

"Oh, I doubt it." She sloughed off my concerns. "They're an odd bunch, but they're really harmless."

"I'm sure they are, but if we've got funerals scheduled—"

"That's what Security is for."

"And visitors coming through—"

"There isn't another tour scheduled until the end of the week. You remember, the one you're leading for that fourth grade class that's doing a project on the freed slaves who are buried here."

I remembered, all right, and remembering, I shivered in my Jimmy Choo kidskin ankle boots. Not that I didn't think the lives of freed slaves were fascinating. But, honestly, fourth graders? It was almost enough to make the County Archives sound like a walk in the park.

Almost.

I thought about the last time I'd ventured into the cemetery's own archives and how I'd needed not one, but two deep pore cleansings and an aromatherapy bath to get rid of the grime that ground its way into my skin. The county facility was bound to be eons bigger. I did the math (sort of) and convinced myself that by the time I was done, I'd need to add a hot oil hair treatment and a manicure to my clean-up-after-research routine.

Don't get me wrong. I'm as much into pampering as any other twenty-five-year-old woman. But I'm not a daredevil. I knew better than to tempt the cosmetic fates. In my book, cleanliness was right up there next to keeping myself from getting embroiled in any more murders.

I couldn't explain the bit about homicide to Ella. Not without confessing the whole PI-to-the-dead-but-not-departed thing.

And something told me she wouldn't get my aversion to boring research, either. When it came to doing anything to advance Garden View's image, Ella was as tenacious as a bulldog.

Come to think of it, with her short, stocky body and in the brown suit she was wearing that day along with a white blouse, she looked a little like a bulldog, too, albeit a warm and fuzzy one. Maybe that was because of the multistrand yellow and blue beads around her neck that added a touch of unbulldoglike color. And the two dozen or so colorful beaded bracelets that shared space on her wrists.

Thinking of dogs made me think of kids. And thinking of kids, I just naturally glommed onto the subject of the fourth graders.

I hopped out of my desk chair. Even without the previously mentioned ankle boots and their two-and-a-half-inch heels, I was a whole head taller than Ella. I hoped the height advantage would make me look authoritative and thus help my cause. "The fourth grade, huh? Is that tour this week? Boy, I should go through my notes again. And visit each of the grave sites just so I'm sure where they are. And—"

"Pepper, Pepper, Pepper." Ella had gone from nodding her head to shaking it, and the writing was on the wall: I was in for the kind of motherly lecture I'd heard her deliver to her three teenaged daughters. She tugged at the hoop earring that dangled from her right lobe. "I think we know each other well enough to be honest, don't you? Stop beating around the bush and just tell me the truth. Do you not want to go to the archives and do this research for me?"

It was my big opportunity to come clean.

"Of course I want to do your research," I said.

I know, I know, lying through my teeth doesn't exactly qualify as coming clean. Call me a softie, but I didn't have the heart to burst Ella's working-here-is-the-best-thing-in-the-world bubble. See, in addition to being my boss, Ella is my friend.

Of course, she was also the one who, just a few

short months earlier, had sold me into indentured servitude to the meanest author in the history of the *New York Times* best-seller list.

For that, I owed her paybacks. And in a weird way, I suppose, my thanks.

If it hadn't been for my stint as secretary to über-author Merilee Bowman, I wouldn't have solved her sister, Didi's, murder.

Or ended up with an extra thousand a month from Didi's granddaughter who was grateful for my help and not reluctant to spread around some of her newfound wealth.

I kept all this firmly in mind. Which was the only thing that enabled me to speak with a straight face. "You know I love doing research. It just doesn't seem fair for me to spend the whole day having fun while you're back here doing something mundane and boring like—"

"Oh, don't worry about me!" Ella grinned and headed for the door. "I won't be bored today. Not for a moment. I'm writing an article for the next edition of the Garden View newsletter. About Albion Cade Mitford. He's buried here, you know. Talk about fascinating! He's the man who invented the bottle opener."

There wasn't anything I could say to counter that. And nothing I could do but gird my loins (figuratively speaking, of course) and head out to the County Archives building on the other side of Cleveland.

As soon as I stepped outside, climbed into my Mustang, and started toward the main gate, I decided that maybe it wasn't such a bad assignment after all. The sun was shining and the air was crisp with the tang of fall. One of the things Garden View prides itself on is its landscaping, and I glanced at the trees that dotted the cemetery lawns and lined the streets that wound their way through nearly three hundred acres of headstones, mausoleums, and tombs. The leaves were just starting to change color, and all around me, the air was bright with tinges of gold and the beginnings of red and orange that, in just a few weeks, would be our last hurrah before another long, bleak winter on Lake Erie's shores.

I guess I was so busy admiring the trees, I wasn't watching where I was going. When I looked back at my windshield, there was a group of people on the road directly in front of me.

I slammed on my brakes just short of slamming into them.

I don't think they noticed. There were four men and one woman in the group. Each of them was carrying some sort of weird-looking piece of equipment, and every single one of them was so busy concentrating on their instruments and sharing their readings with each other, they never even looked up at the sound of my squealing brakes.

I stuck my head out of the window and said, "Sorry!" anyway because, let's face it, I would have been sorry if I smashed them to smithereens. I waited until they were safely on the other side of the road before I continued on my way.

"Ghost hunters," I said to myself. When I stopped at the main gate that led out onto the city streets, I glanced in my rearview mirror. The ghost hunters were walking around a particularly gaudy mausoleum, their gazes trained on their instruments, their expressions so serious, I had no doubt they considered what they did Science with a capital S.

The irony of the situation struck, and for the first time since I found out I would be spending the day getting up close and personal with a whole building full of immigration records, I smiled. I knew the ghost hunters couldn't hear me, but I couldn't resist. "I know something you don't know," I said in a singsong voice. Still grinning, I rolled out onto Mayfield Road and flicked on my radio.

Though I never listened to it, my radio was tuned to an oldies station, and a baritone voice washed over me. Appealing. Exciting.

And all too familiar.

It was Damon Curtis, the bad boy/poet/legend of hippies-vintage rock and roll, along with his band, Mind at Large, and when I heard his voice, my fall-foliage good mood suddenly soured. With a grunt, I turned off the music.

"I know something the ghost hunters don't know, all right," I grumbled. See, a few months earlier I walked passed Cleveland's Rock and Roll Hall of Fame and Museum one night and saw Damon Curtis standing outside watching me. Since then, I hadn't had a moment's peace.

These days, every time I turned on the radio, or stopped at a store, or walked through a mall, they were always playing a Mind at Large song.

Coincidence?

I think not, and here's why.

Damon Curtis is dead. He has been since 1971.

Yep, that's right. Dead, but not gone. Not by a long shot.

As a matter of fact, I'd spent my entire summer trying to avoid him.

I know it sounds impossible. I mean, how can I avoid a ghost when a ghost wants to find me?

Honestly, I don't have the answer. All I know is that even though Damon Curtis is buried at Garden View (he died during a trip—and I do not use that word lightly—to Cleveland for a concert), he had yet to show hide nor ghostly hair of himself around the cemetery.

For this I was grateful.

But I'm not dumb. I'd seen Damon outside the Rock Hall and nowhere else, and since that night, I'd made sure I didn't go anywhere near the place.

So far, so good. Except for Damon's music always popping up—impossible to dance to and so full of what I could only imagine was symbolism, I was never sure what any song was about—I'd managed to keep myself from getting embroiled in any more adventures with anyone from the Other Side.

I actually might have been cheered by this thought if I wasn't so busy being frustrated by the traffic that jammed Euclid Avenue, the main artery between the cemetery and the County Archives. Too impatient to wait out the bumper-to-bumper nightmare, I inched close enough to the nearest viable-looking cross street, turned—and found a utility crew had the street dug up directly in front of me.

"This way, honey!" A guy in a hard hat and a reflective neon orange vest waved me around the mess. I followed where he pointed and tried to get my bearings, but this was an unfamiliar part of town. Maybe if I turned left at the next main street, circled around downtown and . . .

My best-laid plans went up in smoke when I found myself hemmed in by the results of an earlier accident involving a van and a utility pole. Power lines were down across the sidewalk, and one side of the street was completely blocked by huge utility trucks and a crew of guys restringing the lines.

I grumbled my displeasure, but at this point, there was little else I could do. I waited my turn to get by the mess, my teeth clenched around my frustration. Eager to get my mind on something else, I tried the radio again.

A song by Mind at Large—and Damon Curtis—was playing.

Like I was going to let that stop me?

I switched stations.

The same song blared out at me over the airwaves.

When I screamed my opinion of this, the cop directing traffic in the middle of the next intersection thought I was talking to him. I smiled and waved as a way of letting him know not to take it personally, and when he stabbed his hand to the left, I turned. It was that or risk getting on his bad side.

By the time it was all over, I found myself directly in front of the Rock and Roll Hall of Fame and Museum.

"No way," I told myself, but hey, it's hard to argue with facts, and the Rock Hall in all its glass and chrome glory was one large and unmistakable fact. In the morning sunshine, the building sparkled like a beauty queen's smile.

I refused to be tricked; I looked the other way.

"No," I said, my voice as firm as my conviction. "No way am I getting suckered in by another ghost and another case that means putting my life in jeopardy because of somebody who's already dead anyway. No way am I even thinking about it. No way am I looking at the building. No way am I stopping. Or—"

My rant was interrupted when my car bucked and pulled to the right as sharply as if another pair of hands had taken over the steering wheel. I careened toward the curb, and if I hadn't jammed on the brake's, I might have gone right over it. Curious, I turned off the ignition and got out of the car.

It didn't take a mechanical genius to see that my front right tire was as flat as a pancake.

"Son of a bitch!" I moaned, and a couple of people walking by turned to stare. They probably thought I was complaining about the tire.

They couldn't possibly know that the flat was the farthest thing from my mind.

Still grumbling, I fished a handful of change out of my purse and dropped it into the nearest parking meter. When I strode to the front doors of the Rock Hall, there was fire in my eyes and mayhem on my mind.

Neither was slaked by the huge poster hanging outside advertising a reunion concert for Mind at Large. *Still rockin' after all these years,* it said, and it featured two pictures of the band, one recent (and the guys in it, old and tired-looking) and one taken forty years ago when Damon Curtis was still young, hot, sexy—and very much alive.

Chapter 2

From where I stood just inside the front doors of the Rock Hall, I could look up at the glass structure that surrounded me and see the fat, white clouds that floated above the building. They weren't the only things that attracted my attention. The place is, after all, a testimonial to everything innovative, fun and rebellious about rock and roll. I shifted my gaze from the great outdoors to the indoor funk. There was a display of huge guitars next to me, all painted in striking colors. Across from where I stood, two giant neon signs that had once been used as the backdrop to some group's concert scenery were suspended high above the floor. Dangling nearby was a humongous hot dog (complete with bun and relish). This, I didn't have time to wonder about.

My eyes on the brightly lit marquee that advertised the upcoming Mind at Large concert, I paid my admission fee and headed off on a ghost hunt of my own.

Easier said than done.

The hall is a maze of sound and color, and the more exhibits I wound my way through, the more lost I got. Fortunately, I ran across a guy wearing a Rock Hall shirt.

I asked for the Ancient History Department.

He gave me a blank stare.

Until I explained that I was looking for Damon Curtis.

Normal person that he was, he thought I was looking for the exhibit about Damon Curtis.

I left him to his delusion, followed his directions, and got down to business.

Turns out, Damon Curtis has one entire wall devoted to him, and nearing it, I slowed my steps and waited for the cleaning woman who was wiping down the glass exhibit cases to finish her work. She didn't look like she belonged in the same class as the hall employee who'd directed me to the exhibit. Which is a kind way of saying that he was well-groomed and dressed in khakis and a polo shirt. And she . . .

The woman was wearing a pink and purple filmy skirt that skimmed her bony knees, and an orange T-shirt that was a couple of sizes too small. Maybe that was intentional; she had no figure to speak of, and with the shirt being that tight, it was impossible not to notice that she wasn't wearing a bra. She was probably in her sixties, and believe me when I say this: It was a wise fashionista indeed who once advised women of a certain age to cut their hair. This woman's hair was poker-straight and hung to the middle of her back. It was the color of a field mouse, shot through with gray, and it framed a long, bony face that on a good day might have generously been called homely. Her cheeks sagged. There were dark circles under her eyes. The overall impression was of a particularly sad donkey. Even if she was singing a Mind at Large song as she worked.

She took a last swipe at the glass case. That's when she noticed me and stopped singing. Her eyes lit. "Death is my confidant," she said. I figured it must have been a lyric from a Mind at Large song.

"Go death!" I gave her the thumbs-up but I have to admit, when she finished and walked away, I was more than a little relieved.

Dealing with my Gift was challenge enough. I didn't need to throw odd living people into the mix.

Finally with the exhibit to myself, I was able to stand back and take in the overall picture.

DAMON CURTIS: AMERICAN IDOLATER is what the sign above the exhibit said. Displayed all around it in frames and in the glass exhibit cases that were now officially sparkling clean were bits and pieces of the rock star's life.

Handwritten snippets of song lyrics shared space with album covers. A leather jacket that sported enough fringe to make a cowboy proud hung next to an old photo of the guys in the band standing with an older man. Compared to their shaggy tresses, his bald head stuck out like a . . . well, like a bald head. There were stage passes, concert tickets, and even some of Damon's elementary school report cards on display. In the center of it all was a black-and-white photo of Damon, larger than life. I took one look and sucked in a breath. Stared. Oh yeah, and drooled just a little.

The one and only time I'd seen Damon, it was

from a distance. I'd noticed that he was good-looking, of course. I would have had to have been blind not to. But there's a difference between simply good-looking and oh-my-god.

Damon Curtis fit into the latter category.

He had dark hair, and it tumbled around his shoulders in the sort of arty disarray that made me think the picture had been taken just as he got out of bed.

I wondered what he was doing while he was in there. And who he'd been doing it with.

He had dark eyes, too. Even in the colorless photo, they looked like they were lit with fire.

His body . . . well . . . that was to die for.

He was standing in front of a window draped by gauzy curtains that diffused the sunlight until it was as soft as a watercolor. It caressed Damon from behind, outlining the tattered jeans slung low across his hips, his bare chest, and his slim, athletic body. There was a sprinkling of dark hair on his chest that arrowed down toward his waist, and a tiny tattoo of a star near his heart. Just over his left shoulder, the curtain was torn, and a stab of sunlight grazed the left side of his face and rushed toward the viewer like a comet.

It was hokey in a sixties, psychedelic-poetic sort of way. It was also self-indulgent, egotistical, and just about the sexiest thing I'd ever seen.

The Rock Hall was chilly.

I was suddenly hot enough to self-combust.

I didn't even realize I wasn't breathing until my lungs screamed for air. The momentary oxygen deprivation shook me out of my stupor. I gasped, told my hormones to behave, and reminded myself that sexy or not, Damon Curtis was a big ol' ghostly nuisance.

One I needed to deal with ASAP. Before he took up any more of my time.

"I'm here," I said. There was nobody near the exhibit but me, but I looked around anyway, just to be sure no one heard and thought I was a loony. "It's what you wanted, isn't it? You wanted to see me? To talk to me? Well, here I am."

In spite of the way those shows on TV portray things, real ghosts aren't much into grand entrances. At least not the ghosts I've run into. They show up. Just like that. And they look just like regular, living people, too. They're not see-through. There's no glowing aura around them. Actually, except that no one can see them but me and that they're incorporeal and so can't do anything for themselves that involves this world (like open doors or turn the pages of a book), the dead aren't all that different from the living. Well, except for the fact that they're dead, of course. And that if they happen to touch a living person, that person freezes like a Popsicle. I ought to know. My first dead client, Gus Scarpetti, had once pushed me out of the path of a speeding car, and just that bit of contact left me chilled to the bone for days.

Grand entrances aside, there was no sign of Damon Curtis.

Was this good news? Or bad?

I wasn't sure, and while I digested it, I inched nearer to the exhibit to take a closer look.

Damon is a smarter-than-average little boy, the notation on his second grade report card said. *But he sometimes has trouble controlling his behavior.*

"Rock star in training," I mumbled.

Your thesis shows a spark of originality. This was a note from his English 101 professor, written at the top of a paper about some Shakespearean play and displayed right next to a sign that said Damon had flunked out of college soon after he'd gotten this particular failing grade. *Sadly, your ideas are often disjointed and not followed through to their logical conclusions. You have the tendency to rely too heavily on simile and metaphor even when it is not appropriate, and often your symbolism is ambiguous and thus, perplexing.*

"That explains the songs that make no sense," I told myself.

Medical Certificate of Death.

Though I am in the business of the dead (both at the cemetery and in my private investigator's life), this next bit of memorabilia threw me for a loop.

I looked up at the photo of Damon Curtis that stood watch over his exhibit. As I might have mentioned, in it he was young and vital, as tempting as sin and very much alive.

I looked down into the exhibit case, at the facts about his death laid out in cold, hard terms by the Bureau of Vital Statistics.

Shivering, I wrapped my arms around myself.

Cause of Death: heart failure.

Though my father is a doctor (I should say *was* a doctor, since he lost his medical license because of a little matter of insurance fraud), I had never aspired to follow in his footsteps. Still, it didn't take a medical wunderkind to know that every death is ultimately caused by heart failure. One second it's working, the next, *nada*. So this bit of info didn't tell me much about Damon. The sign next to the death certificate, though, did.

On June 22, 1971, while in Cleveland on a Mind at Large concert tour, lead singer Damon Michael Curtis, age 27, died from an overdose of drugs. Though the Cleveland Police Department conducted an extensive investigation, they were never able to determine if the overdose was accidental or if, like the tormented souls who inhabited so many of his dark lyrics and his grim poetry, Curtis made the conscious decision to end his life. His parents, who lived on a farm in Illinois, were strongly religious. Throughout Mind at Large's meteoric rise to fame, they refused to acknowledge their son's stardom. After his death, they declined to take responsibility for the body or the burial. Damon Curtis was laid to rest in Cleveland, at Garden View Cemetery.

Laid to rest. But not in peace.

I thought this over as I moved on to the next part of the exhibit where some of those "dark lyrics" of Damon's were displayed. The first of them looked as if it had been scribbled in the heat of inspiration. The words were written on a pizza box in green Magic Marker. The resulting song, the museum information card said, had sold more than two million copies in less than a month and catapulted Mind at Large past the Beatles, the Stones, and the Doors on the charts and into the forefront of the psychedelic pop movement.

"Dragon's Breath."

The song was popular way before my time, but I knew it, anyway. It was the one that had been playing on not one, but two radio stations while I was in the car earlier. Like it or not, the tune pounded through my head as I read the lyrics.

Lizard scales and devil's wings.
Bloody, spoiled soul.
I'll leave you, love, in your heat, in your sweat.
Sated, gorged.
My black butterfly body,
Wet from the chrysalis.

I wasn't so sure about that whole lizard-scales-and-devil's-wing thing, but similes and metaphors aside, I think I knew what was what when it came to the butterfly body in the wet chrysalis. No wonder the world knew Damon Curtis as an iconoclast. Back in the late sixties when "Dragon's Breath" was recorded, the lyrics and the driving music that accompanied them must have put more peoples' knickers in a twist than just Mr. and Mrs. Curtis back on that farm in Illinois.

"I'll leave you, love, in your heat. In your sweat. Sated, gorged. My black butterfly body, wet from the chrysalis."

The words tickled their way through me. That was because someone had whispered them in my ear.

It didn't take a genius—dark or otherwise—to recognize the blistering, baritone voice.

"It's about time you showed up," I said, rethinking the whole grand entrances thing. But then, I guess a rock star would be more into drama than most other ghosts. "We need to talk about the way you've been bugging me."

Only we couldn't.

Because when I turned around, there was no one there.

I grumbled a curse Farmer Curtis and his wife would not have appreciated.

It was met with a chuckle that came from somewhere on my right.

But there was no one over there, either.

"Fine." Just to show I'd had it, I emphasized my point by slapping a hand against the glass display case in front of me. "If that's the way you want to be, have it your way. I came here to talk to you. But hey, if you're going to play hard-to-get, I guess there's nothing we have to say to each other. I'm leaving, and here's the scoop. I'm not going to tolerate any more of your songs on the radio. And no more flat tires. So you might as well stop trying to get my attention. Nothing you do is going to bring me back here. You had your chance. You blew it."

I stomped away from the exhibit without so much as another glance.

None of this helped soothe my temper. Annoyed, I moved through the museum, heading in what I figured was the direction of the escalator that would take me back to the first floor.

My bad luck, by the time I was halfway there, a long line of patrons was just heading into the exhibit area. They were part of a tour, and when they all stopped to gawk at the costumes that had once been worn by the likes of David Bowie and Elton John, I was trapped. I couldn't get through them. I couldn't get around them.

Never let it be said that I believe in stereotypes. There's absolutely no truth to the fact that I have a low threshold of patience because I'm a redhead. Any right-thinking woman would have tapped her foot and mumbled at the inconvenience. Right-thinking woman that I am, I did just that.

None of which made them move any faster. When they were finally done ogling, they shuffled by. I flattened myself against the nearest display case to allow them to pass, a tight smile my only greeting.

Unshaken by my expression, a white-haired lady chirped at me, "Good morning!"

"Thanks, honey," said the man behind her.

"So nice of you to let us by," another lady said.

I scarcely spared them a nod. That is, until I saw the next person in line.

This was no senior citizen although, come to think of it, had he lived past 1971, he just about would be. He was dressed as he had been in the smokin' photo, in tattered jeans slung low across his hips. His chest was bare, and though I hadn't seen the detail in the photo, there was a delicate blue teardrop at one point of the golden star tattooed near his heart. He wasn't as tall as I expected. When he paused in front of me, we would have been eye-to-eye. That is, if Damon's eyes were on my eyes and not taking a long, slow look at my body.

For way too long a time, I was so mesmerized by the smoldering look, I was tongue-tied. Me! Ms. Cool in Any Circumstances. Ms. I Was Engaged Once and After My Weasely Fiancé Broke Up With Me, I Swore Never to Let Myself Fall Under the This-Is-Love Bullshit Spell Again.

Which was all good to remember. And not so easy to do.

Not when heat rushed up my neck and set fire to my face. And my legs suddenly felt as if they'd turned into Silly Putty. Then again, I'd never had this kind of up-close-and-personal encounter with a legend, living or otherwise. Maybe it was the whole rock star bigger-than-life-persona thing. At that moment, if Damon Curtis had asked me to run off to Africa, or fly to the moon, or drop down right there on the floor with him and—

The thought just about knocked me off my feet, and to get rid of it, I reminded myself that hot or not, this was one cold dude. One cold, dead dude.

If I was smart, I wouldn't forget it.

I remembered my mission. And how I'd done my best to avoid Damon all summer. And ended up here at the Rock Hall anyway.

"Damon Curtis, you son of a—"

"No, not looking for that exhibit." Of course, there was no possible way the man in line behind Damon could know there was a ghost standing between him and the person in front of him. He thought I was talking to him. "We're looking for Elvis."

"Ooo, Elvis!" Damon grinned. "That guy's a god."

"Not what we need to talk about."

"It isn't?"

I dodged both the question and the man in line behind Damon, who had asked it, and excused my way through the crowd. I didn't bother to check and see if Damon followed. Now that he'd made contact, so to speak, I knew he wouldn't disappear again. In fact, I was counting on it.

I ducked into a small theater where a black-and-white movie about the history of rock and roll played in a continuous loop. I was the only one in there, and I took a couple of seconds to orient myself. The walls and bench seats in the theater were black, and the video threw splashes of light and shadow against them. When Damon appeared next to me, the light flashed like a strobe against his bare chest.

"Last chance," I said. I was talking about Damon's last chance to tell me why he was bugging me, not my last chance to jump his bones. I told myself not to forget it. "No more hocus-pocus. We talk now, or we don't talk at all."

Though something in Damon's expression told me he didn't expect me to be so frank, he didn't bite at my offer. At least not as quickly as I would have liked. His lips thinned with concentration, and, one dark eyebrow raised, he cocked his head, the better to study me. A laid-back hippie to the very end. And beyond.

"So talk," he said.

"Hello!" Just to get his attention, I waved my hands in front of his face. "In case you forgot, you're the one who showed up looking for me." Whatever was happening in the movie playing behind me, the music got louder and the flickering speeded up. Light and shadow pulsed against Damon's face. It was making me dizzy, and I plunked down onto the nearest bench.

"I don't need any more clients," I told him.

He sat down next to me. We were both facing

the movie screen, and the play of light and shadow made Damon's face look gray. "That's not what I heard," he said. "I hear that when it comes to special cases . . . well, there's this dude who told me you're an expert."

Gus Scarpetti. It had to be. I was tempted to ask how Gus was doing, but rather than get off track, I stuck to the matter at hand. "Gus has been known to exaggerate."

"He said you solved his case. And that other one, too. The one about the chick and that book of hers."

"So you want me to take your case? No thanks, not getting suckered into a dead-end investigation again. Been there, done that." I stood up and turned my back to the movie screen. Partly because it was less distracting to talk without the flicker of the video flashing in my eyes. Mostly because I needed to dispel the uneasiness that touched me like a clammy hand when I thought about the rest of what I had to say. "Every time I poke my nose where somebody thinks it doesn't belong, people try to kill me," I told Damon and reminded myself. "Not exactly my idea of fun."

"Oh baby!" Damon reached out a hand. But apparently he knew how these things work. He stopped just short of grabbing my arm. "I can see why you'd be uptight. Peace out! I'm not asking you to do anything dangerous. What I want you to do, it's easy."

"Murder investigations are never easy." I knew this for a fact, and I turned my back on Damon and paced to the other side of the theater. Another thought struck, and I spun around again. "You overdosed," I reminded him. "That's what that sign over at your exhibit says."

"You read it, huh?" Damon stood and stretched. His body was lean, and he moved as smoothly as a panther.

I turned back toward the movie.

Damon came up behind me. I didn't have to turn around to know it. The air changed. It didn't get cold, not the way the ghostbusters on TV say it does when a spirit is around. Oh no. Suddenly my temperature shot up and my throat locked. It felt as if all the oxygen had been sucked out of the room.

"That sign you saw at my exhibit, it's right about me overdosing," Damon said. His voice skimmed my ear. "I was careless. Thought I knew my shit . . . but hey, I was jonesing. I wasn't as careful as I should have been."

"So it was an accident?" I'd already had one client with suicide issues. I was grateful Damon wasn't another. My relief didn't last long, though. I spun to face him. "But if you weren't murdered, what do you want me to investigate?"

He stepped away from me, and suddenly I found it easier to breathe. "This has got nothing to do with me being . . . well . . . you know."

"Dead?" If he wasn't going to say it, I would.

As if I hadn't spoken, he went right on. "It's all about something that's happened since. That's what I want you to take care of for me. All you have to do is talk to Vinnie."

I went through my mental Rolodex of the facts I'd learned about Mind at Large ever since I realized Damon was haunting me. The way I remembered it, Vinnie Pallucci was the band's keyboard player. After Damon died he also wrote most of their songs.

"You want me to walk up to a perfect stranger and talk to him about how you accidentally killed yourself?"

"You're not listening!" Damon drew in a breath and let it out slowly. "That doesn't matter anymore. My songs, though . . . My music is the only thing that matters, you know?"

I didn't. Then again, I suppose no one who's not a musician can really understand. Before I could tell him this, the movie ended and the doors at the far end of the theater opened automatically. There were people waiting to come in to see the next show, and I knew we couldn't stick around. We headed for the doors opposite the crowd and ducked into the nearest empty hallway.

"All I want you to do," Damon said, "is to go tell Vinnie to stop stealing my songs."

"Isn't that what attorneys are for? I mean, aren't there copyrights or whatever on songs? Don't people know which songs you've written?" I answered my own question. "God, there's so much about you on the Internet, people who know every little detail of your life and people who interpret your lyrics and people who say you're not really dead at all, just hiding on an island somewhere in the Pacific, or living as a Buddhist monk or—"

"So you've been checking me out!" Damon rolled back on his heels and grinned. "You like what you see?"

"I like being left alone." This was a far better answer than the truth, which was more in line with melting into a puddle of mush at Damon's feet. "You won't leave me alone. That means that whatever's bugging you about Vinnie and the songs, it's important. At least to you. So let's get this over with, why don't we. You tell me what you want, and I'll tell you I don't want to do it. Then you'll disappear into a puff of smoke, and that will be that."

"It turns me on when a girl talks tough."

"I'm not a girl. I'm a woman." I shouldn't have had to remind him, but then, maybe because he was from way-back-when, he wasn't clued in to the whole equality-of-the-sexes thing. "And that's not what we were talking about."

"It's always what people are talking about!" Damon laughed. The sound tickled its way up my spine. "Politics, religion, the stock market, and the price of cantaloupes. It's really all about sex."

He was starting to sound like one of his songs. Better to stick to the matter at hand, which, as far as I could remember, was the songs in question. "You want me to call your attorney?" I asked. "No problem. I can do that. I'm just not sure how I'm going to explain that a client who's been dead for more than thirty years is wondering about copyright laws."

"Not the songs I wrote back then." Damon shook his head. "The new songs. The songs I've been writing in my head since . . . well, you know, since back in '71. Since the night I took that hit of orange sunshine."

Boy, for a guy whose lyrics were as full of death as Garden View Cemetery, he sure was reluctant to say the word. I supplied it for him. "The night you died, you mean?"

He didn't confirm or deny, and I was tired of beating around the bush. "Are you saying that this Vinnie guy's been stealing your songs even though you didn't write those songs when you were alive? What, this is like E.T., phone home? Vinnie gets in touch with you and you sing him your songs and—"

"No. That's not it at all. Vinnie doesn't just get in touch. He's got this hold on me. He's channeling me, that's what he's doing."

Chapter 3

"Huh?"

Okay, so it wasn't the most probing question, but it was all I could think to say before I blurted out, "Channeling? Like changing the channels on TV?"

"Channeling like capturing my spirit and making me do what he wants me to do."

I thought this over, but it didn't make a whole lot of sense. Then again, I was a woman who didn't believe in ghosts until they started butting in on my life. I was quickly finding out that taking a walk on the spooky side meant learning about a whole bunch of things I never knew existed and never would have believed in before my Gift reared its ugly psychic head.

"You mean Vinnie makes you write songs for him?" I asked Damon, trying to get it all straight. "Even though you're dead?"

"Sort of." Damon may have been a genius when it came to dark lyrics, but it was clear this was hard to explain, even for him. "As far as I can see, this is how it works. The body is sort of like a car, and a car needs energy from a battery to run, right?"

I knew as much about cars as I used to know about ghosts. Still, I couldn't argue with this. I nodded.

"But a car doesn't care where that energy comes from. You could buy a battery anywhere, from any manufacturer, and your car would still work."

"And this is the same as channeling because . . ."

"Because it's the same thing as what happens when Vinnie channels my spirit. His body still works, but the energy comes from me."

I was getting dizzy again. To chase away my confusion, I started walking and since I didn't have a whole lot to say, this worked out perfectly. We walked. Damon talked.

"Vinnie's been doing it for years," he said. "He's got it down pat. He calls on my spirit, and like it or not, when he calls, I have to go. I get drawn into his body, and I become the energy that runs it. When I do, he makes me write songs for him."

I thought about the green Magic Marker lyrics on the pizza box. "So why isn't this a good thing?" I asked him. "I mean, you're a songwriter, right? And songwriters are all about hearing their words come to life. Shouldn't this make you happy?"

"You actually get it." He said this like it was something exceptional, and I basked in the glow of the compliment. "There aren't many people who understand. You must be an artist yourself."

Only when it came to accessorizing fashion. I would have pointed this out if I didn't remember that back in Damon's day, *fashion* was pretty much defined by how many love beads a person wore with dirty jeans and raggy T-shirts. Needless to say, I shivered at the very thought.

"I'm making you cold."

Damon's comment caught me off guard, but I answered instantly. "No. That's not it."

"Then maybe I'm making you hot?"

When he said this with a little growl in his voice, it wasn't easy to deny. I tried, anyway, with a tight smile and a quick detour back to the original subject. I was helped out because by that time, we were back in the lobby of the Rock Hall and face to face with the poster of Mind at Large that advertised their upcoming concert.

"Which one is Vinnie?" I asked.

The Rock Hall employee standing nearby—a young, perky blond whose nametag said she was Sarah—naturally thought I was talking to her. She pointed at the poster, left to right. "Vinnie, Ben, Alistair, Mighty Mike, Pete. I think."

I scanned the poster and the five guys on it. Every single one of them must have been at least sixty, and I thought about how different they looked on the poster outside the building, the one that showed Mind at Large back in Damon's day, before they had forty years of hard rockin' under their belts.

Back then, Alistair had been the cute one. Now his hair was silver, his jowls drooped, he wore glasses as thick as soda bottles. Mighty Mike (I'd heard tell the nickname came from female fans who couldn't get enough of his wide shoulders and broad chest) had a stomach that pouched over his belt, and Pete was so thin, I'm pretty sure a brisk wind could blow him away. As for Vinnie . . .

I shifted my gaze and took a closer look at the dark-haired guy who sat at the outside of the picture. His hair was as long as Damon's, but on Vinnie, the style was more grungy than appealing. He wore a tattered T-shirt, beat-up jeans, and a wide smile.

"I've got to tell you, I'm not a big fan." Sarah said this in hushed tones. Like she couldn't afford to let anyone at the Hall know it, but she didn't want me to get the wrong impression. "I mean, their stuff, it's pretty hokey, isn't it? I guess a lot of people like it, though. You know, old people. Somebody told me that Vinnie writes all the band's music. But then, you probably know that. Not that I think you're old or anything," she added, before I even had a chance to get offended. "I just figured everyone knows that!"

"Everyone in this world and beyond," I told her.

She thought I was kidding. "They're going to set up the stage right out there." She pointed toward the plaza out in front of the building. "We figure there will be tens of thousands of people here. They say it's going to be the biggest thing to happen in Cleveland since I don't know when."

I remembered the last biggest social event to happen in Cleveland and how I'd attended it so that I could investigate. That investigation led to the debunking of one of the biggest icons in the literary world. It was a little intimidating to think that if Damon had his way, I would have the same effect on the music industry.

Speaking of investigating, this struck me as a good time to start. "Has Vinnie always written the band's music?" I asked Sarah.

Sarah got big points for honesty. She shrugged.

"I guess. Vinnie Pal—that's what they call him, not Vinnie Pallucci, just Vinnie Pal—I've heard people around here say that he's a genius. You know, that his songs are brilliant."

"His songs are shit."

Since the songs in question were allegedly Damon's songs, this comment from him surprised me. I knew better than to question him within earshot of Sarah, so I excused myself, hurried into the gift shop, and ducked behind a rack of Rock Hall lunch bags.

"I'm getting confused," I told Damon. "I thought the songs were your songs."

"They are my songs. Or at least they're versions of my songs."

I didn't bother with the *huh* this time. My expression said it all.

"It's like this," Damon explained. "Vinnie channels me, and whether I want to or not, I gotta go. Wherever he is. When I get there, I slip into his body, and he makes me write songs for him. But when he does . . . hell . . ." His mouth thinned with disgust. "Inside my head, every single one of my songs is damned near perfect. But when they come out of me and pass through Vinnie, somehow they get all watered down. It's a bummer, man, and it's just plain embarrassing."

"You're dead, you can't be embarrassed!"

A mom and her little boy were just about to check out the lunch bags. She put a hand on her son's shoulder and ushered him away.

Damon hardly spared them a look. "I can be sick and tired of the whole thing. And I am. I want you to go and talk to Vinnie. I want you to tell him to stop. Maybe if he does . . ." Damon looked away.

I guess I was getting good at reading between the lines. Case in point. I sensed that there was more going on than Damon was willing to talk about.

Being the polite person that I am, I knew to leave well enough alone and allow Damon his privacy. But it would take more than civility to get me in on this case. Honesty, for one thing. And a little R-E-S-P-E-C-T for another.

If Damon wasn't telling me the whole truth and nothing but, then I wasn't getting either.

"Maybe if he does . . ." I jumped back into the sentence, hoping Damon would finish it for me, and when he didn't, I narrowed my eyes and pinned him with a look. "You're leaving something out, and you should know this right now. I won't work for you. Not if you keep secrets."

Did I know one of the gift shop employees was refilling a shelf nearby? He heard me and glanced over. "You want to work here? Applications are up at the cash register."

I smiled my thanks. And turned my back on him. There was a stage nearby, one of those makeshift ones that looked as if it was set up and taken down as needed. I scrambled over to it, eager to finish my conversation in private.

I turned to face Damon and made sure I kept my voice down. "Maybe if Vinnie stops channeling you . . . what? What will happen then?"

Damon twitched his shoulders. "I don't know for sure."

"But you have a hunch."

He looked away and back into the lobby with its wild displays. When he looked my way again, his face was as gray as it had been back in the movie theater. "He's the reason I'm still here, Pepper," he said. "Vinnie Pal has this hold on me, and he won't let go. Because of him, I can't leave this plane and move to the Other Side." A young couple passed by near where we stood. They were holding hands and singing along with the music that blared from overhead speakers, bumping hips to the beat of the music.

"It's different being . . . you know . . ."

"Dead?" When I supplied the word, the young man and woman gave me weird looks. They walked in the direction of a security guard, and call me paranoid, I didn't like the thought that they were going to report me as the resident weirdo. I moved away from the stage and toward the front doors.

"We've got to talk somewhere else," I said, my teeth clenched around my words. "You're buried at Garden View. We can just meet there. Tonight after work."

Damon's face, already ashen, got a shade paler. "You could just come here."

We were close to the front doors and the security guard, who, I noticed, was watching me a little more carefully than he was anyone else. I grabbed a brochure about the hall, held it up in front of my mouth, and kept my voice to an impatient hiss. "Except the Rock Hall isn't open late tonight. And before you can suggest it, no, I'm not going to try my hand at breaking and entering. I work until five. I'll make some excuse to stay late. That will make my boss very happy. Let's say seven. Your grave."

"But—"

"Do you want me to take your case?"

"Yes, but—"

"Seven tonight," I said, and I punched my way through the revolving doors. "Your grave."

I can't say for sure, but I think right before he disappeared in a puff of smoke that smelled a whole lot like pot, Damon nodded.

And a new thought struck.

For the first time in as long as I could remember, I had a date. A date with a hot, sexy guy.

Too bad he was dead.

I did actually make it to the County Archives that day, though by the time I waited for someone from a nearby garage to change my tire, it was pretty late when I got there. Still, I managed to do a smidgen of the research Ella had lined up for me, and when I arrived back at Garden View, I had a pile of copies of immigration papers to prove it. My fear and loathing of research aside, they were the perfect excuse I needed to explain why I was still hanging around when Ella stuck her head into my office a few minutes after five.

"That's my Pepper!" Ella beamed me a smile from across the room. "You're staying late to enter all the information you gathered today into our resident database, aren't you?"

I might be willing to take a little credit where it wasn't due, but I wasn't delusional. I looked from the pile of papers on my desk to Ella. "Well, maybe not *all* the information."

"I'd love to help." She wasn't kidding. I prayed that by the time I was her age, I'd have more of a life than that. "But we've got Meet the Teacher Night at school. The girls say I should just forget it, that there isn't anything any of their teachers can tell me that I don't already know, but you know I'm not buying into that."

I did. Ella was the most conscientious parent I knew, and I told her so. She said good night and left me to my database entering, and I checked the clock against the size of the stack of papers. If I didn't make too many mistakes, I could get at least some of it out of the way before I had to leave for my date with Damon.

I caught myself and grumbled a stern lecture. "You have to stop calling it a date. Dead men don't date." And live women who think they can date dead men? It was too sick to even consider.

Rather than think about it, I got down to work. I turned on my computer and accessed the cemetery database. I was about halfway through the stack of immigration records when my phone rang.

"It's after five. I'm surprised you're still there."

For a couple of seconds, the comment caught me off guard. Until I recognized the voice.

Then my throat closed. And my heart stopped. And the hormones I'd been telling to behave since the moment Damon spooked his way into my life sprang back into action, jumping up and down and shouting hoo-ray!

It was Quinn Harrison on the phone, a man I'd last seen the night a few months earlier when a goon with more muscles than brains tried to throw me off a bridge.

Did I say *man*?

Well, there's no denying that Quinn is certainly that. And a gorgeous one, to boot. But he's also a cop. A Homicide detective, to be exact.

Hence our penchant for running into each other.

Not that I'm complaining. In the great scheme of things, running into Quinn is right up there on my wish list along with a trust fund, an end to the annoying hauntings caused by my Gift, and a red Jag that arrives with no strings attached. Trouble is, Quinn thinks I should mind my own business when it comes to investigating murders. And me? I'm not exactly in a position to explain that murders *are* my business because I'm working with the dead victims.

The results are predictable.

Though he is as hot for me as I am for him (and believe me when I say this is plenty hot), in his heart of hearts, Quinn believes I'm a meddler who sticks her nose where it doesn't belong, gets in trouble, and thus, gets in his way.

Hotness aside, I think Quinn is hide-bound, bullheaded, and too quick to judge. Okay, so I do have the tendency to get in his way. And he does have the tendency to show up now and again and save my life. That doesn't mean I owe him explanations, does it? Especially when any explanation I could offer is only going to make him think I'm certifiable.

After our last encounter there on that bridge, he'd handed me his card with his home phone number and told me to call when I finally decided to come clean about what was going on in my life. Believe me, since then, I'd brought out that card a dozen times or more, my cell phone in my hand.

But I never made the call.

Crazy, I know. But Quinn wanted answers. And answers were exactly what I couldn't give him.

Which made me wonder why he was calling now.

I erased the surprise from my voice. "If you didn't think I'd be here, why did you call?" I asked him.

"You got me there." His chuckle was deep-throated. "You're the one who likes to pretend she's a detective. So get to work! You tell me, why did I call?"

I hated playing games. But then, I suspected Quinn did, too. He didn't have the temperament for it. Quinn was more the take-no-prisoners type. He didn't just not like to beat around the bush, he refused to acknowledge the bush even existed. And if he ever did admit it, he'd sooner plow straight through the middle of it than worry about going around.

All of which made me think that whatever was going on, it wasn't something he was comfortable with. I latched on to the clue like my aunt Sally's terrier with a bone. Quinn was uncomfortable, huh? Well, too bad. For all the sleepless nights he'd caused me when I sat there staring at his phone number, I owed him.

"Why did you call me?" I said this in a thoughtful way designed to make him believe I was actually wondering about it. "Maybe because you've finally decided you can't live without me? That's it! You've spent months thinking about me, dreaming about me. You've been waiting for me to call, waking up at night in a cold sweat, wondering when the phone is going to ring. You just can't stand it anymore."

Typical Quinn. He didn't confirm or deny. "You wouldn't have said that if it wasn't exactly what you've been going through these past months."

"But I'm not the one who made the phone call."

I could just about see through the phone to the way he smiled in response. It wasn't an oh-boy-am-I-happy smile. Quinn didn't own that expression. This was more like you-got-me-there-but-I'm-never-going-to-admit-it.

I couldn't hold it against him.

I'd never admit it, either.

"So . . ." I stood because sitting still while I was talking to Quinn was next to impossible.

To get rid of the nervous energy that suddenly buzzed through my bloodstream like a drug, I did a quick turn around my pint-size office. While I was at it, I took a second to move the phone away from my ear and hit the button on the receiver that showed the caller ID. It said "private caller" which meant he hadn't called from the Justice Center where the Cleveland Police Department was headquartered and where Quinn had his office. He was calling from his cell. Or from home. Either way, this wasn't business. It was personal.

The buzzing got louder.

"You have been thinking about me, haven't

you?" I made sure I kept my words oh-so-casual so I didn't give away the fact that I'd been thinking about him, too.

"Did I say that?"

"You didn't have to say it. You proved it. You called me."

"I called you because . . ." Like a man prepared to jump into the deep end of a pool, he took a long breath. "I've got this CI, see."

He paused, waiting for me to ask what a CI was and thus prove myself a rookie when it came to the detective game. Little did he know that when I wasn't out hunting evildoers, I was home in front of the TV. I'd watched my share of *Law & Order* and *CSI* reruns, and none of those hours had been wasted; I'd learned my share of cop jargon. "A confidential informer, huh?" I said this like it was no big deal, even though I expected him to be impressed. "A Homicide cop doesn't have much use for a CI. That's for cops who work Vice. Or Narcotics."

"Well, I used to work Narcotics." It was the most he'd ever told me about his past, and I considered that a minor victory of sorts. "He's not my CI now. He used to be my CI. And he still comes in handy once in a while."

"So let me see if I've got this straight. Your CI called and he told you to call me."

"He didn't tell me to call you. He doesn't know you exist."

"So you don't talk about me at the office, huh?"

"He never comes to the office."

"So why did he want you to call me?"

"He didn't." This time when Quinn drew in a

breath, it was one of pure annoyance. "He called to tell me he had some tickets. To the baseball game. The Indians are in the playoffs, you know."

This was news to me. But then I wasn't much of a sports fan. In fact, I wasn't a sports fan at all. I didn't point this out simply because this was the aha moment. Finally I had it figured out, and I knew what was coming. Tickets to a game and a phone call I'd been praying for practically since the moment Quinn finished putting the cuffs on the perp and walked off that bridge.

I was about to get asked out on a date.

By a guy who was actually alive.

It wasn't easy, but I played it cool. "Your CI gave you tickets, huh? What do they call that? Graft? Or a bribe?"

"It wasn't graft or a bribe. I paid for the tickets. Full price."

"And you're looking for someone to take to the game."

Quinn was glad to get the messy do-you-want-to-go-out-with-me part out of the way. I could tell from the relief that swept through his voice. Which doesn't mean he was about to confess to undying love. Or even affection. "I could have called a dozen different people over at the Justice Center, you know. Any one of them would have been glad to go with me. The game's sold out."

"But you didn't call any of them. You called me."

"I thought—"

"What? That I'm a sports fan?" The way I laughed pretty much told him the possibility was a long shot at best.

"Give me some credit! I knew you weren't a sports fan. But that doesn't mean we wouldn't have a nice time. Dinner downtown before the game and drinks in the Warehouse District after . . . I'm thinking that will help sweeten the offer."

"Considerably."

"You'll come with me?"

Up until this point, things were going pretty well. Of course I had to go and open my big mouth and ask the logical question. "When?"

"Tonight." The sound of my gulp was drowned by Quinn's voice. "I know it's short notice. I just got the call about the tickets. But since you're still there at the office, it's obvious you're not busy. I can come by and pick you up there, and—"

"I can't."

There was a nanosecond of silence on the other end of the phone. "You're blowing me off again."

"I'm not. Really. I just can't go. Not tonight."

"Because . . ."

I debated about telling him the truth. For about a second and a half. "I've got a date," I said.

This, of course, may not have been the complete truth, but it was a version of the truth, and the least Quinn could have done to show his appreciation for my candor was to say something.

"What?" When it cut into the silence, my voice was a little sharp. Who could blame me for being defensive? I'd just come clean. Sort of. The least Quinn could do was be gracious about it. "You don't think I have dates?"

"I don't think you have a date tonight. If you did, you wouldn't still be at the office."

"Maybe I'm at the office waiting for my date."

"Waiting at the cemetery? Don't tell me, let me guess. Your date is dead."

He thought he was being funny. Or sarcastic. He couldn't have possibly known how close he'd come to the truth. Call me a glutton for punishment, I decided right then and there that if Quinn wanted me to come clean about my after-hours investigating, this was as good a time as any.

"As a matter of fact," I said, "he is. Dead, that is. And since I don't know how to contact him, I have to wait for him to show up. So you see, I'm going to have to pass on the ball game. But if the offer of drinks in the Warehouse District after is still open . . ."

Any self-respecting guy would have caved at the little purr in my voice. I guess Quinn wasn't self-respecting. "I'm not looking for a part-time date," he said. "Or bullshit excuses. You've got a date tonight. I can accept that. You don't need to try and humor me with silly stories."

"Stories that might not be so silly after all."

"Whatever."

Quinn had been willing to swallow his pride and call me. I figured the least I could do in return was meet him halfway. "Look," I said, "we could do it another time."

"I thought this was the other time."

"It would have been the other time if you gave me time to make time."

"Whatever."

"You said that before."

"You make me lose track."

"We can do it again?"

"Sure." Before my ego and those pesky hormones could rejoice, he qualified the response. "But next time, you're going to have to call me."

"But—"

"I'm erasing your number from my cell phone."

"But—"

"I'm taking you out of my Rolodex at the office."

"But—"

"Goodbye, Pepper."

"Goodbye," I said, the reply automatic even though the sound of the dial tone was already blaring in my ear.

So that was that. One live guy down and one dead guy to go. Could my love life get any more pathetic?

There was only one way to find out.

I checked the clock, grabbed my sweater, and went out in the pitch-dark cemetery to look for my date.

Chapter 4

I had recently observed my six-month anniversary as an employee of Garden View Cemetery. On my own, this is not something I would have noticed, and if I did, it sure wasn't anything I would have celebrated. But Ella being Ella . . . well, she made a big deal out of it. She took me to lunch and gave me a mini-review. In it, she pointed out that although I still had a long way to go when it came to mastering the ins and outs of the cemetery business, I had made what she called "great strides." According to her, every day I knew more about the history of Garden View and the folks buried there and, she pointed out, I'd already planned and researched two tours on my own, written articles for the newsletter, and been an all-around team player. She even went out of her way to mention that ugly period the summer before when I'd been laid off from my cemetery tour guide job and still stepped in to do her a huge (and, as it turned out, dangerous) favor.

I was learning a lot, she told me, and though I wasn't nearly as jazzed about all this as she was, I couldn't dispute any of it.

One of the things I'd already learned was that I didn't like to be in the cemetery by myself after dark. Don't get me wrong. I'm not a chicken. It's not the *dark* part that bothers me as much as it's the *myself* part. I have my Gift to thank for that. After all, I know better than anybody: Just because I'm by myself doesn't mean I'm alone.

I thought about this as I listened to the main door to the office building swish closed and lock behind me. Automatically I checked the parking lot and the long, silent stretch of cemetery I could see beyond the glow of the nearby security light. One ghost at any one time was more than enough, and I already had Damon to deal with; I didn't want to be waylaid by some other specter who needed my services.

The coast was clear, and breathing a sigh of relief, I hopped into my Mustang and locked the doors. I wasn't fooling anyone but myself; I knew from experience that if they wanted to, ghosts could get past the locks and materialize in my car. But hey, whoever said hope springs eternal must have known something about avoiding pesky spooks.

There are no streetlights in the cemetery, and the roads through Garden View are as picturesque as the rest of the place. They sweep over stone bridges and curve through groves of trees. The road I was on wound its way through the newer sections of the cemetery, and I followed it for a while, then turned. I wasn't headed for the front gate and the older sections where Cleveland's once rich and powerful are buried with pomp, circumstance, and elaborate monuments, but down into the valley that borders one little corner of Garden View.

"Creepy." The word whooshed out of me as, both hands on the wheel, I maneuvered the Mustang through a hairpin turn on a narrow stretch of road and went down, down, down. At the bottom of the hill, the valley opened up to a field where people from the surrounding neighborhoods brought their dogs to run. On my right was a line of tombs built into the side of the hill. Once upon a long time ago, they'd been showplaces. But years had passed since anyone was buried in any of them, and the families that had once carefully tended to their dearly departed were now dearly departed themselves. The Garden View grounds crew took as good care of these tombs as possible, but as Ella had enthusiastically pointed out, I'd learned a lot in the six months I'd been there. One of those things was that there would always be a certain amount of natural decay in a cemetery (no pun intended). The other was that no matter how hard anyone wished it would stop, it was impossible to eliminate vandalism. The tombs I passed had seen better days. Their front steps and pillars were cracked and patched. Their stained glass windows were missing or broken. The gaping holes left behind had been filled with cement, and in the gloom, the squares of lighter-colored material stared at me like unblinking eyes.

I told my overactive imagination to shut up and crept along carefully, following the map to Damon's grave that I'd printed out at the office and left on the front seat next to me. It was dark and way too quiet in the valley. Exactly, I reminded myself, why Damon had been buried there, far from the hustle and bustle of the more active parts of the cemetery. According to what I'd read in our archive files, Damon's business manager and agent, who'd arranged the burial, decided that the more out-of-the-way his grave was, the less likely it was to be overrun by fans.

In theory, it was a good idea. But that agent should have known that it's hard to keep wild and crazy rock fans down. When I cruised up to the grave, there was a group of people standing around. I saw in a moment that these weren't die-hard fans, though. They were carrying flashlights, cameras, and, oh yeah, Geiger counters.

Since the ghostbusters seemed hell-bent on looking at their instruments and nothing else, I slammed my car door to announce my presence.

"Cemetery's closed," I said. My voice echoed through the valley like a disembodied thing. "You aren't supposed to be here."

"You're just saying that so you can do some ghost hunting on your own, right? You want to get the scoop yourself." A guy who was apparently the leader of the merry band approached me, his hand out. "Brian," he said. "And this is John, Theo, Angela and Stan." The other ghostbusters barely spared me a look, which was fine by me because though I waved to be polite, I really didn't care about them, either. "You must be investigating, too."

"I work here," I told him. "I'm not investigating anything."

If I didn't get rid of the ghost hunters, it would be true. No way could I chat with Damon while they were around. "I stayed late at the office and decided to leave the back way." I waved in some vague direction to make Brian think I just happened to pass by on my way out. "What are you guys up to?"

"Looking for Damon Curtis, of course." The answer came from Stan, who was holding a yellow Geiger counter. He pointed it right at me and took a reading. It didn't beep or buzz. I was grateful. Stan lost interest. He did a circuit around the simple headstone I saw illuminated by Theo's flashlight.

Damon Michael Curtis, it said. There were no dates listed and nothing about Mind at Large or platinum albums, world tours, and the adoration of millions of screaming fans. Behind the stone where Damon's name was carved was another stone. This one was flat and as large as a twin bed, and over the years, the fans who'd been plucky enough to make the pilgrimage down there had turned it into a shrine. Candles winked from colorful glass cups, their light glinting off a bottle of Johnny Walker Black, a dozen Mind at Large CDs, a Styrofoam cup with the words *City Roast* printed on the side, and a bong.

"I've worked here for like forever," I told Brian. "I've never heard one story about Damon Curtis haunting this place."

"But he has to." Angela caught wind of the conversation and hurried over. "A young rock star. A tragic death." She was carrying a digital camera that she held to her heart. "This is the stuff great hauntings are made of!"

"Maybe, but—"

"You mean you haven't heard anything about Curtis? From anybody?"

The question came from Brian, so I turned back to him. He was wearing one of those vests I'd seen fishermen wear, the kind with about a hundred little pockets all over it. Even as I turned, he patted down his pockets. He took out a notebook from one and put it back, a pen from another and put that away, too. Finally he found what he was looking for, a couple of AA batteries, and he handed them to John, who was standing nearby with a tape recorder that was apparently out of juice.

I did a double take. "Tape recorder?" I wondered out loud, and maybe ghostbusters are used to this kind of skepticism; John didn't take offense.

"For EVP," he explained, slipping the old batteries out of the recorder and popping in the new. "That's Electronic Voice Phenomenon. Sometimes you don't see a ghost or get any readings from the other equipment, but if you talk to them, they talk back. Not that you can hear them while it's happening. But later, when you play back the recording . . . well, let me tell you, it's wild. We've recorded some amazing things!"

A few months earlier, none of this would have worried me. Like most people of sound mind, I figured ghostbusters were nothing more than nutcases. Sure they were dedicated, and some were scientific, too. But in the months I'd worked at Garden View, I'd seen my share of them, and I knew what they were really all about was the equipment. Yep, techno-junkies, every last one of them.

And like I said, I wasn't worried. I knew ghosts were real, but finding ghosts with the help of things that went beep in the night? Not a chance!

Or so I thought.

Until Dan Callahan bushwhacked me at a party.

Okay, a quick explanation is in order here. Dan is a brain researcher. At least I thought he was a brain researcher. I met him at the hospital after I clunked my head on Gus Scarpetti's mausoleum and Dan told me that my brain scans were odd and that he wanted to study me. I thought he was nothing more than a nerd, but that was before the fateful day he saved my life. After that, he started following me around. Only I could never catch him at it and ask what he was up to. Until the aforementioned party.

That's when Dan showed up out of nowhere and shoved a photograph under my nose. It was a picture of me, and in it I was standing with two misty white blobs.

They were ghosts.

I knew that, but Dan shouldn't have, and though he didn't come right out and say it, it was clear he did.

Disturbing, yes? Especially when I didn't know there was a camera sophisticated enough to take a picture like that. When Dan left me at the party, he gave me some cryptic advice: I was messing with powers I couldn't possibly understand, and it was dangerous, he said. More specifically, he told me that if I was smart, I'd back off.

Oh yeah, and that it was the only warning I'd ever get.

Good thing a shiver scooted up my back. It forced my mind away from worrying about what Dan was up to these days and back to the matter at hand.

Ghostbusters.

Who, if past experience meant anything, just might be lucky enough to capture evidence of a certain ghostly client of mine.

John and his tape recorder were already headed back toward Damon's grave, so I turned back to Brian. "You haven't recorded anything here, have you?" I asked him. "You've never seen anything or gotten any of these ESPs—"

"EVPs," he corrected me. "And unfortunately, you're right. We haven't been lucky enough to catch anything here at Curtis's grave. Yet. That's exactly why we have to keep trying! If we're the first to record some kind of evidence of his ghost, we'll be famous. I figure they'll put us on the cover of *Rolling Stone*."

It was dark so he didn't see that I crossed my fingers as I said, "There's not one ounce of evidence of Damon hanging around." Another thought struck and I added, "Not here, anyway."

I was, of course, referring to the fact that though Damon had never been seen in Garden View, he had definitely been seen at the Rock Hall. By me, anyway. I hadn't intended to distract them, but as it turned out, my offhand comment worked like a charm. As one, the ghost hunters' ears pricked up. I found myself in a center of the circle of them and realized they were waiting for me to say more. The way I saw it, this put me in something of a pickle:

a. I could tell them the truth and swear no one had ever reported a Damon sighting in the cemetery. But I'd already tried that, and they weren't listening.

b. I didn't want to mention the Rock Hall, partly because if I did, they'd ask too many questions about how I knew Damon's spirit was there and mostly because it hardly seemed fair to the nice folks at the Hall to sic a bunch of ghostbusters on them.

And

c. I had to get rid of them if I had any hopes of meeting with Damon without them catching wind of it.

I wracked my brain for a plan.

"It's President Garfield's memorial," I blurted out. It sounded ridiculous, even to me, but I suppose by definition, ghost hunters are an open-minded bunch. Instead of telling me I was talking nonsense, they leaned nearer. I scrambled to put substance to my story. "Here's the skinny," I told them. "I've heard that Damon's spirit hangs out over at the memorial just to bug the President. You know how those old hippies were, up against the establishment and all that." I looked over my shoulder, up the hill, and toward the main part of the cemetery and the huge monument that dominated the landscape there. "When I drove by a little while ago, I saw another group of ghost hunters up there. I wouldn't be surprised if they don't run into Damon's spirit. Seems like a good night for it, don't you think?"

Brian and the rest of them apparently agreed. They scrambled for their equipment and jumped in the SUV parked nearby. Before I could say

Electronic Voice Phenomenon, they were gone.

I was alone.

In the dark.

Waiting for a ghost.

It was the beginning of October, and chilly. I wrapped my arms around myself.

"Damon!" I hissed, and in the dark, my voice sounded small and frightened. "Hey, I got rid of the ghostbusters. You can come out now." There was no answer, and I looked all around. "Are you here somewhere?"

"Are any of us somewhere? Or are we lost, amoebae fighting the currents of change and time? Cursed. Driven to despair. Hollow men without morals. Dipped in blood."

I recognized the lyrics of the Mind at Large song. And the voice. But I couldn't tell where it came from.

There was no sign of Damon anywhere near his grave or in the field behind me. I peered into the dark beyond the flickering candles. "Come on, Damon. It's been a long day. It's kind of late for games."

"Too late for laboring love. Or changing zebras into moon-dark creatures. Too long overdue. Pressure. Sin. No remorse for death."

"Yeah, yeah. I recognize that song, too." I wanted him to know I'd just about had it, so I sighed loud enough for him to hear. "Come on, Damon. We've got work to do." A shiver snaked up my back. "And it's getting cold out here."

"I could keep you warm. You could heat my body."

These weren't song lyrics. At least none I knew. I

spun toward the voice that had whispered in my ear, but, big surprise, Damon wasn't anywhere near. Not that I could see, anyway.

"We don't have to go through this again, do we?" I asked. It was better to focus on the fact that he was pissing me off than it was thinking about the way his voice tickled my ear—and my libido. "I thought we got it out of the way this afternoon. I showed up. You played hard to get. I told you I wasn't putting up with the bullshit. Now here we go again, and I just passed on a real, live, honest-to-goodness date with a real, live, honest-to-goodness guy for this, so let me tell you, if you're going to screw around, I'm not going to be happy about it. I mean it, Damon, if you don't get your ghostly butt over here by the time I count to three, I'm gone. One . . . two . . ."

Out of the corner of my eye, I saw a shimmer of white about twenty feet away. I turned toward it, but there was nothing there but darkness. Or was there? Another shimmer, like moonlight on pavement, and Damon appeared. He was wearing skin-tight black leather pants and a white shirt with wide sleeves. It was unbuttoned to his navel, and his bare chest looked as if it had been chipped from marble.

"It's about time," I said. It was a less indiscreet greeting than *hubba-hubba*. "Get over here. I don't want to talk too loud. In the dark, my voice will carry, and I don't want those ghostbusters to think there's anything going on down here."

He didn't move.

I groaned and marched over to where he stood. "Come on," I said. "At least we can sit down over there." I was talking about the flat stone behind Damon's headstone, but I don't think he knew it. When I looked that way, he didn't.

In fact, as I closed in on him, I realized he wasn't looking at anything at all. His eyes were blank and glassy. He was staring straight ahead into the dark.

"Hello!" I waved my hands in front of his face. "Earth to Damon! Anybody home?"

His voice was as flat as his stare. "You don't have a joint, do you?"

Had he bothered to look my way, he would have seen that my smile bristled. "Even if I did, you couldn't smoke it. You're dead, remember?"

Damon winced as if he'd been slapped. "Of course I remember," he said. "Let's go. We'll talk in your office."

"I don't want to go all the way back to my office. Come on." I moved toward his grave. "I'll bet that big stone is still warm from the sun this afternoon. We can sit there."

"Or not."

I was halfway to his grave, and I turned to see Damon hadn't budged an inch.

And that's when it hit me. Like the proverbial ton of bricks.

I sucked in a breath of astonishment. "You've never been here, have you?" I asked him. "You've never seen your own grave. That's why you're so reluctant to get close. You've never—"

"I—" Damon's shoulders rose and fell. "No, I never—" He looked away, and when he turned to me again, there was a glint in his eyes, as if he was just daring me to prove him wrong. "My things are at the Rock Hall," he said. "I stayed with my things."

"Your things are at the Rock Hall, sure. But your body is buried here." I listened to my own words and had another aha moment. "You do know you're dead, right?" I asked him.

"I know it." Damon's voice was a growl. "I've known it all these years. It's just—"

"That there's a difference between knowing something in here . . ." I pointed to my head. "And admitting it. In here." I pressed my hands to my midsection.

His silence was all the proof I needed that I'd hit the nail on the head. My anger dissolved beneath some other feeling I couldn't name. It slammed into me, right about where my hands were clutched.

"Come on," I said, strolling back to walk alongside him. "You don't have to look at the grave alone, I'll be with you."

Damon drew in a breath and let it out slowly. Just as slowly, we inched toward the headstone where his name was engraved. Without the ghostbusters' flashlights, it was too dark to see much of anything, so I grabbed one of the candles from the makeshift shrine and held it in front of the letters etched in granite.

"Damon Michael Curtis." His finger followed the light, skimming over the words as he read them. "I guess this makes it official."

It did, and although he'd had more than thirty years, I gave him another minute to get used to the idea.

I took a seat on the flat stone and watched as he

studied the stone with his name on it. "It was a good life," he said. "I had one hell of a time."

"And now?"

When he looked at me, the glow of the candle flame flickered in his eyes and made them spark. He looked very much alive. He wasn't, and when he rounded the headstone and came to sit at my side, I reminded myself not to forget it.

"My life was one constant happening," Damon said. "I got a buzz from performing. And expanding my mind. I loved the women!" He tipped his head back. Whatever he was remembering, it made him grin. "Man, life was a trip! Now . . ." His smile faded. "I'm bored, Pepper. I've been bored for more than thirty long years."

I could have come back with a smart-aleck comment about sex and drugs and rock and roll, but the look of quiet desperation in Damon's dark eyes stopped me.

It also helped me make up my mind about taking on his case.

"Then we'd better do something about it," I said. I thought back to everything he'd told me that afternoon. "It sounds like we need to start with Vinnie."

"Vinnie Pal, right. If we can stop him from holding my spirit on this plane, I can pass to the Other Side."

Let's face it, in theory, this sounded reasonable enough. But on closer examination, there were gaps in Damon's logic.

"Don't get me wrong," I said, "it's not like I don't believe you or anything. But I can't believe Vinnie can just call you and you go whooshing over to wherever he is. If it was that easy, everyone would do it. You know, people would keep loved ones with them. Or somebody would figure out how to make famous scientists and doctors stick around so they could keep doing all the good things they were doing while they were alive. Shit, my mom would have hung on to Louise, her cleaning lady, long after the poor woman was dead. Mom always said no one could clean a bathroom like Louise."

"But if you told people it was possible, that they could call up the power and do exactly what Vinnie's doing, do you think they'd believe you?"

Damon's voice was thoughtful, and it made me think, too. "They'd say it was bull. They'd say it was nutso. Like believing there's such a thing as—"

"Ghosts?"

I had come to accept my Gift, even if I wasn't one hundred percent comfortable with it. "I used to think I was crazy," I told him.

"You mean the first time you ran into one of us."

I nodded. "I thought it was because I hit my head on Gus's mausoleum. After that, that's when he started showing up."

"Then you realized that it was true. That it truly is a Gift."

My laugh was skeptical. "Not a Gift I want."

"You're kidding me, right?" Damon twisted so that he was facing me. "But you should be totally stoked! It's wild, what you do, talking to the dead. And a girl as smart as you—"

"Smart? Yeah, right."

As if it would help him see me better, he narrowed his eyes. "You don't think you're smart?"

"I think most people see my body. Not my brain."

"Your body . . ." We were sitting close, so when Damon skimmed a look from my face, down my neck and lower still, I swore I could feel the heat. "You're awesome," he said, and he made it sound like it wasn't any big deal, just the honest truth. "But come on, every guy you meet must realize that there's more to you than just a dynamite body. You're smart and you're funny and from what I've heard, you're not afraid of anything. You took on the mob for Gus."

Before Damon could see that my cheeks were on fire, I turned to look the other way.

"Come on, little girl, crave the possibilities." They were the lyrics to the most famous of all the Mind at Large songs, and Damon didn't say them, he sang them. His voice was a rumble that tickled my skin with a feather's touch. "Laugh and run, naked in verdant meadows, drunk with your power."

When I turned back to him, I had every intention of making a smart-ass comment about not being a fan of oldies. A better plan than begging him to find a way for flesh-and-blood me to get it on with his ectoplasm. I would have done it, too, if I didn't find Damon's mouth just a hairbreadth from mine.

"You're dead," I told him and reminded myself. It would have been more convincing if my voice didn't choke behind the sudden ball of anticipation that tightened my throat. "We can't—"

"Oh, but if we could!" He backed away, and

though there was a smile on his lips, I couldn't help but notice that his eyes were filled with regret. "So what's the deal with this guy who wants to date you?" he asked.

It took me a second to remember to breathe. And another before I had any idea who—or what—he was talking about. Quinn. I dismissed the whole thing with a lift of my shoulders. "Just a guy."

"And you're not interested?"

"I am, but—"

"He's not your type."

"He is, but—"

"You're afraid to get hurt."

I would have liked nothing better than to argue this point with him, but it was kind of hard considering that it was true. Rather than lay my pathetic love life out on the line, I opted for the quick-and-dirty explanation. "I was engaged once," I said. "He called it off."

"And you're going to let that stop you from enjoying every second of your life?" Damon laughed, but not like it was funny. More like he couldn't believe what a dope I was. "Believe me, you're hearing this from somebody who knows. Grab every bit of life you can hold on to and never let go. Enjoy yourself, girl. You only go around once!"

"And if it turns out to be the wrong thing to do?"

He grinned. "Right or wrong, it doesn't matter. All that matters is the doing."

I wasn't so sure. I'd done the doing and all it had done was do me in. "Joel is a weasel," I said, though why I thought it important to point this out, I'm not sure. "All he left me with is emotional baggage."

"Then you should be sending him a dozen roses to thank him."

When I looked at Damon in wonder, he laughed. "Don't you get it, baby? The emotional baggage, that's what it's all about! It's what gives us our edge. It's what propels us through this lifetime. Without it, you'd be an empty shell."

"A happy empty shell."

"Are you telling me that you wish he would have stayed around?"

Instead of answering right away, I thought about the last time I'd seen Joel. That morning, I'd gotten a voice mail from our florist saying that she was sorry we wouldn't be working together and reminding me that, so close to the wedding date, there was a fifty percent cancellation fee. Baffled, I'd stopped at Joel's office to tell him about the weird call. I was just in time to hear him on the phone, telling the harpist who was scheduled to play at our reception that we wouldn't be needing her services after all.

"He's a liar and a creep." I knew this in my bones.

"And that's why you wanted to marry him?"

"Of course not! I wanted to marry him because . . ."

Try as I might, I couldn't remember why I wanted to marry Joel Panhorst, and when I admitted it, Damon's smile was sleek. "Screw this new guy," he said. "Get it out of your system."

"You're a true romantic."

"Romance is for books. This is real life." Damon rose to stand in front of me.

Call me shallow, but looking at the zipper on those tight leather pants while we were having a conversation about screwing and getting guys out of my system didn't do much for my self-composure. I stood, too. "You're cynical," I told him.

"You're scared to take a chance."

"You're awfully nosy considering none of this is any of your business."

"I know better than you do. After all, I'm dead."

"And you think—" He hadn't come right out and said it, but then I suppose an artistic type like Damon would never simply lay things on the line. We were back to the whole simile and metaphor thing, and I was left to read between the lines again. "You took that overdose because of a woman."

His eyes flashed "I told you, it was an accident. Believe me, I never took a woman that seriously. Not any woman. I just screwed them all to get it out of my system."

"Did it work?"

"No."

I hadn't expected him to be so blunt or so honest, and I wasn't prepared for any more of his advice. I knew it was better to stick to my case. "Is that why Vinnie is stealing your songs? Was he jealous? Maybe you messed with some woman you shouldn't have messed with?"

He shrugged like it was no big deal. "She was his wife. He got over it. That's not why he's channeling me. He wanted to get rich."

"Did it work?"

"Oh, come on!" Damon paced off into the darkness and back again. "Mind at Large was as big as they get. As big as the Stones or the Doors. Bigger than the Beatles for a while. Without my songs, no way they could have stayed on top of the charts that long."

"Which still doesn't explain how Vinnie makes it all happen."

Damon scraped a hand through his hair. "It all started back in sixty-five or sixty-six," he said. "We were touring in California. That's when we met Melicant and Badnor."

"They were a rock group?"

"They were witches."

"Whoa!" I put up a hand and backed away. "You're creeping me out. Are you saying—"

"That we dabbled in magic. Sure. All of us. We tried a few spells and hosted some pagan gatherings. Most of it was mildly interesting; some of it was mind-blowing. But it turned out to be like everything else. After a while, it got old. We all lost interest. Except for Vinnie."

"He's using witchcraft to make you write his songs?"

"Not witchcraft. Not exactly. At least not the kind of witchcraft we played with. Vinnie was best at it, see. We did it for fun and to see women dance naked around bonfires." He gave me a wink. "Vinnie, he was a true believer. He went a step further."

I swallowed hard. "You're talking black magic?"

When he moved, Damon's white shirt shimmered like starlight. "I guess that's what you'd call it. Whatever it is, he's wicked good at it."

"And you want me to tell him to stop?"

"I want you to tell him that whatever happened between me and his old lady, it don't matter anymore. He's got to let me leave. Before . . ." As if there was electricity sparking through them, Damon flexed his hands. "I can't be in the world and not be part of it," he said. "Not for much longer. It's killing me."

"You're already dead."

"It's killing my spirit, Pepper. Don't you see it?" He held his left hand in front of my face, and for the first time, I noticed that it looked a little different than the rest of him. I could almost see through it. "If I can't cross over soon, I'll disappear completely. Not in this world. Not in the Other World. Will you help me, Pepper?"

I didn't have a chance to say I would. An SUV coasted down the hill. The ghostbusters were back.

"Nothing up there at the monument," Brian called out to me before any of his compatriots piled out of the car. "We didn't see that other group of ghost hunters you talked about, either. We figured maybe they headed down here, so we thought we'd give it another shot. Have you seen anything?"

I refused to look at Damon. "Not a thing."

"But something's going on!" Stan's face glowed with excitement. He pointed his Geiger counter right at Damon. It crackled like a son-of-a-bitch.

Brian signaled to Angela to start taking pictures. Her flash went off in my eyes and blinded me. "Here, grab this." He shoved an electronic thermometer in my hand. "Get a reading."

I did. When my eyes adjusted to the darkness again, I saw that the spot where Damon stood was colder than the surrounding area. I flicked off the thermometer. "Not a thing," I told Brian. "And I wouldn't hang around here too long if I were you. Security makes its rounds here in another few minutes. We should all get going."

Damon got my message. While the ghostbusters were stomping around calling out readings to one another and looking as excited as can be, Damon walked off into the dark.

Stan's Geiger counter stopped making noise. He turned it off, then on again, just to see if it was working. "What happened?"

I shrugged and headed for my car and, funny, I wasn't feeling nearly as negative about this case as I had been that afternoon.

Not even the idea of talking to a guy who was really good at black magic discouraged me.

The afterglow of all Damon had told me radiated from my smile. I was smart and I was brave and I never quit.

"Come on, little girl, crave the possibilities." I sang the tune under my breath as I got in my car and pulled away. "Laugh and run, naked in verdant meadows, drunk with your power."

I was already up the hill and out the side gate that led back to the real world when the lyrics to the rest of the song hit me and caused my temperature to soar.

"Open to me. Give your body. Your soul. Your love. Your all."

Chapter 5

The next morning, I was still on top of the world.

Who could blame me!

I was smart. I was pretty. I talked to the dead and the dead talked back. Sometimes, they even sang.

Not to worry. I may have been delusional about guys in the past (Joel Panhorst being the prime example), but I wasn't headed off the deep end. I knew my relationship with Damon was going nowhere with a capital NO. But if nothing else, my little talk with him had been a wake-up call. Thanks to Damon, I remembered that I had a lot to offer, and a lot to look forward to.

I was so sure of all this that when I got home, I called Quinn.

Of course, I'd forgotten about the baseball game, and when his voice mail message clicked on and I heard the blistering rumble of his voice, I hung up. I wasn't in the mood for playing phone tag, leaving a message and waiting for him to return my call. I liked it better when I was in the driver's seat.

After all, that was where a self-reliant, fearless, in-control woman belonged.

Humming a Mind at Large song, I wheeled my Mustang into the cemetery, enjoying the splash of morning sunshine against the road. I had a meeting with Ella at nine, and after, I was doing a run-through on that tour for the fourth graders. Other than that, my calendar was free and clear, and with any luck, Ella wouldn't find a way to fill it and I'd have time to do a little sleuthing. I needed to find out more about Vinnie Pal and come up with a plan as to how I was going to approach him about Damon's problem.

After all that was taken care of . . .

Smiling at the thought, I turned into the employee parking lot and took my usual space at the far end where the shade of nearby trees would keep the Mustang cool all day. I turned off the ignition, grabbed my purse, and reached into the backseat for the plastic grocery bag that contained the Cool Whip container of salad I'd brought along for lunch. By the time I was on my way to the office, I had my plan down pat. After I took care of the details of my business life (both the cemetery part and the private investigation part), I'd get back to the personal side. I'd written Quinn's number on a sticky note and tucked it in my pocket. Later, I'd give him a call.

Old habits die hard, and when I thought about talking to Quinn, butterflies filled my stomach and threatened to erode my aplomb. I ordered them to settle down. As of last night, I reminded myself, I was a new woman, a confident woman, and everything about me said self-assured: The tilt of my chin. The swagger in my walk. Even the authoritative sound of my heels clicking against the flagstone pavement as I approached the building.

Pepper Martin was nobody's doormat. She'd never be needy or scared or wimpy. There wasn't anything in this world—or in the Other one, for that matter—that would change that. Not anything at all except—

"Joel?"

At the bottom of the steps that led into the building, I screeched to a stop and stared in stunned surprise at the man in the gray pin-striped suit who stepped into my path.

"Joel? What the hell are you doing—"

"It's nice to see you, too, Pepper."

Joel's smile was wide and genuine. He leaned in close and gave me a peck on the cheek like we were old friends.

Which, I reminded myself, we never were. Friends, that is. Our relationship had never started with casual friendship, long talks, and the kind of getting-to-know-each-other my mother always told me was essential if a man and a woman were ever going to really get along. Oh no. I'd met Joel at a friend's wedding, and the attraction was mutual, instant, and impossible to resist. Before the night was over, he'd dumped his date, I'd dumped mine, and before anybody could say, *Happily ever after*, we were at the nearest hotel having hot monkey sex.

He was a successful financial advisor who came from a family even wealthier than mine. My parents were over the moon.

I was a girl whose parents belonged to the right country club, lived in the right upscale suburb, and knew how to mingle with the best of them. It didn't hurt that my father was a plastic surgeon or that Joel's mother was something of a cosmetic surgery junkie. His parents saw it as a match made in heaven.

This, of course, was all good news, and it would have stayed that way if not for the fact that just weeks before the fairy-tale wedding I'd planned down to every last flower petal, he called things off.

I told myself not to forget it, but like I said, old habits . . .

My head knew Joel was a first-class creep who was more worried about what my dad's status as a convicted felon would do to the Panhorst reputation than he was about ruining my life.

That didn't keep my heart from skipping a beat.

"Imagine bumping into you here." My voice barely made it past the lump in my throat. Until another thought struck. "Nobody died, did they?" I asked Joel. "Oh my gosh, you're not here to—"

"Buy a plot? No, no, nothing like that." Joel waved away the idea with a dismissive gesture. I looked over his suit—expensive, his haircut—expert, and his tan—not store-bought, which meant he'd recently spent time at the family's home in Jackson Hole. No doubt, he noticed me noticing. He brushed a hand over his sandy hair. It was as thick and as wavy as ever. When he was done, every strand fell back into place. "Actually," he said, "that's not why I'm here at all."

It isn't often that I find myself at a loss for words, but I have to admit, all this came at me out of left field. The first explanation that popped into my head seemed the most preposterous. But it was the only thing that made any sense. "You're here to see me?"

Joel's smile got a little wider. He chuckled, and I remembered that in a lifetime that seemed a lifetime ago, I'd thought that sound was as rich as Joel was. I also thought it was as sexy as sin. Unfortunately, that part hadn't changed. "Of course I'm here to see you," he said. "I wonder if we could talk."

It wasn't what he said, it was the way he said it. That single word, *talk*, contained all the wallop of a lightning strike. Could anyone blame me for taking this scenario to its logical conclusion?

Joel wanted me to take him back.

The thought stuck in my brain like bubble gum on a sidewalk. My stomach flipped. My head spun. I reminded myself that these days, marriage wasn't what I wanted. Joel wasn't what I wanted.

Was he?

I stalled for time and dared another look in his direction. Because I'm so tall, I'd always liked guys who towered over me. The way I remember it, the fact that he's six four was one of the first things I'd noticed about Joel, along with his slim, runner's body and a face that wasn't as handsome as it was distinguished. He had eyes that in some light looked as if they'd been lit with blue neon. His hands were large and strong, and even though I knew this wasn't the time or the place, I couldn't help but remember that he used to give the best massages and that more often than not, what started as a loosen-up-Pepper massage turned into hot sex.

I gulped down the knot in my throat and forced

the hormone-induced bubble of excitement from my voice. "Of course we can talk. There's a picnic table out back where employees eat their lunches. Why don't we—"

"Wouldn't we be more comfortable in your office? You do have an office, don't you?"

I did, and I thought about its size, my uncomfortable guest chair, and the mess I'd left when I raided the cemetery archives for information about Damon. Not exactly the impression I wanted to make. And not exactly the place I wanted to take Joel, not when I looked over at the building and realized Ella had her nose pressed to the window of her office. No doubt, somebody told her there was a man hanging around outside and she'd already figured out that Joel and I weren't strangers. I didn't need her questions; I started toward the back of the building. Joel followed along.

My head was spinning so fast, I couldn't bring myself to say another thing until I tossed my lunch bag and my purse on the table and sat down.

A few feet away, Joel shifted from foot to foot. I could understand why. It wasn't easy for a guy with as much pride as Joel to grovel.

"So?" I leaned forward, egging him on. "How did you find me?"

He sat down on the bench next to me. "I heard you worked here. You know, from around."

The thought of our former friends gossiping about how Pepper Martin was down on her luck and working as a tour guide in a cemetery didn't cheer me. Then again, my guess was that none of our former friends talked to the dead. I was one up on them there.

I smoothed a hand over my brown wool pants and the creamy colored sweater that made my hair look more fiery than usual, and contained a grin when out of the corner of my eye, I caught Joel checking me out. "So, you knew I'd be here. And you wanted to talk," I reminded him.

"Yeah. Of course." His smile was fleeting. He rose to his feet and walked over to where a stone wall higher than his head marked the boundaries of the cemetery. When he came back again, he looked more ill-at-ease than ever. I could have been magnanimous and tried to relieve his discomfort, but let's face it, he deserved to squirm. At least a little.

Joel sat back down. "It's about our engagement," he said.

"Of course it is." I braced myself for his apology.

"You see, Pepper, it's like this . . ." Joel stood and looked down at me. "I want the ring back."

"What?" I was on my feet before I knew it, my fists on my hips, ever so grateful that he'd cut to the chase and saved me wasting any more brain cells on the possibility of getting back together with him. This was exactly what I needed to remind myself what it was I didn't like about Joel—he was a no-good, dirty, rotten rat. "You came all the way here to tell me you want me to return something that was given to me as a gift?"

"No, I came all the way over here to tell you I want back what's rightly mine."

"The ring you gave to me."

"Yes, of course I gave it to you, but Pepper . . ." I'd already turned and walked away, and Joel had to scramble to catch up. Like I said, his legs were longer than mine, and apparently all those years of tennis lessons had not been for naught. He managed to scramble in front of me and angle himself in my path. He refused to budge. "You remember the story about the ring, I know you do. You know how important that ring is to the Panhorsts."

"Yeah, yeah. So I was told. About a million and one times." Just so there was no mistake about me being sick to death of the whole thing, I rolled my eyes. "Your grandfather bought the ring at a little antique shop on the Left Bank and gave it to your grandmother as they stood at the top of the Eiffel Tower. They were married in Paris, and they were unlucky enough to still be there when the Nazis showed up. Your grandmother smuggled the ring out of the country by sewing it into the hem of her skirt. Who cares! And now that I think about it, how stupid could they have been? Who vacations in a country that's about to be conquered, anyway?"

At the risk of crinkling his Italian silk tie (blue, the exact shade of his eyes), Joel crossed his arms over his chest. "That's beside the point."

"There is no point."

"There certainly is. The ring rightfully belongs in the Panhorst family. And you're not a Panhorst."

"I'm not a Panhorst because you didn't want me to be a Panhorst. And—" When I saw him open his mouth to interrupt, I held out a hand to stop him. "Just so there's no confusion about the subject, let's get this straight right here and now. I'm thrilled not to be a Panhorst."

"Which is exactly why you shouldn't mind giving me the ring."

If there was logic somewhere in Joel's argument, I couldn't find it. Tired of even trying, I spun away from him, grabbed my purse, and reached inside. It was three days before payday and I'd already received (and spent) my monthly check from Harmony, Didi Bowman's granddaughter. The only paper money I had was a ten. I wadded it into a ball and tossed it at Joel.

"Here. You need to sell the ring to raise money, I'll save you the trouble."

His cheeks got dusky. He didn't stoop to retrieve the ten. In fact, he didn't even look at it. His voice was as icy as the look he shot my way. "I happen to be doing very well financially, thank you very much."

"And I'm so happy for you." Sarcasm dripped from my every word. "Now if you'll excuse me, I need to get to work, where, by the way, I am doing very well, too."

"Yeah, right. As a tour guide in a cemetery."

Joel's voice chilled me to the bone. Which wasn't easy considering that my temper shot to the stars and my temperature went along with it. I had never been particularly proud of making my living by leading tours through a cemetery, but at least it was an honest living. (Except, of course, for the part about briefly being on the mob payroll.)

Besides, there was more to my life than leading tours. I was a private investigator, damn it. And a damned good one, to boot. I somehow managed to keep my voice to less than a roar. "You've got a lot of nerve criticizing me. If it wasn't for you dumping me—"

"If it wasn't for your father breaking the law—"

"—I'd never be here in the first place."

"—I never would have had to suffer the embarrassment of associating with your family."

"And just so you know, buster, I do a whole lot more around here than just—"

"Leading little old ladies on sweet, little tours! It's such a come-down, Pepper. You can understand why people are talking. I mean, it's incomprehensible—"

"—that you would show up here and demand my ring back. Just because you can't—"

"—that you have to do this to make ends meet. Incomprehensible and strangely, sad. And just so you know that you can keep your money, that I don't need it, I don't want the ring so I can—"

"—sell it? Of course that's what you want to do. So don't try to lay a guilt trip on me about good ol' Grandma and Grandpa Panhorst. You're going to head to the nearest jeweler to make a quick buck. And in case you're wondering how I know, there's no mystery there. All you care about is money. It's all you've ever cared about. Why else would you want the stupid ring now?"

"So I can give it to my new fiancée."

Temper or no temper, this stopped me cold. Not that I cared that Joel was engaged to someone who wasn't me. Honest. If nothing else, this visit from him had served to remind me of all the reasons I didn't want to be engaged to Joel. Or to anybody else. But, damn, even though I knew this on an intellectual level, it was a little hard to integrate it emotionally.

Of course, the fact that I staggered as if I'd been kicked in the stomach was exactly the response Joel was hoping for. When he saw my mouth drop open, his expression was less smile than smirk.

"I see you still care," he said.

"Like hell."

"Which is why you look so upset."

"There's a difference between upset and surprised." I poked a thumb at my own face. "What you see here is surprise. I can't believe any woman would want a creep like you."

"You did."

"Temporary insanity."

"Right. You would have gone through with the wedding. If I didn't call it off."

"For which I am eternally grateful."

"Then you can show your appreciation by handing over the ring."

Before I left the house that morning, I'd pulled my hair back and wound it into a braid. Which was the only thing that kept me from pulling it out. It didn't stop me from screeching, though.

"You are the most annoying man on the face of the earth." I was pretty sure I'd mentioned this to Joel a time or two before, but there was no harm in reminding him. "I told you, the ring was given to me. That makes it mine. You can't take something that's mine and give it to . . . to . . ."

"Simone Burnside." Joel reached into his back pocket for his wallet and flipped it open to show me a photo of the happy couple. Simone looked to be about a foot shorter than me, a tiny blond with a feathery smile, a porcelain complexion, and an outfit that cost what I made in two months' time. When he added the icing to the cake, Joel's smile got wider. "Simone is an attorney. She's a partner at Smith, Hoover, and Burnside."

"I'm so happy for you," I said, even though I didn't mean it. "Now get lost." This I did mean, and to prove it, I aimed a look at Joel that would have frightened off a smarter man.

Joel wasn't dumb, but I should have remembered that when it came to assets, he was as tenacious as can be. It was one of the things that made him such a good financial advisor. And such a bad fiancé.

"The ring is mine," Joel said. "I'm going to give it to Simone. Our engagement party is next month, and come hell or high water, I'm going to present the ring to her there. I promised her, Pepper, and I'm not going to let down my fiancée."

"That's a first."

"And that's a low blow."

"Not as low as canceling a wedding before you tell the bride."

Maybe it was starting to sink in. The color drained out of Joel's face. "You mean you're going to make Simone suffer for what I did? That's unconscionable, Pepper."

I was cheered by the thought. "It is, isn't it?" For the first time since Joel Panhorst ambushed me, I smiled with all sincerity. I gave him a biff on the arm. "Buck up, chum. It's not like I'm trying to ruin your life like you ruined mine. It's just that . . . well, heck! I couldn't give that ring back even if I wanted to. You see, the minute you told me the wedding was off, I sold it."

Tan or no tan, the color drained from Joel's face. Like a walleye pulled from Lake Erie, his mouth opened and closed in silent horror. "S-s-sold?"

"Hell, yes! What else was I supposed to do? My dad was in jail. The man who was supposed to love and cherish me made it clear his reputation was more important to him than I was. My family's assets were gone. But then . . ." I think Joel was too horrified to notice my wide-eyed, innocent expression, but I gave it my best shot, anyway. "But then, you know that part, don't you? After the Martin family reputation and bank accounts were kaput, so was any interest you ever had in me. That's why you dropped me like a bad habit."

"But . . . but sold? You sold my grandmother's ring? Maybe it isn't too late to get it back. Where did you take it? What jeweler?"

Laughing, I grabbed my lunch bag and my purse, and this time when I marched away, Joel was too stunned to stop me. "No place you'd ever shop. No place you ever heard of, either. Stopped at the first jewelry store I could find," I said. "Got a fast couple thousand for the ring, too."

"Couple thousand?" His Adam's apple bobbed. "For a three-carat diamond?"

On my way by, I slapped him on the back. "Hey, a girl's got to do what a girl's got to do."

"But Pepper . . ."

I was already past Joel, and I could afford to respond to the desperation in his voice. I turned.

"But Pepper," he said, "that ring is a family heirloom!"

My smile was firmly in place when I left him with my parting shot. "Lucky for me, it's not my family!"

The authoritative tone of my voice crackling in the air, I walked away as quickly as I could. After all, I didn't want to ruin the moment, and it would have been a real shame if Joel caught wind of the fact that even as the sarcasm was still dripping from my lips, my newly bolstered self-esteem was plummeting.

But then, discovering that the man she was once engaged to has gotten over her and gotten on with his life while hers was as still and stagnant as pond water has a way of doing that to a girl.

So did finding out that the woman who was now the woman in his life was prettier, wealthier, far more successful, and wasn't stuck working in a cemetery.

She was probably better in bed, too.

My self-confidence made a *splat* sound when it hit rock bottom.

There was a trash can near the front door of the office building. Right before I went inside, I wadded up the sticky note where I'd written Quinn's phone number.

I threw it away.

Chapter 6

I spent the rest of that morning reminding myself that Simone the Size Zero Successful Attorney was welcome to Joel.

This was the God's honest truth. I knew it in my heart of hearts.

But try as I might, it was a little harder to convince the rest of me. Especially my ego.

Still, I managed to get by. I deflected her motherly but nosy questions about the man in the pinstriped suit and made it through my meeting with Ella. I slogged through my practice freed-slaves tour. As far as I could tell, no one at Garden View was the wiser about what had really happened out by the picnic table that morning: Pepper Martin had been hit over the head with the ugly truth. Her life was going nowhere. Her job was the object of ridicule, far and wide. Her love life was nonexistent.

And she wasn't willing to take a chance on changing any of it.

Why?

The answer is simple enough.

The visit from Joel had been a sobering reminder

that when I put my heart on the line, it invariably ends up getting smashed, mashed, and bashed.

By the time lunchtime rolled around and I pulled out my salad and a bottle of low-fat dressing I kept in the refrigerator in the employee break room, I knew I needed a time-out from feeling sorry for myself—and there's nothing like a little detecting to take my mind off my troubles.

Salad bowl and plastic fork in hand, I closed my office door, logged onto the Internet, and Googled Vinnie Pallucci's name. I had yet to formulate a plan, so I really wasn't sure what I was looking for. What I got, however, was thousands of hits, from sites that featured Vinnie Pal's baby pictures to ones that recounted his three divorces. In detail. But it was one of the newest listings that caught my eye.

The Granddaddy of Rock, an entry from the Rock Hall site said. *The life and times of Mind at Large with music legend Vinnie Pallucci.*

I clicked over to the proper page, scanned the information, and for the first time since Joel asked for his engagement ring back, my mood brightened.

Because it looked like Vinnie Pal was scheduled to be in town long before Halloween and the big Mind at Large concert at the Rock Hall. In fact, as part of the Hall's community and music education efforts, he'd be spending the next three Wednesday evenings in a classroom setting, talking about the group and its influence on modern rock.

In an effort to prove to myself that my life wasn't as pathetic as I feared, I took my calendar from my purse and checked it against the dates listed for the class.

My calendar was empty. My life was as pathetic as I feared.

But for once, my lack of a social life worked to my advantage.

I grabbed my credit card and signed right up.

I was headed to the School of Hard Rock, and a chance for a little one-on-one with Vinnie Pal.

I'm not sure what I expected. Hippies, I guess. Love bead–laden, barefoot, and smelling of pot and patchouli.

Which was why I was surprised when I walked into the classroom at the Rock Hall designed to seat a hundred or more and found twenty or so nicely dressed, middle-aged men and women who looked like the friends my mom and dad played golf and tennis with at the country club. (That was, of course, before the feds put the cuffs on Dad, every one of their so-called friends vanished, and Mom fled to Florida to put a couple of thousand miles between herself and her disgrace.)

Imagine my surprise ratcheting up a notch when I realized one of them wasn't as stylishly frumpy as the others. It was the long-haired, skinny woman I'd seen cleaning Damon's exhibit the day I met him. She had a seat front row and center, and she was sipping from a cup that said *City Roast* on the side of it.

Yeah, yeah, I know. It was what we in the trade call a clue. Or at least what I should have/would have called a clue if I'd been paying attention. As it was, I was a little late and more than a little preoccupied feeling conspicuous. Earlier in the day I had decided that it was probably best not to look like I was there to try and find a way to destroy the reputation of a man who owned a half dozen Grammys, but by the time I thought of it, I was dressed and out of my apartment and it was already too late. In black pants, a brilliant green sweater, and stilettos that added three inches to my height, I stood out in the crowd.

I excused myself past a couple seated on the aisle and found a chair in the center of a row. I got myself settled just as a hall employee walked to the front of the room to give a brief overview and introduction.

"I always hated school."

I wasn't surprised to find Damon in the empty chair next to mine. This was the first he'd shown himself since the day I signed up for the class, and that was fine with me. With a little time and a whole lot of you-go-girl pep talking, I was finally far enough removed from the sting of Joel's visit to act as if the only thing on my mind was my case. Anxious to present my plan, I pretended I was rummaging through my purse when I answered him.

"Doesn't matter if you like school or not. This is perfect!"

"Vinnie's going to be here?"

"He's the guest of honor." Even if the place wasn't crowded, there was only so long I could keep looking through my purse and mumbling and not attract attention. I pulled out a notebook and a pen and scrawled a message to Damon.

I'm going to try and talk to him after class.

"That's good." Damon didn't have to worry about being overheard. He stretched his legs out in front of him, his arm thrown across the back of the empty chair to his left. Our nearest neighbor was a woman two seats down, and though Damon wasn't close, he was apparently close enough. She shivered and slipped on a sweater decorated with pumpkins and teddy bears in witch hats. "What are you going to say to him?"

This was a question I'd been asking myself ever since I plunked down my hard-earned dollars for the class. I didn't have a fleshed-out plan, but I had the beginnings of one.

I'm going to start by telling him I think he's the most fabulous singer in the whole world.

Damon made a face. "He's not."

A little flattery may get me a long way.

"Or it will swell his head bigger than ever."

He deserves it. He's a star.

"He's a fraud."

I have to tell him I'm a fan. It's the only way.

"Then what?"

My shrug pretty much said it all, but I added, *I have to talk to him. Alone.* I underlined this last word. *I have to show him—*

"Ladies and gentlemen . . ." The man at the front of the room made a sweeping gesture toward the door. "Vinnie Pal! Mr. Vinnie Pallucci!"

I'm not much for standing ovations, but it was join the crowd or miss my first chance for a look at Vinnie Pal.

Who didn't look like the guy I'd seen on the poster out in the lobby at all.

I gave myself a mental slap. The first guy through the door was big, black, and as beefy as a professional wrestler. He was dressed in a dark suit and he was wearing Ray-Bans. He yanked them off and scanned the crowd.

Security. Of course. Apparently, the coast was clear. The security guy waved toward the hallway.

That's when the real Vinnie Pal walked in.

There's a difference between seeing a photo of a star or watching him prance around on stage at the MTV Music Awards and seeing him from just a few feet away. While most of the crowd was clapping politely and some folks were snapping pictures, I took the opportunity to give Vinnie Pal the once-over.

He was shorter than me, wearing jeans that looked as if they could stand a good washing and, in spite of the chilly weather outside, a gray, short-sleeved polo shirt. His gut bulged over his belt. Considering his age, I suspected that his dark hair was more a product of chemistry than it was of genetics. You'd think a guy who had his bucks would spring for a better stylist. A shampoo wouldn't have hurt, either. Vinnie Pal's hair hung limp over his shoulders.

"Black magic, huh?" The crowd was loud, so I didn't have to worry about anyone overhearing me. I turned to Damon. "He doesn't look like a sorcerer."

"What does a sorcerer look like?"

I shook my head. "Not like that. I thought he'd be . . . I don't know . . . scary. Or at least tough and edgy. He looks like somebody's old, drunk uncle."

"Looks can be deceiving."

I had no doubt of that. But before I had a chance to say any more, Vinnie put both arms in the air, a signal to the crowd to settle down.

"Thank you! Thank you very much!" he called out, as loud and as enthusiastic as if he was center stage in some arena and there were thousands of fans screaming for him. He took a seat in front of the room. "You're fabulous!" He glanced around. Was it my imagination? I could have sworn that when he saw the skinny lady with the coffee cup, he paused to give her a second look.

I leaned in close to Damon when I spoke, and with a tip of my head, indicated the cleaning woman in the front row. "Who is she?"

Damon looked. But not for long. He shook his head. "I've never seen her before."

"But Vinnie has. He knows her."

We didn't have a chance to discuss it further. Vinnie went right on studying the crowd. When he came to the spot where Damon was sitting, his eyes narrowed and lit with interest. I wondered if there was something about his black magic that made it possible for him to see Damon. Until I realized that he wasn't looking at Damon at all. Vinnie was staring at me. I slid Damon a sidelong look that told him I suddenly had a plan and sat up a little straighter. The posture played hell with my back muscles, but it gave Vinnie Pal a good look and allowed me to give him a smile.

It wasn't easy to hold the pose, but it was worth it. Time and again while Vinnie droned on and on about the first years of being a member of Mind at Large, his gaze returned to me. He was older-than-middle-aged, overweight, and like I said, the hair left a whole lot to be desired.

Every time he looked my way, I twinkled like a star-struck groupie.

Class ended with the promise to continue with the band's history the next week, and with Vinnie occupied shaking hands and signing autographs, I finally had a chance to relax.

"You're not going to throw yourself at him, are you?"

It was the first thing Damon had said since right after class started, and I couldn't blame him for sounding pissed. Dead or alive, rock stars are all about causing a scene, and Damon didn't like sitting there—invisible—while Vinnie Pal took all the credit for Mind at Large's success. Not that Damon's part in the group's rise had been entirely forgotten. In the question and answer session that followed class, the skinny lady had asked about Damon. Twice. Both times, Vinnie had prefaced his answer with a shake of his head.

"Sad," he'd said, "that Damon wasted his life like that. He had potential. He could have made something of himself."

"He sings in his grave." There was a murmur in response to this comment from the woman. "He shines. Like a sun. And the worms feast on his heart."

Vinnie made a face. Like anyone could blame him? Big points for him, he managed a smile. "You're right, some people are like fireflies. They shine bright, then flicker out. Damon did some good work—"

Damon grumbled a curse.

"—but his talent never had a chance to mature."

Thinking it better not to bring up the fact that Damon might be feeling a little touchy about all this, I grabbed my purse, clutched my notebook to my chest, and stood, waiting for the people nearest the aisle to clear out. After all that talk about Damon and worms—yes, just thinking about it made me queasy—I wasn't surprised to see the skinny woman wait for her chance for a little one-on-one with Vinnie. They exchanged a few words before she hightailed it out the door.

I watched her go, then, my teeth clenched around my words, I turned to Damon.

"I'm not going to throw myself at Vinnie," I told him, careful to keep my voice down. "When I smiled at him during class, I was just being friendly. I'm going to need to keep being friendly if there's any hope of talking to him in private."

I looked at Vinnie, old and bloated and tired.

I looked at Damon, young, gorgeous, and as sexy as any dead guy I'd ever met.

"This would be easier if you weren't around," I told him, and I didn't give him a chance to argue. As I took my place in line to meet Vinnie, I shooed Damon to the door.

I can't say for sure if he left or not, I only know that when it was my turn to step into the glow of Vinnie's fame, Damon was nowhere around.

Vinnie stuck out his hand, and when I shook it, he held on to mine a little too long. "So, what's a hot little chicky like you doing here?" As pickup lines went, it was lame, but when I had to, I could simper with the best of them.

It worked. Vinnie looked me up and down. I guess he approved because his smile got as wide as his waistline. "You a rock and roll fan?"

"I'm a Mind at Large fan."

"Come on." He tried for modest, but years in the spotlight had eliminated any chance of that. "We were big before you were ever born."

"You're still big." How I managed to make it sound like I was talking about Vinnie's reputation and not his stomach, I don't know. "I have every one of your CDs," I added. "I know the lyrics to every song you've ever written. Especially the new stuff. You're a genius."

Vinnie didn't disagree. He signaled to the bodyguard who was over near the door tapping his foot and looking at his watch that we'd be another minute. "So . . ." He skimmed another look from the top of my head to the tips of my shoes, pausing at where I had my notebook pressed to my heart. "You ever meet a rock singer before?"

"Not one as famous as you." I made sure my voice was breathy with excitement. "Mind at Large . . . you guys are gods!"

Okay, so I was laying it on a little thick. That didn't justify Damon hissing in my ear. Since I assumed he was long gone, I flinched. My shoe caught on the leg of the nearest chair, and I would have gone down like a stone if Vinnie didn't grab by arm to keep me from falling.

He settled me and made sure he gave me a thousand-watt smile before he bent to retrieve the notebook that had tumbled to the floor. "You're not going to faint or anything, are you?" he asked. "I mean, girls sometimes do that when they meet me, but you don't look the type who . . ."

Vinnie's comment faded. That was because when he picked it up, my notebook opened to the page where I'd written my replies to Damon.

"Hey! You write poetry." He grinned. "And son of a bitch! It looks like it's about me."

Out loud, he read the comments I'd made to Damon. "*I'm going to try and talk to him after class.*

"*I'm going to start by telling him I think he's the most fabulous singer in the whole world.*

"*A little flattery may get me a long way.*

"*He deserves it. He's a star.*

"*I have to tell him I'm a fan. It's the only way.*

"*I have to talk to him. Alone.*

"*I have to show him—*"

The smoldering look in Vinnie's eyes intensified. He shuffled a little closer and lowered his voice. "Hey there, sugar baby, you didn't finish. You didn't say what you're going to show me when we're alone."

It wasn't easy, but I giggled like the star-struck fan I was supposed be. "We're going to have to be alone before you know that," I said.

That pretty much sealed the deal; we agreed to go for drinks.

Vinnie said he'd have his driver (he indicated the bodyguard, who apparently did double duty) take us over to Synergy, a popular Warehouse District bar, but I wasn't ready for that much up-close-and-personal. I made up an excuse about getting my car out of the lot where it was parked before ten when the lot closed and promised I'd meet him in thirty minutes. I was already out of the classroom and on my way to the bar when the enormity of what had just happened hit me.

For the second time in a week, I had a date with a rock star.

Only this one wasn't dead.

Because it was a weeknight, Synergy wasn't nearly as crowded as I'd seen it on Fridays and Saturdays. Still, the music was loud and the folks who were there—well-dressed young professionals, for the most part—needed to shout at one another to be heard. When Vinnie came back from the bar with our drinks, he slid into the booth next to me.

The charitable Pepper liked to believe he was being considerate, that he knew we'd have to sit close to hear each other. The practical Pepper knew it was no accident when his thigh rubbed up against mine.

I scooted a little closer to the wall on my right.

Vinnie didn't take it personally. But then, something told me he was biding his time. He knew better than anyone that rock stars didn't have to beg. Not for anything.

He took a drink, and when he was done, he stared at the scotch—straight up—in his glass. "If my doctor saw me with this," he said, sliding an arm across the back of the booth, "she'd have my head."

It was one thing pretending to be a fan, but I was willing to sacrifice only so much. I managed a sympathetic smile and slid a bit farther away. "Something tells me you're not the type who worries about what doctors say."

Vinnie took a long gulp. "Used to be true. These days, doctors and attorneys, they're the ones I spend most of my time with."

"Not an attorney named Simone, I hope."

I was going for funny, but of course, Vinnie didn't know that. He swallowed down the rest of his drink, and when the bartender looked our way, he signaled for another. When he was done and turned back to me, his smile inched up a notch. "But then, a gorgeous girl like you, you don't want to hear about things like doctors and lawyers, do you?" He leaned nearer. I leaned back. "You want to know all about me."

I hoped he wasn't talking *know* in the biblical sense, but hey, who was I kidding? I deflected the thought with a little fan rah-rah. "I've got tickets for the big concert," I told him. Yes, it was a lie, but Vinnie didn't know it, and I didn't want him to think I was angling for a trade, a couple of his backstage passes in exchange for—

I gulped back my disgust at the picture that popped into my head and told him, "I know so much about the band! I'm thrilled you're all going to be in town."

"Not going to be." The waitress who brought his drink over was years older than the bartender. She recognized Vinnie right off the bat, and her eyes went wide. Vinnie grinned and gave her a wink. "We're already here," he told me. "All of us. Since we're scattered all over the universe these days, it seemed easier to meet up here before the concert. You know, so we could do some promotions. We're recording a new CD, too." He wiggled his eyebrows. "I can get you a copy before it hits the shelves. And it won't cost you hardly anything at all." He slid a look to my green sweater. "And what you'll get in return . . . baby, I can promise you a time to remember!"

If I sat there doing nothing, I was going to barf, so I grabbed my sour apple martini and took a sip. A very small sip. The vodka helped lubricate my smile. "A copy of the new CD, wow. Maybe I can pick it up at class next week."

"Maybe you could come back to the place I'm staying. Bernie's waiting out in the car, and it's got a big mother of a backseat. He won't watch us in the rearview mirror. At least not too much." By now, I had no room left for retreat, so when Vinnie lowered his voice and leaned even closer, I was trapped like the proverbial dirty rat. "It's a short drive to Winton Place," he said. "You know, over on the Gold Coast. Once we're done in the car, we'll do it again up in the penthouse."

"That would be terrific." Was that my voice? I wondered if Vinnie recognized the difference between breathy/bowled over and breathy/disgusted. I'd have to keep him guessing for a little while longer if I hoped to accomplish anything. "If not tonight, maybe I can stop by sometime and—"

"Any time, baby. Day or night." He gave me a wink. "I'll leave word with the doorman to let you up."

I took another drink and skimmed a finger over the table in a lazy, figure-eight pattern designed to attract his attention so Vinnie would stop staring at my chest. "Before we do that, though, I'd like to talk about something. Something important."

"You talk, I'll listen. Right after I'm done kissing you."

I braced myself, but before Vinnie had a chance to make good on the threat, I was saved thanks to the arrival of the waitress who'd brought over Vinnie's drink earlier. This time she came with one of the cooks and a couple of other patrons who were apparently old (or drunk) enough to be convinced they were in the presence of rock and roll greatness.

Believe me, I didn't mind one bit when all those blubbering fans made Vinnie forget all about me. In fact, I sat back and breathed a sigh of relief.

While I wondered how to get Vinnie back on track and talking about Damon, I watched the circus. The waitress kissed Vinnie. The cook slapped him on the back. Both the other patrons asked him to autograph their cocktail napkins, and one of them had a digital camera and insisted on sitting next to Vinnie for a picture. Glory and hallelujah! I saw my way out.

"You don't want me in the picture!" I chirped and made a move to slide out of the booth. I should have known Vinnie wasn't going to make it easy. Instead of moving, he just grinned and patted his lap. My only way out was over him.

I won't elaborate on the experience; let's just say that I was grateful to fight my way through the crowd. I managed not to shudder until I was over near the bar, where I grabbed the nearest empty stool and decided to get going while the getting was good.

Was I giving up on my investigation?

No way, but something told me Vinnie would be too busy with his fans for a while to talk about Damon, and besides, I thought it best to catch him another day. Like when he wasn't drinking. Or when he wasn't all set to toss me in the sack.

I had just reached into my purse for my car keys when I caught a movement just on the other side of the big window that looked out onto the street. On a weekend, I never would have noticed, but like I said, it was pretty quiet around there, and it was the first I'd seen anyone walk by. When I swiveled to get a better look, my breath caught in my throat.

"Holy shit!" By that time, the man I'd seen had already walked by. No matter, I'd recognize that face anywhere. It was Dan Callahan. Yes, the same Dan Callahan who had me believing he was conducting brain research at a local hospital—until I found out no one there knew him and the space I thought was his office was really a broom closet. He was the guy who had bushwhacked me at a costume gala and shown me that photograph of me talking to two ghosts.

I hadn't seen Dan since the fateful event, but of course, that didn't mean he hadn't been around. If I'd learned nothing else in the last months, it was that people were always following me. Some, because they liked me. Some, because they wanted something from me. Some of the others wanted to kill me. At this point, I wasn't sure which category Dan fell into, and I wasn't willing to take any chances. I slid off the barstool and headed toward the ladies' room.

But I didn't go inside.

Just as I hoped, there was a back door nearby. My fingers crossed that opening it wouldn't set off some kind of alarm, I slipped outside and down an alley that led to the street. My timing was perfect. I stepped onto the sidewalk just as Dan got there.

Was he surprised? It was kind of hard to tell. The light of a nearby street lamp winked against the lenses of Dan's wire-rimmed glasses and made it impossible for me to see his eyes.

"Hello, Pepper." Dan and I are just about the same height, but in my towering stilettos, I had the advantage. He backed up a step to get a better look at me. "You look terrific. Imagine running into you here."

"Yeah, imagine. I don't know why you'd be surprised since you've been following me around."

"Have I?" He pushed his glasses up the bridge of his nose.

One of the things I haven't mentioned about Dan is that he's as cute as they come. He's also a mighty good kisser. These were things I tried not to think about as I took a gander at him in his tight jeans and black leather jacket. I had enough on my mind without adding lust into the mix. I told myself not to forget it, and in an effort to look intimidating, I crossed my arms over my chest. "What are you up to?" I asked him.

When he shrugged, his jacket made a crinkly sound. "Out for a walk." He slipped his arm through mine. "You want to go for coffee?"

"No." I untangled myself and stepped back and out of his reach. "What I want is answers. What do you want?"

"Me? Nothing."

"Something. You're the one who showed up at that party and showed me a picture of me talking to two ghosts."

There was no mistaking the smile that tugged at the corners of his mouth. "Did I ever say they were ghosts?"

Dan was right, and I could have kicked myself. I clambered to hide the faux pas beneath a little righteous indignation. "You implied it," I told him.

He grinned. "Never happened."

"You meant to imply it."

"Never did."

"Then why did you bother to show me that photo in the first place? And how the hell did you even take a picture like that? Nobody has the equipment to take pictures of gh—" He wasn't going to catch me in my own words again. I backed up and started again. "Nobody has the equipment to take pictures that good through windows. And you did take it through a window, didn't you? When I was in the library at the Bowman house. You were spying on me."

"Don't be ridiculous." Like when I first met him at the hospital when I went to the ER after I clunked my head on Gus Scarpetti's mausoleum, Dan's hair was past needing to be cut. It was shaggy, and when he shook his head, it fell in his eyes. He brushed it back with one hand. "I'm not spying on you, and I'm not following you."

"Which is how you got that picture. By not spying on me and not following me."

"I had to take the picture, Pepper. You wouldn't have listened to me otherwise."

"I'm not listening to you now."

"But you should be. You're messing with things you shouldn't be. You're dealing with—"

"Powers I can't possibly understand. Yeah, yeah. Whatever. That sounds like a line from a really bad horror movie. So instead of wasting your time and mine, why not just cut to the chase. You think I know something about ghosts, and you wouldn't think I know something about ghosts if you didn't know something about ghosts yourself. Is that why you're following me? To find out what I know? Or are you just planning to show up now and again to mumble cockamamie warnings, then disappear into the night?"

"My warnings aren't cockamamie. I know what I'm talking about."

"Really?" My voice was suddenly thoughtful, and that was no surprise. An idea had just occurred to me. Maybe running into Dan was a good thing, after all. "Do you know anything about black magic?"

It was Dan's turn to be surprised. He took a minute to think about my question. "You're not messing with—"

"I'm not messing with anything. I'm looking for information. If you know so much about the Other Side—"

"Which I never said I did."

"And you never said you didn't."

Dan groaned. Like he had a headache, he tipped his head back and rolled it from side to side. "We need to talk," he said. Once again, he wrapped his arm through mine.

And once again, I so wasn't in the mood to be treated like I had to be led around. I batted his hand away.

As confrontations went, it wasn't much, but at that moment, a black-and-white police patrol car just happened to cruise by. The cop riding shotgun rolled down his window. "You all right?" he asked me.

"I'm fine," I assured him, and I knew I would be, too, because even before the cops left, Dan was back-stepping his way into the alley.

"Magic isn't a game," he said. "You've got to be careful, Pepper. Very careful. Or somebody's going to get hurt."

And with that cockamamie warning, he disappeared into the night.

By the time I got home, I'd had it. With my investigation. With my failure to get any useful information out of Vinnie Pal. And with men.

Especially with men.

I kicked off my shoes just inside the front door, flicked on the living room light, and wished I'd finished the rest of that sour apple martini. Maybe it would have helped drown the niggling voices in my head. The ones that reminded me I was too chicken to call Quinn. And too confused by Dan and his messages of doom. And way too grossed out to try and contact Vinnie any time soon.

And then, of course, there was Joel.

It wasn't like I cared, I told myself, but that didn't keep me from sighing. Or from heading into my bedroom. I didn't like to mire myself in the past, but there were some nights just made for a little self-pity.

This was one of them.

I turned on the light and sat cross-legged on the floor in front of my dresser to open the bottom drawer. Under my wool sweaters and a pair of silk long underwear my mother insisted I'd be happy to have once the icy winds of a Cleveland winter started to blow, was a wooden box decorated with a smiling, yellow sun. I pulled out the box, opened it up, and reached inside.

I sat back and stared at the object in my hand.

The light of my lamp glinted against Grandma Panhorst's three-carat, Nazi-defying diamond. That's right, my engagement ring.

Chapter 7

"You told him you sold that ring."

You'd think by now I'd be used to people (or at least people who used to be people) popping in and out of my life. And I was. Mostly.

Unless they happened to pop up in my bedroom.

At the sound of the voice, I leaped to my feet and spun around. My mouth dropped open and I stared at the woman who was standing near my bedroom door.

I'd know that pink housecoat anywhere, the cigarette dangling from between two fingers, and the nails that were polished a shade of red that rivaled the color of a city fire truck. There was no mistaking the steel gray hair that had been rolled and teased and sprayed into submission, the face, as wrinkled as an old blanket, or the vivid red lipstick applied, as always, with an expert hand and a dare-to-tell-me-this-doesn't-look-good attitude. The color was as thick as clotted cream and shaped into an impossible point where her top lip bowed.

She was the last person anyone would have suspected had millions, but I knew better. Her own family had started in the grocery business selling vegetables out of handcarts and had ended up owning a mega-chain of stores on the East Coast. Her husband had made a killing going door to door back in the days when aluminum siding was synonymous with the American Dream. The frowsy housewife look was a cover-up for a razor-sharp mind, a determination that gave *iron-willed* a whole new meaning, and a personality that was as pragmatic as her taste in clothes was dubious.

"Grandma Panhorst?" My voice was sharp with disbelief. I blinked my eyes, but of course, that didn't change anything. "Grandma, what the hell are you doing here? You've been dead for nearly a year!"

"As if that makes a difference?"

She was right. Which didn't keep me from stammering, "You're . . . you're buried in New York."

"New York, Schmoo York." She waved away the info. Cigarette smoke tickled my nose. "I was bored."

"So you came to Cleveland?"

"I stayed with my ring."

It was the first I remembered that I still had the diamond ring clutched in my hand. I looked down at where it sparkled against my palm and immediately went on the defensive. "I meant to sell it," I told her.

In typical Grandma Panhorst fashion, her only reply was a stare that had been known to cut folks down at twenty paces.

I had seen the look so many times, I was immune. Almost. "I did mean to sell it," I insisted, and I lifted my chin in an attempt to convince her—and myself—that there was at least a chance of standing up to her. "I would have done it, too, but I've been busy."

"Too busy to make a fast buck? Even when you really needed it?" Grandma plunked down on my bed. She tapped the ash from her cigarette, and I saw it drop away, but instead of hitting the floor, it simply disappeared. "You should know better. You can't bullshit me."

"I'm not trying." I was. She knew that. I knew she knew. It didn't stop me from making one last valiant effort to cling to my dignity. "I would have sold it in a heartbeat, but—"

"But you didn't." There was that look again.

I could withstand it only so long. I flopped down on my bed, grabbed one of my pillows, and hugged it close, trying to figure out how to explain to Grandma what I couldn't explain to myself.

She didn't give me a chance. Grandma took a long drag on her cigarette and let the smoke out through her nose. "You're better off without him, you know," she said. "Joel, he was never good enough for you."

"You couldn't have told me that before you died?"

Just like when she was alive, her face was coated with foundation a couple of shades darker than her skin tone. When she grinned, the makeup left a fissure on each side of her mouth. "Even if I told you, you wouldn't have listened. You had to find it out for yourself."

"And I found out the hard way."

A little pity would have been appreciated, but Grandma never expected any, and she sure never doled out any. She chuckled. "You never would have believed me if I told you my only grandson was a son of a bitch."

"You're right." I squeezed the pillow a little tighter, thinking of everything that had happened since Joel walked back into my life. "Do you think I should give the ring back to him?" I asked her.

She lifted one shoulder. Her version of a shrug. "Give it back. Sell it. Keep it tucked away and never wear it. Nobody can tell you what to do. This is another thing you have to figure out for yourself."

"You came all the way back from the dead to tell me that?"

Grandma was indifferent. "I told you, I stayed with the ring. You never even would have known I was here if you left it alone and didn't bring it out so you could feel a little sorry for yourself."

When I didn't dispute her take on the situation, she breezed right on. "And by the way, just for the record, I never kept the ring anyplace so conspicuous. A pretty little box hidden under your sweaters? It's the first place a burglar would look. Me?" Grandma lifted one leg. She was wearing the pink, fuzzy slippers she used to slip on to shuffle around the house. "When I wasn't wearing the ring, I kept it in the toe of my right slipper. When I was wearing my slippers, the ring went into the pocket of the robe I hung behind the bedroom door!" She laughed and coughed. "Good thing I gave the ring to Joel to give to you before I died. My slippers went to the Salvation Army with the rest of my things. The ring would have gone with them. So . . ." She sucked in the last drag from her cigarette and flicked the butt away. I knew I wouldn't find it lying around. "What are you going to do?"

"About the ring, you mean?"

Grandma raised brows that had been plucked into a thin line, then darkened with eyebrow pencil. "About the ring. About Joel. About that rock star you've been hanging around with."

I didn't ask if she was referring to Damon or Vinnie Pal. It didn't much matter. My silence pretty much said it all.

"Listen . . ." Don't ask me where they came from, but Grandma suddenly had a new cigarette in one hand and a green plastic Bic lighter in the other. She used the cigarette to point my way. "You've got to make some pretty important decisions, Pepper. Don't rush into anything."

I looked down at the ring. "You mean about this."

"I mean about everything. Not just about the ring, about your life. You don't think it's going to get any easier, do you?"

This was not something I wanted to hear and I told her so, but instead of trying to bolster my spirits, Grandma just flicked her Bic and lit her cigarette. "Not up to you," she said, dragging in a breath. "Never is. It's the one thing I've learned since I passed. That and the fact that life is a messy business. A lot like love."

"Love?" As far as I knew, that wasn't something we were talking about. "You don't think I'm still in love with Joel, do you?"

She smiled, and even as I watched, she shimmered, as if I was looking at her through the heated air around a fire. "I told you, he was never good enough for you."

"Then if not Joel, who? Quinn? Dan?" Confused, I plunked my head down into my pillow. As far as I knew, Grandma Panhorst couldn't have had the inside track on my relationship with either Quinn or Dan. Even I didn't have the inside track. Quinn was impossible to read. Dan was a complete mystery. And she couldn't have been talking about—

"Damon?" My head came up.

I looked over to where Grandma had been sitting.

Had been being the operative words.

Didn't it figure? Just when I needed answers, she was gone in a *pouf*! I pounded my pillow and grumbled my opinion of my Gift.

Because of the first ghost in my life, the mob had tried to kill me. Because of the second one, I almost got tossed off a bridge. The third one filled my head with song lyrics and fired my imagination, and my libido. A couple of others had just been pests.

And this one?

Shit, this one was bound and determined to make me think about my life, the choices I'd already made and the ones I still had in front of me.

You'd think talking to the dead would be good for something useful like getting the inside track on lottery numbers. Or advance notice of what was going to be on the sale rack at White House Black Market.

What did I get?

Advice that wasn't exactly advice.

Oh yeah, and a bedroom that smelled like cigarette smoke.

"So, how was it?"

I had been thinking about my visit from Grandma Panhorst and the can of Oust I'd used to clear the air in my bedroom before I left my apartment for the office.

What Damon was talking about was anybody's guess.

I tossed my purse down on my desk along with my lunch bag (today's entrée was peanut butter and jelly, a cup of applesauce, and all the pretzels that remained in a bag I'd bought the weekend before), and turned to where he was sitting in my guest chair.

"How was what?"

"Very cute." I had to agree with him there. In a red and white plaid skirt and a red sweater cropped just above my hips, I was not only cute, I was fashionable. And looked like a million bucks. But though Damon's eyes lit when he looked me over, something told me my excellent taste wasn't what he was referring to. He gave me a look nearly as penetrating as Grandma Panhorst's. "Vinnie. How was Vinnie?"

"You mean in class? Boring as hell. You know that. You were there."

"I'm not talking about how he was in class. I'm talking about how he was in bed."

The face I made pretty much said it all, but in case he didn't get it, I choked out a protest. "You're kidding me, right? You think Vinnie and I—"

"Hey, I understand. He's a star."

"He's an old, fat guy."

"Who happens to be famous."

"A famous, old, fat guy."

"And has millions of dollars."

"A rich, famous, old, fat guy."

"So you're telling me . . ." Damon cocked his head. I don't think it was my imagination. He actually looked relieved. "You didn't—"

I screeched my frustration. "This isn't the Free Love generation," I said. "And yes, that's exactly what I'm telling you. I didn't go home with Vinnie. I didn't—" Too gross. I couldn't even speak the words. Instead, I remembered my mission, and my shoulders drooped. "I didn't talk to him about channeling your songs, either. I'm sorry."

"Mellow out! It's no big deal. You'll get another chance."

"I suppose. I could go to class next week and—"

What I was going to say was that I could try and talk to Vinnie again. But my words dissolved in a gurgle of surprise. Even as I watched, Damon flickered and got fuzzy, like the TV picture when the cable goes out.

I'd never seen anything like it, and when he flickered back a second later, I was already halfway over to where he was standing.

"Stay cool!" Damon's breaths came in shallow gasps. He staggered back against my bookcase. "It's nothing."

"Nothing?" I dared a few steps closer just as he blinked out again. He blinked back in. "It's something," I said. "Vinnie? Is he—"

"Channeling me. Yeah." Damon's voice was

fuzzy. Just like his body. He winked in and out a couple of times before he winked out completely.

But not before I saw a flash of pain—and a look of stark terror—cross his face.

The doorman said Vinnie was expecting me.

Since I'd made the trip across town to the high-priced, high-rise condo complex on the lake called Winton Place for the sole purpose of talking to him, this should have cheered me right up.

Instead, it gave me the heebie-jeebies.

Less than twenty-four hours after we'd sat side by side, he guzzling scotch and me barely tasting my martini, and Vinnie was so sure I was a conquest, he'd already rolled out the red carpet. Literally.

The doorman ushered me to the elevator and assured me he'd call Mr. Pallucci so that he was ready for me when I arrived upstairs.

Oh joy.

I controlled the spurt of disgust that soured my stomach, ignored the wink the doorman gave me as the elevator door closed, and hit the button for the penthouse.

I am not a philistine. I had, after all, been raised in a family that valued material goods and had the wherewithal to afford the best. But when the elevator doors whooshed open, even I was impressed. And confused.

This was not at all what I expected from Vinnie Pal.

The hallway was sedate and sprawling. It was paneled in cherry and lit with spots recessed in the ceiling and trained on oil paintings of exotic flowers. Even if I don't like to admit it, I do have a degree in art history, and though I had never exactly set the academic world on fire, I know good when I see it. Just like I know expensive. These were both.

So was the huge Oriental rug on the floor, the round table in the center of it, and the humongous vase of lilies, roses, and tiny purple orchids arranged on top of it.

I sneezed, sniffed, and looked around some more. Through the veil of flowers, I saw a closed door to my right. I pressed the bell and waited.

Not for long.

The door opened, and when it did, a wave of music came crashing out at me. It was so loud, my bones vibrated.

"Vinnie! Hi!" I had to scream to be heard above the noise, and when Vinnie bowed and made a broad gesture, I stepped into the apartment. This, I realized, was more of what I'd been expecting.

In order to make the most of the floor-to-ceiling windows that looked out over the lake to the north and downtown Cleveland to the east, the room was open, with clean lines, a freestanding fireplace where a small fire sparkled in the grate, and a black marble floor that glimmered in the morning light. There was a grand piano in one corner and a drum set along one wall, as well as three guitars (two electric and one acoustic) that had been tossed on a leather couch. There were also pizza boxes everywhere—along with a few empty coffee cups, a couple of bottles of Jack Daniel's, a case of beer on ice in a decorative, claw-foot bathtub, and a pair of jeans draped over one shoulder of a life-size cardboard cutout of a naked woman.

"You want some?" Lucky for me, Vinnie was talking about the pizza. He grabbed a piece of pepperoni, double mushroom and olive, and offered it to me, and when I shook my head, he bit into it himself. "I figured you'd show up eventually."

"I—" A particularly enthusiastic guitar riff split the air. I cringed. Maybe Vinnie wasn't such a bonehead after all. He held up a finger in a gesture designed to tell me to hold on a minute and hurried into another room. When he turned off the music, I breathed a sigh of relief.

My head cleared. It was the first I saw that Damon had come into the penthouse apartment with me.

Another sigh of relief. Except for his left hand—the one I could practically see through— Damon looked like Damon. No fuzziness or flickering. There was no trace of pain in his eyes, either. I hadn't realized how worried I was until I wasn't worried anymore. "You're okay!"

"I'm fine. Really." His come-and-go smile wasn't exactly convincing, but I didn't call him on it. There wasn't time, and besides, something told me he was putting on a brave face for my sake. "You came to talk to Vinnie? About the channeling?" Damon asked.

I nodded, but it was all I had time to do before Vinnie came back into the room.

"Better?" He'd already finished his piece of pizza. He wiped his hand against his jeans. "Can't understand why the music bothered you. It wasn't all that loud. Then again . . ." He grinned, grabbed a beer, and popped the top. "My doc says that after all the years of standing so close to the amps, my hearing's practically gone. You sure you don't want something? I mean . . ." He wiggled his eyebrows. "Something other than me?"

"Always the kidder!" My smile was stiff. "Actually, what I'd like to do is talk to you." I glanced over at Damon. By not confronting Vinnie the night before, I'd let him down. I wanted him to know I wasn't going to let it happen again. "It's important."

"Sure, sure." Vinnie was hardly listening. He grabbed my arm and piloted me over to the piano. "But first, you gotta hear this song. It's a new one I'm working on. I'm gonna have it done in time for the concert, and I'll tell you what, baby, it's got platinum written all over it."

He plunked down on the piano bench and patted the space beside him, but I declined, and not because Damon was looking daggers at Vinnie, either. I was there to talk, nothing else, and I didn't want to send the wrong signals.

That is, until I took a closer look at the piano. There was an old, beat-up guitar on top of it, just to Vinnie's right. And a candle. It was nothing like I'd ever seen before.

The candle was fat and black, about six inches tall. There were strange symbols carved on its surface. And a piece of twine wound all the way around it. Tucked below the twine was a lock of dark, silky hair, a guitar pick, a feather, and, oh yeah, a wallet-size photo of Damon.

I've never been interested in weird, magical things. I never believed any of it was real. I didn't know anything about the occult, either, but believe me, after all that had happened to me in the past months,

I knew creepy when I was face-to-face with it. And this was just about as creepy as it got.

My stomach went cold. Good thing the piano bench was nearby. I dropped down onto it. "You're writing a song!" I don't know how I pulled it off, but when I turned to Vinnie, I sounded impressed rather than suspicious. I ruffled my fingers over the piano keys. "Go on," I said. "Show me how you do it."

"All right!" Vinnie cracked his knuckles and played a couple of chords. "Here's the setup. We'll start with a killer guitar solo, you know, something mournful and high drama. That always gets to the chicks and hey, chicks buy a lot of music. Then we'll bring Alistair in on the drums. Nothing too heavy, just slow and steady. You know, like a heartbeat. Little by little, it will pick up speed. Like my heartbeat when I'm close to you."

When he leaned a little nearer, I hardly noticed. My gaze was still on the black candle, the picture of Damon, and Damon himself, who was standing at Vinnie's right shoulder, watching the whole thing.

"Then the melody starts up," Vinnie said. He played it, and when he was done, he turned to me. "So, what do you think?"

"It's . . . good." The song sounded more Barry Manilow than it did Mind at Large. The look of disgust on Damon's face told me he wouldn't be caught dead (if he wasn't already, that is) within a mile of that song.

And that made me wonder . . .

Maybe the guitar and the candle were nothing more than some weirded-out tribute? Maybe Vinnie wasn't channeling Damon after all?

There was only one way to find out.

I slid a little closer to Vinnie and tried for the kind of sultry rumble I figured would appeal to him. "Show me how you do it," I said.

It worked. He practically melted into a puddle of mush. "How I do what, baby? Because let me tell you, I can do all kinds of things. And I do them all real good."

None of which I wanted to know about. My smile was coy. "We'll get to all that later. First show me how you write a song."

He hesitated.

Clue number one: If he didn't want to show me how it was done, maybe he really was doing something he shouldn't have been doing.

Then again, sex is a powerful motivator.

And I could tell from the glow in his eyes that Vinnie was convinced if he only did this one thing for me, he'd finally get me in the sack.

"I have a little ritual." He gave me a wink and reached for the lighter that was on the piano near the candle. "You know, a little something to get me in the songwriting mood." He lit the candle.

Damon blinked out. He was back again in a second, and I sat up and watched him carefully.

"I have this sort of mantra I repeat, too," Vinnie said, and from the way he tried to make it sound like it was no big deal, I knew it was a line of bull. This was no mantra, it was a spell. Vinnie was counting on the fact that I was too dumb to know the difference. "It's sort of a tribute. You know, to my old friend, Damon Curtis."

Vinnie closed his eyes and laid both his hands on the battered guitar.

Damon got fuzzy.

Okay, it wasn't exactly subtle, but I couldn't help myself. Watching Damon fade out, the question just sort of popped out of me. "The same Damon Curtis who you've been stealing songs from all these years?"

Vinnie's eyes flew open.

Damon came back into focus.

"What are you smoking?" Vinnie laughed. "That's crazy."

"But it's something I've heard. You know, one of those urban legend things. I've seen it on the Internet."

"Well, that doesn't keep it from being crazy. I wouldn't do that to Damon. He was my friend." Vinnie needed a shave. He scraped a hand over the stubble on his chin. "What I'm doing now is honoring him." He glanced away.

Clue number two: Why would a man who thought he was honoring a friend look so guilty about it?

I had to know for sure.

"Go ahead," I said, and when I did, I was looking at Damon, not at Vinnie. "Show me."

Again, Vinnie closed his eyes. Again, he touched the guitar. He sat in quiet contemplation for a couple of moments, and all the while he did, Damon didn't flicker.

I had just about convinced myself I was barking up the wrong black magic tree when Vinnie jerked up as fast and as straight as if he'd touched a finger to an electrical line. His eyes flew open. They were wild and they burned as if a fire had been lit inside Vinnie's brain. When he started to chant in a language that was thick and guttural and use words that had way too many syllables, his voice was distant and hollow. Like it came from another world.

Did I pay attention to what he said? Not a chance! I didn't understand a word of it, and besides, I was too busy watching Damon writhe in pain. Don't ask me how I thought I could help, but I sprang from the piano bench and rushed toward him. Before I got there, he winked out completely.

I heard music, and it wasn't in my head or even in my ears. It wasn't coming from Vinnie, either. His hands were poised above the piano, not touching the keys. The music was all around me and I was part of it. Driving guitars, and Damon's sexy baritone singing in words loaded with symbolism. They made no sense. I didn't care. It was pure poetry and it flowed through my bloodstream and tangled around my heart.

I am a shape-shifter, a creature of the night.
Overgrown and elder, too big for your world.
Unquiet, foreign in your accidental lands
Disdaining human life.
Existing on nothing.
Feeding on your love.

No sooner did the words and the heartrending emotion tear through me than Vinnie picked up the beat. His hands came down on the keys, and the resulting chords drowned Damon's music.

It was Damon's song but it wasn't. It was watered-down, mushy. I could practically hear the violins that would be part of Vinnie's final recording.

I've changed, baby.
Don't need you no more.
You're strange, baby.
Don't want you for sure.

No wonder Damon was pissed. Vinnie was taking the songs inside Damon's head and turning them into lite rock.

That was bad enough. Even worse was that all the while Vinnie sang, Damon's image came through behind him like a snowy picture. It buzzed and flickered and broke apart. In fact, the only thing constant was the look in Damon's eyes.

A look of total, mind-numbing torment.

"Stop!" I screamed the word, but a lot of good that did me. Vinnie didn't hear me. I don't think he could. His eyes were fiery and fixed on the flame of the candle. And the candle?

The flame didn't flutter like a regular candle. It sizzled like a Roman candle, and sparks shot out and sprinkled the piano keys where Vinnie's fingers danced, machinelike.

"Stop!" I tried again, but I was wasting my breath. Even when I grabbed his arm and shook him, Vinnie didn't respond.

I had to do something, and I didn't know what. I blew out the candle.

As if he'd been dropped from a high place and landed hard, Vinnie jerked. He stopped singing and playing. Behind him, Damon came into focus. I don't think ghosts breathe, but he looked like he was trying, and struggling for each breath.

I didn't even realize I was crying until I wiped tears off my cheeks. My knees were rubber. I sank down on the bench. "You have to stop," I told Vinnie. "You can't do this anymore."

He rubbed his eyes. "Not do what? What the hell are you talking about, woman? This is great shit. Why would you want me to stop writing songs?"

There was probably a more polite way to broach the subject, especially if I wanted Vinnie to agree to leave Damon—and his songwriting spirit—alone. At this point, I didn't really care.

"Not the songs," I sobbed. "I'm not talking about the songs. You have to stop channeling Damon. Don't you realize what you're doing? You're destroying him!"

Chapter 8

Clue number three: Vinnie didn't laugh when I said this. He didn't tell me I was nuts, or ask what I was talking about, either.

In fact, his spine folded, his shoulders sagged, the air rushed out of him with a *whoomp.* His hands shook and his eyes, lit with the fire of inspiration such a short time before, were cold and empty. The blood drained out of his face, and when he hung his head, his hair fell in his eyes. Even that didn't hide the lines on his face that accordioned into a network of wrinkles. He looked tired, worn out, and older than ever.

His shoulders heaved, and Vinnie wept softly. "I couldn't help it. You're not going to tell anyone, are you? You've got to understand, I couldn't help it. I had no choice, Pepper. I had to channel Damon. I needed those songs."

I guess I wasn't expecting him to come clean so fast or so easily. I looked over to where Damon was still struggling to catch his breath. "You're admitting it?"

"Yeah. Yeah, it's true." He dropped his head in his hands, sobbing harder than ever.

Vinnie might have been a dirty old man, and he was stealing Damon's songs. But I couldn't stand to watch him suffer. I rubbed his back until he settled down.

When he did, he sniffled and dared a look at me. "How did you know?" he asked. "I mean, about Damon? About the songs?"

Since we were already discussing black magic like it was the most ordinary thing in the world, I didn't see any harm in telling him the truth. "He's here," I said, and I looked over to where Damon was standing. He was pale and as burned out as Vinnie's candle. The air around him, though, still crackled and fizzed, like the distant lightning that foretells a summer storm. "I met Damon at the Rock Hall. Or at least, I met his ghost. He told me what you were up to."

Vinnie looked over his shoulder. "I don't see him."

"I'm the only one who can."

"And he told you—"

"About you stealing his songs, yeah. He's pissed about it and I don't blame him. But it's not just that, Vinnie." I had a feeling Damon wouldn't like me to reveal this part of the equation, so rather than sit there and watch him look unhappy, I stood. "You're hurting him," I told Vinnie, pointing to the place where Damon was standing. "Every time you channel one of his songs, it causes him excruciating pain."

I didn't think it was possible for Vinnie to get any paler. He swiped a hand over his cheeks. "I didn't know. I'm sorry. I thought—"

"And you're holding him here," I added, because

I figured he might as well know the whole story. "As long as you're channeling his songs, Damon can't leave to go to the Other Side. He's fading, Vinnie." I refused to look at Damon when I said this. I didn't want to see his left hand and the way it was blurry, as if an eraser was slowly wiping away every trace of him. "Pretty soon, there's not going to be anything left of him, and then he'll never be able to cross over."

Vinnie drew in a calming breath and turned. He was looking at an empty spot six feet to the left of where Damon was standing, but I didn't bother to point that out. When it comes to talking to ghosts, I figured close counts. "I'm sorry, buddy," he said, his voice rough with tears. "I never meant for any of that to happen. You get it, don't you? Shit, I just thought . . ." Vinnie pushed both his hands through his hair. "When I first tried channeling you . . . well, man, I gotta tell you, I was scared shitless. But I was high so I tried anyway, and when it actually worked, man, it was better than sex! And it saved my butt. It saved the band. Without you, man . . ." Shaking his head, Vinnie turned back to me.

"Damon was the lifeblood of the band. You know that, don't you? When he died, we were in the crapper. Our old stuff kept selling but the band . . . shit, nobody wanted us. We used to fill stadiums! Without Damon, we couldn't even get a booking in a bar. We needed songs and we needed them bad."

"So you got that first song from Damon and Mind at Large recorded it."

It wasn't a question. Vinnie nodded, anyway.

"That song put as at the top of the charts again, even without Damon. It made us millions. I got all the credit for writing it, and the chicks, well, let me tell you . . ." His eyes were red and swollen but he managed to wink anyway. "Chicks will do anything for songwriters."

Not something I wanted to think about.

My arms wrapped around myself, I went over to the couch. Though I hadn't noticed him move, Damon was already there. When I sat down, I made sure I kept my distance even as I thought about what a shame it was that I had to. What with watching Damon suffer and listening to Vinnie spill his guts, I needed a hug and I needed one badly. I sure didn't want to encourage Vinnie, and I couldn't get close to Damon or I'd freeze up like a snow cone. The realization left me chilled.

I chafed my hands over my arms. "So you recorded that song and—"

"And then I couldn't stop!" As if this was all the explanation he needed, Vinnie nodded. "I mean, it was like a drug, you know? Not just the songs, but the power. Imagine it, Pepper! Think about how cool it is to call on a dead man and actually have him come to you. Especially somebody like Damon." Vinnie's laughter was rough with tears. "The great Damon Curtis! The face and the voice everyone thought of when they thought of Mind at Large. The guy every chick wanted. We were all stars, sure. But Damon, he was a supernova. We had groupies, as many as we wanted. But they only stayed with us so they could have the chance of getting close to Damon. And then . . ."

Like they had when he was deep in his trance

and channeling Damon, Vinnie's eyes lit with an otherworldly fire. "And then I found out that I could actually raise his spirit, this guy who was the supreme being of music. I could make him obey me! For a while, I channeled him just because I could. The songs, they were a bonus. But then the songs turned into hits, one after another. And not just with our usual crowd. I was able to take us one step further, and we got popular with the middle-of-the-road crowd. Hey, they may not be as hard rockin' as the kids, but they've got plenty more money to spend. After that, well, then everyone just expected me to keep writing hits. You know, Ben and Alistair, Mighty Mike and Pete. Even Gene Terry, our agent. Especially Gene. He was thrilled. He said he'd been paying so much attention to Damon, he never realized I had it in me to write great songs, too. The band, our agent, our fans. How could I stop when everyone was counting on me? I couldn't. I didn't. Not until . . . Not until now."

I gave him a penetrating look. He didn't even notice, so I spoke up. "Pardon me for sounding like the voice of reason here, but what I just saw, that didn't look like you stopping."

"But that's just it!" Vinnie hurried over to where I was sitting. He shuffled from foot to foot, his voice tight with desperation. "This was going to be the last time. Honest. The last song. I just need one more, one new song for the big concert. I swear . . . I swear, even before you told me about what I was doing to Damon, I was never going to channel him again."

It was the whole thing about me sitting and

looking at a guy's crotch again. Considering the crotch in question belonged to Vinnie, it was pretty gross. I got up and stepped to the windows. "I don't believe you," I told him, and when Damon mustered up the energy to shake his head, I added, "Damon doesn't believe you, either. Something tells me maybe you've promised before."

"I have tried to stop before. You're right. I just never . . ." Vinnie's shoulders rose and fell. "I couldn't help myself."

"And you expect me to believe that this time is different?"

"It is." Before I even saw him coming, Vinnie raced over and clasped his hand around my arm. He pulled me down a hallway, opened a door, and dragged me inside a room. There were no windows in there and the walls were painted black. It took a minute for my eyes to adjust, and after they did, I saw that there was a pentagram painted on the hardwood floor in glowing white paint.

Creepy, creepier, creepiest.

Even I didn't know I could move that fast. In a heartbeat, I had myself untangled from Vinnie's grasp and was back out in the hallway.

"Hey, not to worry, babe!" When he gave me an anemic smile, Vinnie's teeth glimmered in the gloom. It wasn't very comforting. "It's only my magic room. I have one everyplace I stay. Nothing bad can happen to you just from coming inside."

"And that's supposed to make me feel better how?"

"Because, don't you see? There's nothing left in here." Like Vanna in front of the letter board, Vinnie waved his arm.

I kept my feet firmly planted in the hallway and took the chance of leaning into the room for a better look. He was right. The walls were bare and there wasn't a speck of furniture in the room. In fact, there wasn't anything in there at all except that glowing pentagram and two big cardboard boxes.

"I've packed it all away," Vinnie said. "I'm done with magic."

Call me skeptical. I couldn't get what Vinnie said out of my head, that stuff about how the songs had earned the band millions, and the rush he got from channeling, and, oh yeah, how chicks will do anything for songwriters. "You're done with magic because you're tired of being the center of attention, is that it?" I'd seen more than enough; I headed back into the living room. "I'm not buying it, Vinnie. Why would you quit now when you haven't quit in the last forty years? Why should I trust you?"

"How about because I'm dying?"

That got my attention. I screeched to a stop and turned. "You're—"

"Dying. Yeah, that's right." Vinnie poked his hands into the pockets of his worn jeans. "I told you, I spend all my time with doctors and lawyers these days. That's because I'm getting everything in line, you know? That concert at the Rock Hall? My docs say it's going to be my last one."

My morbid curiosity got the best of me. "Are you sure?"

He nodded, and I had to give him credit, he didn't look as resigned to his prognosis as much as he looked at peace with it. "Pancreatic cancer," he said. "They say I've got a couple of months. If I'm lucky."

"I'm sorry."

"Me, too!" Vinnie grinned. "But I'm grateful, too. I mean, I found out a couple weeks ago and since then, I've had time to get things in order and hey, maybe I've helped my cause a little, too. See, I gave away just about every cent I have to that hospital where they take care of kids with cancer. Told them they couldn't say where the money came from, either, or I was taking it back. And if you're thinking that I'm a great guy for doing it . . ." A soft smile touched his lips. "I'm just trying to oil a few palms. You know, so that when I hit the Pearly Gates they don't send me packing for hell."

Did I still look dubious? I guess so, because Vinnie went back to the magic room, and I heard him messing around with those packing boxes. When he came back, he had two manila envelopes in his hands. He shoved them at me.

"Here," he said. "Take these. This will prove that I mean it when I say I'm not going to channel Damon again."

Neither envelope was sealed, and I peeked inside. The larger of the two had a couple of guitar picks in it, along with a string of love beads and a beat-up old bandana. The other, smaller, envelope was filled with snippings of dark hair.

"It was Damon's," Vinnie said. "All of it. The guitar picks and stuff, that was easy to get. Damon always left stuff lying around."

I saw the flaw in Vinnie's logic and called him on it. "And the hair?"

"Damon was screwing some hairdresser chick.

She used to love to trim his hair. You know, to make him look good before every show. Once, when she was done, I swept up the hair and kept it."

"But if you never planned to channel Damon—"

"I didn't. Not then. The hair . . ." He glanced away. "That was for something else."

"A different spell?"

He nodded. "The hairdresser chick . . . I don't remember her name . . . but she was mine first and a fine little piece of ass, too. Before Damon set his sights on her. I wanted her back. And see, that's one of the first things they tell you when you learn magic. If you're going to put a spell on somebody, you need something that belongs to them. Don't you get it? None of it matters now. What matters is that I've had this stuff of Damon's for years. I use a little bit of it each time I need a new song. And I had it all packed away. I was going to get rid of it. Once it's gone, I can't call on Damon's spirit anymore. You've got to believe me!" Eager to prove he was telling the truth, Vinnie plucked the two envelopes out of my hands and looked around the room for a place to get rid of them. His gaze fell on the fireplace and the fire that sparkled there, and he hurried over to it and tossed the envelopes into the fire.

For a second, nothing happened, and I wondered if the envelopes had smothered the fire. But then a finger of flame licked the side of the smaller envelope. A hiss of steam went up and a second later, a sound like thunder filled the room, so loud and so powerful that Vinnie and I both staggered back. Flames erupted and filled the fireplace, throwing a light show of orange and yellow against the walls.

The next second, the fire burned itself out. All that was left was a small pile of ash and a plume of smoke that scrolled to the ceiling and disappeared.

Vinnie swallowed hard. "See? It's gone. All of it. Now do you believe me? There's nothing more I can do to Damon now. I've got nothing left that belonged to him. I never meant to hurt him."

Softhearted or not, a private investigator does not have the luxury of letting somebody off the hook just because they grovel a bit. "You didn't have anything to do with Damon's death, did you?"

"It was an accident. It had to be." Vinnie spoke to the empty space over near the windows. "You had a lot to look forward to, Damon, so I know it wasn't suicide."

"There's one way for you to prove you're sincere," I told him.

"Anything."

I knew Vinnie meant it and took him up on the offer. "Give me the candle and the guitar."

"Sure. Sure." Vinnie went over to the piano and retrieved the items. "Like I said, I'm not going to need them. Not anymore. Once you get rid of that stuff . . ." He drew in a shaky breath and let it out slowly. "That's the last of it. I won't have a hold on Damon anymore. Once you get rid of this stuff, that should free him."

It was what Damon wanted. And exactly what I wanted, too.

Wasn't it?

I asked myself the question as I tucked the candle into the crook of my arm and grabbed the guitar, and I was still wondering why it unsettled me as Damon and I rode the elevator down to the lobby in silence.

Back outside in the late morning sunshine, I didn't head for my car. Instead, I crossed to the far end of the property where the parking lot overlooked the lake. I set the candle and the guitar down on the waist-high wall that surrounded the lot and glanced down to the water, some twenty feet below.

Maybe I wasn't as tough as I liked to pretend I was. When I asked Damon the question, I didn't have the nerve to look at him. "Are you sure?"

"Hey, baby, you're not changing your mind about helping me out, are you?"

Maybe Damon wasn't as committed to heading to the Great Beyond as he claimed to be, either. There was an undercurrent of emotion in his voice, and anxious to understand what it was, I turned to him.

I was sorry I did. Regret shimmered in his eyes and in the smile he gave me. Was it for the life he'd led? Or because he'd been shackled to this earth long past his time? Or was there some other reason he was sorry to leave? Someone he was sorry to be leaving behind?

My heart lurched, but before I had a chance to say anything, Damon spoke.

"It's time," he said.

"I know." Which didn't explain why I was so reluctant to make the final move. "It's just that—"

"What?"

I bit my tongue. It was better to keep my mouth shut than to tell a guy who'd been dead since before I was born that I was going to miss him.

Rather than take the chance of confessing my feelings and looking like a chump, I did exactly what I was supposed to do—I threw the candle in the lake. Damon stepped up to the wall, and side by side, we watched the candle bob. In my head, I imagined that Damon's spirit was doing the same thing, hovering in some unnamed space between this world and the next.

The candle finally went under the water. And Damon?

I gave him a sidelong glance.

Damon didn't flutter or fizz or fade.

As one, we turned our attention to the guitar.

"I don't think you can just toss it in," he said. "I mean, someone might fish it out. Or it could just sink to the bottom and stay there and maybe that would mean I'd have to stay here, too, at least until it rots away."

He was right. I picked up the guitar, and maybe I was a little emotionally strung out and maybe my imagination was playing tricks on me. I swear I could feel Damon's essence in it. I closed my eyes and cradled it, close to him in a physical way for the first time.

But hey, strung out or not, I knew the feeling couldn't last, so I clutched the skinny end of the guitar in both hands, backed up, and brought the guitar down on the wall as hard as I could.

It shattered, and the *boing* of all the strings snapping at once echoed through the parking lot. A couple of people getting into their cars not far away stopped and stared and pointed.

I didn't care. Before anyone could stop me, I scooped up the pieces and tossed them into the lake. The guitar was the last connection Vinnie had to Damon. There was no way he could channel him again, no way he could hold Damon's spirit to earth, and I knew it. I knew I couldn't watch Damon fade and blur into nothingness, so I kept my eyes on the water, watching until I saw every last fragment of guitar sink.

"Well . . ." Big points for me, I was pretty good at fooling myself. Even though I was talking to nobody but me, I managed to sound like my throat wasn't clogged with emotion. "That's that. It's over. It's done. Damon's—"

"Still here."

When I heard Damon's voice behind me, I jumped and squealed.

As if he was just as surprised as I was, he looked down at himself and held his hands out to examine them. His left hand was still washed-out, but other than that, he looked the same as ever.

Okay, so it wasn't the most politically correct thing to say to a dead guy who was hoping to move on to the trip of all trips, but I couldn't help myself. I blinked and stammered, "What the hell are you still doing here?"

Chapter 9

Much to Ella's delight, I stayed late at work that day. What Ella didn't know was that I wasn't combing through the cemetery files looking for more immigration information like I said I'd be doing. I was down at Damon's grave, and he and I . . . well, we were trying to figure out why he wasn't wherever he should have been now that Vinnie's power over him was gone.

We got nowhere together, and when I finally gave up and went home and thought about it some more, I got nowhere alone. Except, of course, for the nagging and uncomfortable feelings that kept me awake half the night—the ones that made me wonder what the hell was wrong with me. And why I wasn't sorry that Damon hadn't crossed over.

By the next day, I was so tired of thinking (and feeling what I had no business feeling about a dead guy), that my brain hurt. "It doesn't make any sense." I dropped my head down on my desk. It helped with the pounding. "Vinnie's not holding you here anymore."

"Unless he is, and he's lying."

This was, of course, one of the first theories we'd discussed the night before. Now, as then, I dismissed it. I sat up, and because my hair was loose, I shoved it out of my bloodshot eyes so I could look across my desk to where Damon was sitting in my guest chair. "I believe him," I said. "Don't ask me why. But if he's really sick like he says he is, if he really gave away all his money . . . It's pretty clear that Vinnie's trying to turn over a new leaf. And he does feel really guilty about the channeling. You saw how upset he got when I told him what it was doing to you. It seems impossible, but it all adds up. I believe him."

Damon sighed. "So do I."

All of which, of course, put us right back where we started.

I didn't dare breathe a word about what I'd been thinking the night before. I mean, about how maybe it wasn't so bad that Damon was sticking around after all. But I didn't dare not mention it, either. If I didn't say anything, and if Damon had already thought the same things I was thinking, then I'd not only look obvious, but stupid, to boot.

When I brought up the subject, I wanted it to sound less like an obsession and more like an oh-yeah-I-forgot-to-mention-this-P.S., so I moved around the piles of papers on my desk to make it look like I was busy. Since I wasn't known for my filing skills and there were plenty of papers and plenty of piles, I had a good excuse for not meeting Damon's eyes. "I don't know, I think maybe there's nothing we can do. Maybe . . ." Was that me sounding like a love-struck teenager? I gave myself a mental slap and gulped down my mortification. "Maybe you'll just have to stick around for a while."

"Pepper . . ."

It wasn't Damon saying my name, it was the way he said it that forced me to look up.

I don't think I ever knew exactly what *bittersweet* meant until that moment. Because that's what the smile Damon gave me was, gentle and warm at the same time it was filled with emotion so sharp that I sucked in a breath and collapsed back in my chair, as if a hot knife had sliced my heart into little pieces.

"Wish I could stay around." He didn't elaborate. All he did was hold up his left hand.

I could barely see it. Or part of his arm.

I don't panic easily. At least not unless I have a really good reason. This was a really good reason.

I sat up straight, and my brain froze. All I could think about was what might happen if I didn't help Damon cross over before he disappeared completely. If he was never allowed on the Other Side, and he disappeared from this one . . .

A terrible vision filled my head. It was of a lonely place where the spirits who didn't belong anywhere spent eternity lost and all alone. Yeah, I wanted Damon to stick around. For purely selfish reasons. But not at that price.

I slapped my hand against the desk and stood. I hoped that moving around the office would kick my brain into gear, so I paced to the door and back again.

"We've got to do something," I said. It was an understatement, but I couldn't think of anything profound. "It was easy with my other cases," I grumbled. "Gus and Didi both had unfinished business, and once we finished it, they were able to go to the Other Side. But you died of an accidental overdose. Everyone knows that. But if you're still here, maybe you do have—"

Call me slow. Or maybe I was just so caught up in thinking Damon was going to vanish, and then so relieved when he didn't, that I hadn't been able to think straight.

"Unfinished business." Damon and I said the words together, and now that we were finally getting somewhere, I hurried over to my desk and sat back down.

"If the overdose wasn't accidental then maybe what's holding you here isn't the channeling. Maybe you're being held here—"

"Until we find out what really happened that night I died."

"Shit."

At my vehement reply, Damon raised an eyebrow. "This is good news, isn't it? I thought this was exactly what we were trying to figure out."

"It is. But you see what it means, don't you? I've just talked myself into another murder investigation."

The most logical place to start was with Vinnie. I bought myself some time by telling Ella I needed another trip to the County Archives. It wasn't a total lie. Number one, because I did need more information if I was ever going to add to all those files Ella had pulled out. Number two, because the

County Archives was in the same direction as Vinnie's Gold Coast penthouse. Sort of.

With Damon riding shotgun, I headed back to the suburb of Lakewood.

I only had to endure a couple of winks and one comment from the doorman about how he bet Vinnie Pal couldn't wait to see me again. It was a small price to pay for being allowed up to the penthouse unannounced. A short while later, I was in the wide, elegant hallway that led to Vinnie's apartment.

The door was open.

"Hey, Vinnie!" There was no loud music playing that morning, so when I toed the invisible line between the apartment and the hallway and rapped on the door, I figured Vinnie would hear me. "It's me, Pepper. Can I come in?"

I wasn't sure, but I thought I heard a muffled response.

I took it as an affirmative and stepped inside. Except that it was messier, the place looked like it had the day before: pizza boxes everywhere, coffee cups and beer cans (open and empty) strewn all around, and of course, the cutout of the naked woman. But there was no sign of Vinnie.

"Vinnie?" I tried again, louder this time, and again I heard what sounded like a muted reply. It came from Vinnie's magic room.

I headed that way, and at my side, Damon grumbled his disapproval.

"Vinnie didn't lie to us," I said, reminding him of what we'd both decided back at the office. "He's trying to go straight. He promised not to channel you again. Nothing's going to happen to me if I go in there. He's not messing with magic anymore."

"What if he is?"

I paused, my hand on the doorknob of the magic room. "I'll open the door, but I'll stay out here. And if I see anything weird, I'll run."

I yanked open the door. And I did see something weird. And I did run. Only not away from the magic room. In fact, I raced into the room and dropped to my knees.

Right next to where Vinnie was lying on the floor, moaning.

"Vinnie, are you all right?" After what Vinnie had told me the day before about his cancer and how much time the doctors told him he had to live, I assumed he'd taken some medication and gotten dizzy. Or had an attack of some kind. Until my eyes adjusted to the dim light in the windowless room and I saw the knife sticking out of his chest and the stream of blood that gurgled up around the edges of it and flowed to the floor.

"Holy shit!" Instinctively, I jerked away. But just as quickly, I had a full-blown attack of guilt. This was not the compassionate way to respond to a dying man.

And I knew beyond a doubt that Vinnie was breathing his last.

His eyes fluttered and opened. I couldn't tell if he was able to see me or not. Still, a smile touched his lips. "Must . . . already be . . . in heaven," Vinnie said. "You're an angel."

"Or not." To prove it, I grabbed Vinnie's hand and held on tight. "What happened?"

He managed to shake his head, but when he moved his lips, no words came out.

I told myself to get a grip and promised Vinnie help was on the way. I rummaged through my purse, grabbed my phone, and made the 911 call. When I was done, I took Vinnie's hand in mine again.

"It's going to be okay," I told him. I was lying, but let's face it, at a time like that, a little white lie provides a whole lot more comfort than the truth. "The paramedics will be here in a couple minutes. They're going to take care of you, Vinnie."

He rolled his head to the side and looked to where Damon was kneeling on the floor opposite me, and I don't know where he found the strength, but Vinnie raised a hand in greeting.

That's when I knew for sure that Vinnie didn't have much time. One thing I'd learned in the paranormal PI game was that when living people (other than me) see a ghost, it means the end is near.

With that in mind, I knew I had to get Vinnie to talk.

I cradled his hand in both of mine. "What happened?" I asked him. "Who did this to you?"

"Who?" Vinnie drew the word out in one, long syllable. His voice was like the whisper of the wind. His chest rose and fell, and so did the knife stuck in it. It was too terrible to watch. And too horrifying to take my eyes off.

Even as I knelt there, frozen with horror, Vinnie dragged in a shallow breath and let it out slowly.

Then he went perfectly still.

"Vinnie?" I poked his shoulder with one finger,

but he didn't respond. "Vinnie, just hang on. They're coming to help." I heard the pulsing sounds of a siren out in the street. "Just a couple more minutes, Vinnie."

But it was too late.

Vinnie's hand still in mine, I sat back on my heels. "What's going to happen?" I asked Damon.

He shrugged. "Since I never crossed over, I can't say for sure. Unless Vinnie's stuck here, too. By the look of that knife in his chest, I'd say he's got some unfinished business for sure."

No doubt, but before I had a chance to wonder what it meant and how I'd be involved, something weird happened.

As if a white light had been turned on behind it and its glow seeped through the plaster, one of the walls of Vinnie's magic room began to shine. Little by little, the light intensified until I couldn't see the wall at all. I squinted and covered my eyes with my hand.

That is, until I saw Vinnie rise out of his body. He walked over to the wall, and at the place where the light was its most blinding, he paused and turned. Smiling, he raised his hand and waved goodbye.

Right before he disappeared into the light.

I don't know how long it took. I only knew that while it was happening, I didn't move a muscle. I stared at the light, filled with emotions I didn't understand and couldn't name. I do know that it was all over by the time the cops and the paramedics burst into the apartment and hurried down the hallway and into the magic room.

That's where they found me, kneeling on the floor next to Vinnie Pal's lifeless body.

Word of a celebrity's death travels fast.

By the time I answered questions from the cops, filled out forms for the paramedics, and made my way downstairs, there was a crowd gathered out in the parking lot. I counted four vans from local TV stations and a dozen or so reporters. One of them was talking to the doorman, and believe me, I made sure I snuck out of the building so he didn't see me. I didn't want to be fingered as the last person to see Vinnie Pal alive. Not on the six o'clock news, anyway.

By the time I got back to Garden View, I felt as if I'd been wrung out and hung up to dry. I dragged myself out of the car, fully prepared to hightail it to my office, shut the door, and hide out for the rest of the day.

I was on my way to do exactly that when I saw the ghost hunters gathered around one of the cars parked in the lot. They were listening to the radio.

"Did you hear?" Brian, the chief dork, accosted me where the sidewalk met the parking lot. "Vinnie Pal is dead."

I stepped around him. "I heard."

"You know what this means, don't you?"

I knew, all right.

It meant that though the Lakewood cops who came in response to my call told me I was free to go, I was in for a whole bunch more questions, a thorough background check, and a close examination of my motives and what, exactly, I'd been doing in Vinnie's apartment when he met his untimely end.

It meant that I wouldn't get rid of the memory of that knife sticking out of Vinnie's chest any time soon. Or, from the looks of it, the bloodstain on my good gray linen pants. Sad but true, and another thing I'd learned thanks to being PI to the dead: Blood does not easily wash out of natural fibers.

Of course, the news wasn't all bad. I'd learned something helpful, too. I knew for certain Vinnie couldn't have had anything to do with Damon's death.

How?

No murderer could possibly cross over that quickly. Even one who had tried to buy his way into the Promised Land.

None of that was information I was willing to share with Brian, so I shrugged in response to his question.

"It means there's even more reason to find evidence of Damon Curtis's ghost," he said, and how anyone could look so excited about a murder, I couldn't say. Then again, Brian wouldn't spend the next I-don't-know-how-many-years trying to fall asleep with the image dancing through his head, the one of blood and knives and the way a person's face gets chalky just before he buys the farm. "Vinnie's mysterious death is really going to add to the Mind at Large mystique. Hey, maybe we can even find Vinnie's ghost!" This was, apparently, a new thought, and anxious to share it with his fellow dorks, Brian hurried over to tell them.

That's when I realized that one of the dorks looked awfully familiar.

Dan Callahan didn't stay with the group to hear what Brian had to say. His hands tucked into the pockets of his black leather jacket, he strolled over, and even though he gave me a smile, I couldn't help but notice that his gaze dipped down to the bloodstain on my pants.

A preemptive strike was in order. I asked questions before he could. "You taking up a new hobby? Or do you just like hanging around with the geek crowd?"

"You mean them?" Dan tipped his head toward where the ghost hunters were plotting strategy. "Just being friendly. Thought I'd give them a few pointers."

"Because you know how to hunt ghosts."

"If you're asking, does that mean you believe in ghosts?"

"If I'm asking, it's because I'd like to know what you're up to. Do you know a lot about ghosts?"

"I know a lot about a lot of things." There was a twinkle in Dan's eyes that I would have found irresistible. If I was in the mood.

Maybe he sensed it. Or maybe he just put two and two together and realized that bloodstains on a girl's pant leg tend to blunt her good humor.

Before he got daring and decided to broach the subject anyway, I turned to head into the building.

"I could offer you a few pointers, too."

Dan's words stopped me in my tracks. I rolled my eyes. Which he didn't see since I didn't bother to turn around. "Let me guess, dark prophecies and vague warnings. Ghosts that go bump in the night. Been there, done that today, thanks very much."

"I'm not talking about ghosts. I'm talking about

that cop who's waiting for you in your office."

Just like he knew I would, I spun around.

Just like I knew he would, Dan didn't stick around to elaborate. He was already walking away, and I wasn't about to run after him. It was less humiliating and far more satisfying to grumble a word that shouldn't have been used where the dead are supposed to be resting in peace. Childish? Sure, but it made me feel better and a little more ready to deal with the suburban cop who I knew was going to grill me about Vinnie.

The second I stepped into my office, I knew I was right about the grilling.

And wrong about the cop.

"For a woman who's supposed to work here, you don't spend a lot of time in your office."

Quinn Harrison, looking like a million bucks in a charcoal suit, a crisp shirt, and silk tie the same impossible green as his eyes, was perched on the edge of my desk. Since Quinn didn't have a politically correct bone in his body, he wasn't embarrassed to have some of the papers from my desk in his hands. Even as I stood there, he thumbed through them one more time.

"Doesn't your boss ever call you on the carpet for not being more industrious?" he asked.

Like the rest of the junk on my desk, the papers were nothing important, but I had my standards. I plucked the papers out of Quinn's hands and tossed them back where they came from. "Don't they teach you guys civility at the Police Academy?"

His thousand-watt smile lit up my office. "I missed that day."

"And today?"

I crossed my arms over my chest and stepped back. Not that I was afraid of Quinn or anything, but when he stood, I didn't want to be too close.

He stood.

I didn't want to be too close. I took another step back.

"Today I got an interesting phone call," he said. "It was from a buddy of mine. We're supposed to play racquetball tonight and we needed to double-check. You know, to make sure one of us reserved a court."

"Fascinating." Everything about Quinn was fascinating, from the aroma of his expensive after-shave to the lock of coal black hair that fell over his forehead. And because I couldn't let him know I thought so, I made sure I packed all the tartness I could into the word. "So you came all the way here to tell me that you're as fit as a fiddle. It makes me feel guilty for eating that pint of Chunky Monkey last night."

One corner of Quinn's mouth pulled into what was almost a smile. "I like Cherry Garcia myself. And I didn't tell you about the racquetball because I think you care. I told you because the guy I'm playing with is a friend of mine. Another cop."

"If you're looking to fix him up, I'm not interested. I don't date cops."

"A fact you've made perfectly clear."

"Have I?" Is that what this was really all about? Was Quinn here about another date? Knowing Quinn, it seemed unlikely, but I wasn't going to take any chances. I tried for a sexy smile and hoped it wasn't coy. "Maybe you just haven't asked at the right time."

"Maybe you've got blood on the leg of your pants."

My hopes melted along with my patience. "You're a pain in the ass." I pushed past Quinn, opened my bottom desk drawer, and tossed my purse inside. When I was done, I sat in my desk chair, pulled the papers Quinn had been looking through closer, and tapped them into a neat pile. If he wanted to talk, he'd have to turn around.

He did. "My buddy was on a call today. There was a homicide. In Lakewood. Unusual for a suburb as nice and quiet as that."

My hands stilled over the papers.

"He said he interviewed a woman at the scene. A stunning redhead, that's how he described her. Call me an incurable romantic, I heard the words *stunning*, *redhead*, and *murder* in the same sentence and I just knew it was you."

"No one has ever accused you of being an incurable romantic."

"You got that right." Quinn laughed. "I am incurably curious, though. Professional hazard. And right now, I'm wondering about this Vinnie Pal guy. Is he the one you stood me up for the night I called you about the ball game?"

So we weren't talking about murder. We were back to talking about sex.

I didn't want Quinn to see me breathe a sigh of relief, so I kept busy with the papers. "You came here in the middle of the day to ask about my love life?" I asked Quinn.

"I came here in the middle of the day because it looks like your love life and a murder might be connected. It's that whole incurable romantic thing again. I can't help myself. I'm worried."

"You're nosy."

"I'm nosy and worried."

"Vinnie and I weren't involved, if that's what you're being nosy about. I took his class down at the Rock Hall, and he loaned me a CD. I was returning it. That's when I found him." It was the story I'd told the Lakewood police, and I was sticking to it.

The least Quinn could have done is pretend he believed me. He pursed his lips and tipped his head back, thinking. "It's funny how you're always around when people are dying," he said.

"Not technically true. This is the first time I've actually been around someone who was dying. All the rest of them were dead by the time I got to them. As for me being there when Vinnie died, that was nothing more than a coincidence."

I was saved from elaborating when Quinn's cell rang. He listened for a moment, barked a quick "I'll be right there," and flipped it closed.

"Coincidence, huh?" Quinn started for the door. "Then maybe what just happened down at the Rock Hall is a coincidence, too. Alistair Cromwell, the Mind at Large drummer, he was down there and one of the spotlights on the stage fell. Practically took his head off."

Chapter 10

"I can come with you, can't I?"

Since I'd followed Quinn out of my office and down the hall to the main door, he shouldn't have been surprised by my request.

Just like I shouldn't have been surprised by his answer.

"No."

"But I'm going to go anyway. You know I am. Since we're both going to the same place—"

"No." When he punched through the door and walked into the parking lot, I was right behind him. I stayed there while he unlocked the door of his unmarked police car.

"But you've got this whole car to yourself," I said. I wanted to be in on the investigation and I knew that wasn't going to happen unless I walked into the Rock Hall with Quinn, so I didn't curl my upper lip when I peered inside the car. Utilitarian black vinyl seats, stripped-down dashboard . . . this was not the kind of ride I pictured for him. Then again, I suppose the car was standard issue for public servants. And since I was one of the public, it was time for Quinn to start serving.

"There's no reason you can't give me a ride," I told him.

He yanked open the door and slid behind the wheel. "I don't need a reason. The answer's still no."

I stabbed a finger toward where my Mustang was parked. "It's not like you can keep me away. If you don't take me, I'm just going to get in my car and drive to the Rock Hall myself. And have you seen the price of gas?"

I can't say for sure because the sun reflected off his windshield and just about blinded me, but I think Quinn smiled. Then again, maybe it was a sneer. "Take the bus."

"In this outfit?" Honestly, I'm amazed at men. They can miss the most obvious things. I side-stepped around the open driver's-side door. Quinn couldn't close it while I was in the way, so like it or not, he was in for a lesson in high style. "The sweater's from White House Black Market. The pants are Nanette Lepore, from Saks, and good thing they were on sale, since I'm going to have to toss them. The shirt . . ." I fingered the collar of my white cotton blouse. "Well, I can't remember where I bought it, but I know it cost me plenty. I'm much too well-dressed for the bus-riding crowd."

Quinn stuck his key in the ignition. "Don't worry about it. Mingling with the masses builds character. Believe me, I mingle all the time, and I've got plenty of character."

"Which is exactly why you're going to let me come with you."

"Which is exactly why I know better than to let you." He gave me a level look and I don't think he was sizing up my outfit. He wanted me to move.

I planted my feet. "Think about it . . . I was with Vinnie when he died. Your friend, that other cop, he told you that, didn't he?"

"So?"

"So, don't you get it? Vinnie's murder and the attack on Alistair . . . they might be related."

While Quinn thought about this, I beefed up my position.

"Something Vinnie said to me before he died might be important. Only you'll never know unless you talk to me about it. And I'm not going to talk to you about it unless you let me go with you. That means you'll do it, right?"

When Quinn didn't cut me off at the knees, I knew I was finally getting somewhere. He sat back and took his hands off the steering wheel. "You didn't kill Vinnie, did you?"

Did the police really suspect me?

My heart lurched into my throat. My blood ran cold. "Is that what your friend said?" My voice wobbled. So did my knees. One Martin in prison was one too many, and Dad already had that slot all to himself. Besides the food (less than first-rate, I imagined), the girl gangs (I was so not into following the crowd), and the shared showers (need I say more?), I couldn't picture myself in an orange jumpsuit.

I blurted out the same explanation I gave Quinn's friend when he questioned me back at the condo. "I told your friend the whole story. The door to Vinnie's apartment was open when I got there, and I walked in. That's when I found Vinnie." The memory of the knife sticking out of Vinnie's chest, rising and falling with every labored breath, caught me off guard. I'd been pretty good about the whole thing. Up until that moment. Suddenly my stomach went wonky, my head spun. If I didn't grab on to the door of the unmarked police car, I would have toppled right over.

"You don't really think I could kill someone, do you?" I asked Quinn. My voice was as breathy as Vinnie's when he breathed his last. "Your friend, he doesn't think—"

I was obviously upset, and I expected that a little understanding was in order. Laughter was not.

Quinn grinned up at me. "My friend knew Vinnie Pal was staying there. And he knew all about Vinnie's lifestyle and his reputation. He took one look at you and decided right then and there that you were a high-priced call girl who happened to be in the wrong place at the wrong time."

A new kind of horror gripped me. "You set him straight, didn't you?"

"About the wrong time, wrong place thing? Or about the call girl thing?"

I wasn't about to dignify the question with an answer, so I stuck to the matter at hand. "None of it changes a thing. Quinn . . ." Still hanging on to the door of the car, I bent to look him in the eye. "I was the last one to see Vinnie alive. And now Alistair's been attacked. Two Mind at Large band members in one day? Even I can see that it's a little weird. And suspicious, too."

He didn't agree or disagree. He just leaned over and opened the passenger door.

Before he could change his mind, I hurried around to the other side of the car and climbed in.

We were on our way to the Rock Hall in no time.

Good thing it wasn't too far away.

The vinyl seats were lumpy and uncomfortable, and the police car smelled like . . .

I sniffed, and this time I couldn't have controlled my reaction if I tried. I made a face.

Quinn wasn't a detective for nothing. He slid me a sidelong look. "Cigarettes. The guy who uses this car on night shift. He says he's going to quit, but you know how it is."

"You should get one of those air freshener things. You know, the kind you hang off your rear-view mirror."

"A hula dancer, what do you think?" Quinn's smile was wicked. "That would send my lieutenant into a state of feminist-induced furor."

"At least the car would smell better."

He drew in a breath and let it out slowly. "Smells better already. But then, you don't smell like stale cigarettes."

I was glad he noticed. Happy Heart isn't cheap, and I'm not rolling in dough. "You see, giving me a ride is a good thing. I've already made your day better. So, what's our strategy when we get there?"

"*My* strategy . . ." He made sure he paused so I didn't miss the emphasis, "is to check out what happened and talk to everyone involved. Your strategy is to look inconspicuous and stay out of the way. Then again . . ." He sighed, and, call me egotistical (or maybe it was just hopeful), but I swear he didn't sound nearly as annoyed as he had earlier. *Wistful* was too poetic a word. Maybe *hopeful* worked for Quinn, too. "You couldn't look inconspicuous if you tried."

Now we were getting somewhere! More comfortable flirting than I was when we were at each other's throats, I settled myself as best I could against the stiff vinyl. "What you're saying is that I could be mistaken for a high-priced call girl. Is that such a bad thing?"

Quinn pursed his lips. "Not that I can see." We were nearly to the Rock Hall, and he stopped at a red light and raised a hand in greeting to the cop who was directing traffic there before he looked my way. His eyes sparked, and maybe it was my weakened condition that made me susceptible. When he looked at me that way, I felt as if I was about to melt.

Quinn's left hand was on the steering wheel. He moved his right hand across the seat until the tips of his fingers were just barely touching my thigh.

The melting factor rose a few degrees.

He kept his eyes on the road, and I did, too. That didn't mean I wasn't keenly aware of the heat of his skin and the touch that was almost not a touch. My insides quivered and my outsides . . . well, let's just say it was too bad Quinn was clocked in on the payroll. I could think of better things to do with our time.

He pulled up in front of the Rock Hall, and unlike the rest of us mortals, he didn't have to wait for an open meter. He angled his car right behind an ambulance with its lights spinning.

Once he had the car in park, he turned to me. "So . . ." He moved his fingers a fraction of an inch. A feeling like liquid fire spread up my thigh. "What *did* Vinnie say to you before he died?"

The whole touch-but-don't-touch thing? It was a

dirty trick and Quinn knew it. That's why he grinned when I shot daggers at him. "You're underhanded," I said, and I didn't wait for him to deny it. I got out of the car.

"No more underhanded than you." Who the hell would have the nerve to steal a cop car, I didn't know, but when Quinn got out, he locked the door. He tossed the keys in the air, caught them in one hand, and shoved them into his pocket. "You played me for a sucker. That's how you got a ride out of me. So I figured—"

"You'd play me," I snarled.

He didn't notice. He was busy flashing his badge at the uniformed cop stationed outside the revolving doors that led into the lobby. I breezed in on his coattails, so to speak, and nearly ran smack into him when he stopped just a couple of feet inside the lobby.

"Keep quiet and stay out of the way," Quinn instructed me, and before I could remind him that I was always quiet and I was never in the way, he was striding across the lobby toward the makeshift stage set up outside the gift shop and the crowd gathered there.

"He's really into you."

It had been a long day. And it wasn't even three. When Damon popped up right next to me, I jumped and pressed a hand to my heart.

I didn't lose my cool, though. Before I said a word, I made sure I turned my back on the action. With everyone focused on the stage area, nobody was going to pay attention to the lone woman over by the front doors who was clutching her chest and talking to herself.

My smile was sour. "He's a jerk."

"Maybe, but he's crazy about you."

I grunted. "He's got a funny way of showing it."

Damon laughed. "All guys have a funny way of showing it. You should have figured that out by now."

First Grandma Panhorst and now Damon. Did every dead person within a hundred-mile radius have an opinion about my love life?

I crossed my arms over my chest. "So now you're an expert? From what I've heard, you weren't exactly Mr. Commitment."

"You got that right, baby!" Damon's grin was as dazzling as the sunshine that streamed through the glass lobby. "I had a thousand chicks and a thousand good times and I'll tell you what, I wouldn't trade a minute of it. But I've also had nearly forty years to do nothing but think. And thinking about it . . ."

Damon's eyes lost their luster. "Back then," he said, "it was a game, and the name of the game was having them all. Young, old. Short, tall. Fat, skinny. I didn't care. I preferred my women young and gorgeous, like you . . ." He gave me a wink. "And it was always easier if there wasn't some jealous boyfriend or husband who wasn't getting all bent out of shape because I was screwing his old lady. But I'll tell you what, I wasn't particular, and stealing some other guy's chick, well, that was all part of the fun. I wanted any woman any other guy had. When I had her, I had the time of my life. But once I had her, I didn't want her anymore. Now . . ." He scraped a hand over his jaw and glanced across the lobby to where Quinn was talking to one of the dozen or so uniformed officers who had responded to the emergency call.

"That cop of yours, he's gonna get what I can never have, and I'm not just talking about the sex. It's you, Pepper. It's everything you are." Damon's voice sizzled with emotion. His eyes glimmered, not just with reflected sunlight, but with a heat that came from within. He leaned closer, and okay, I knew better. I knew I couldn't make contact with a ghost. Not without turning into a female frosty.

Try and tell that to my hormones.

When Damon stepped nearer to look into my eyes, I tipped my head back.

When he got even closer, my eyes fluttered shut.

When he brought his mouth down on mine—

"Ouch!"

Good thing there was such a hubbub going on in the lobby. When I yelped, nobody heard me. When I jumped back and away from the icy cold touch of Damon's lips, nobody noticed.

My mouth stung. Like I'd smooched an icy piece of metal, my lips were raw.

"I'm sorry." Damon raised a hand to touch a finger to my mouth, but hey, it was the old once-burned, twice-shy thing. Only burning wasn't what I was worried about. I ducked out of the way, and then I was sorry I did; Damon looked as if I'd slapped him.

"I couldn't help myself, Pepper," he said. "I've never felt this way before! Not about any woman. Man, can you believe it? This is a first! Damon Curtis is jealous!" He looked back to where Quinn was talking to one of the paramedics, and I looked that way, too. "Jealous of a cop!"

There was a time I thought a broken heart was nothing but a metaphor. Or was it a simile? No matter, I swear I felt mine crack in two. There wasn't anything I could do, and nothing I could say. No worries. When I turned back to Damon, he was nowhere in sight.

And wonder of wonder, when I looked around to see where he went, I saw Quinn instead, just as he raised a hand to wave me over. I moved fast. Before he could change his mind.

I'd been so busy concentrating on Damon, I'd pretty much blocked out everything going on around me, but as I crossed the spacious and wide-open lobby, the commotion got louder and the crowds got thicker.

I stepped around a group of Rock Hall employees watching the action. And a couple of paramedics standing around wondering what to do with the empty stretcher they were carrying.

The acoustics in the lobby were great for music, but they amplified the uproar of voices and the crackle of police radios until it all blended into one giant nightmare of noise. Still, through it all, one voice rose above the racket. Alistair Cromwell was sitting on the top stair of the steps that led up to the stage. He was dangling his smashed glasses in one hand, and there was a gash across the bridge of his nose. One of the paramedics was trying to dab a gauze to the wound, but Alistair would have none of it.

"Get your bloody mitts off me, you bloody little ponce." Alistair slapped the man's hands away. "I'm right as rain, and if you can't see that for yourself, then you're in the wrong business."

Quinn turned his back on the scene. He acknowledged me with a nod, and he was just about to turn to the short, bald man who stood at his side when he stopped and squinted in my direction. "What happened to your mouth? Your lip is bleeding."

"My lip . . ." Until I tried to talk, I didn't realize that in addition to being raw, my lips were swollen. Like I'd gotten a whopping dose of Novocain, my mouth was numb. I tried to answer Quinn again, slower and more carefully this time. "I wan into . . ."

A dead man's lips?

Couldn't exactly say that, so I waved a hand in the direction of the revolving door where we'd entered the hall. If Quinn wasn't so preoccupied, he might have noticed that there was nothing over there I could possibly have run into. The way it was, he took my story at face value.

He reached into his pocket for a handkerchief and pressed it into my hand before he turned back to the man at his side. "This is Gene Terry, Mind at Large's business manager and agent," Quinn said. "I was just telling him that you saw Vinnie this morning."

"Talk about bad luck!" Gene had a Brooklyn accent as thick as a deli pastrami on rye and really good taste in clothes. His navy blue suit was Armani. His white dress shirt must have been made-to-order or it wouldn't have fit so well over his broad shoulders. Unfortunately, the effect was lost when he paired the outfit with black-and-white sneakers. He was a head shorter than me and completely bald. Since I had the hankie in my right hand, he grabbed my left hand and pumped it. He looked at my chest before he looked me in the eye. "Officer Harrison here tells me you were with Vinnie this morning when he kicked it. Did he say anything? I mean, anything for the boys in the band? Anything for me?"

Carefully, I touched the hankie to my lip. When I lifted it away, it was stained with red. "Vinnie was weally woozy," I said. "I twied to talk to him but as for wesponding . . ." I screeched my frustration and chose my words carefully. "He didn't say much."

Terry had a round body and heavy jowls. When he frowned, his face folded in on itself. "Did he tell you who—?"

"Bloody hell!"

Alistair's shout split Gene's question in two. I spun around just in time to see him grappling with two strapping paramedics. He was far older than either of them, but he was having one heck of a hissy fit, and he had rock stardom on his side. He pushed himself to his feet and stood, and the paramedics backed off to give him plenty of distance. When he walked over to where we stood, he wobbled.

"Get rid of these bleeding idiots, Gene. I can't take it anymore. They're fussing over me like I'm a bloody retard. Call my personal doctor."

"We've done that, Al." I could tell Gene had been through this song-and-dance before. He moved in on Alistair and took charge, lowering his voice like he was talking to a child. Or a wild animal. "Dr. Brighton is in L.A. He's canceled his appointments for the rest of the week and he's going to be on the first plane."

"As if there are planes between L.A. and this bloody place!" Alistair's face was red. A vein bulged at the side of his neck. "Who the hell ever thought of doing a concert in this hellhole? It's a death trap, that's what it is."

"It was an accident." Gene put a hand on Alistair's arm, made eye contact, and refused to look away. I'd seen one of my uncles do the same thing with a cocker spaniel that was impossible to train. "One of the lights fell. You just happened to be under it at the time. It's not going to happen again. This isn't even the stage you'll be using for the concert. That will be outside. What were you doing here anyway, Al? You told me you were going to be home this morning."

"Shit." As if he didn't realize he was holding on to them, Alistair looked at the bent and twisted glasses in his hand. He tossed them on the floor. "I thought it would be fun just to pay a visit. You know, see the place and get the lay of the land. I couldn't resist jumping up on that stage. You know, for a look. It's going to be hell getting the sound right in this place."

"That's what the sound team is for. They'll get it right."

"And the crowds . . ." Alistair looked past the soaring windows to the plaza beyond. "How the hell many people do they think they can get out there? It won't be like Shea."

I don't know if Quinn had heard enough or if he had a legitimate place to go. Either way, he didn't bother excusing himself before he moved toward where a couple of guys in blue windbreakers were looking over the wreckage of lights and wires that littered the stage.

Gene Terry watched him go, then returned to the matter at hand. "Shea was a long time ago," he reminded Alistair. "You know we don't get the crowds we used to."

"Well we bloody well should," Alistair grumbled. "And who the hell are you, anyway?" he asked, turning on me. "I told them, no damned reporters."

"I'm not a weporter." I winced "My name is Pepper. I was with Vinnie this morning and when I heard what happened to you . . ." I tasted blood on my lips and held the hankie to my mouth again. It was the first I noticed that Quinn's initials were embroidered on it. "It seems stwange, doesn't it? I mean, it's awfully cuwious . . . Vinnie was murdered. And then this."

Something told me this was something Alistair had yet to consider. He squinched up his eyes and stared at me hard. "What the hell is this woman jabbering about?" he asked Gene, as if I wasn't even there. "Is she interrogating me?"

"She's concerned."

I tried to thank the agent for his support with a smile, but it hurt too much.

"I'm not intewwogating . . ." I clenched my teeth. "I just think we need to talk about it. That's all."

"The cops say Vinnie's place was burglarized." This came from Gene, and I was grateful. It was more than I knew when I left the condo.

"If it was a wobbery—"

I grimaced.

"If it was wandom—"

I counted to ten, searching for patience and words that didn't include any Rs.

"We can't dismiss this," I said and congratulated myself when I managed to not sound like Elmer Fudd for a whole sentence. "What if it isn't a coincidence?"

It was my turn to come under Terry's ministering care. He dropped his hand from Alistair's arm and patted mine. "You're right," he said. "We do need to talk. Hearing about Vinnie's last moments will help give us all closure. But you're jumping to conclusions as far as what happened to Alistair is concerned. It was an accident."

"Pwobably."

I'd been so busy concentrating on my vocabulary, I didn't notice that Quinn had joined us. He looked over his shoulder back toward the stage and the crime scene technicians who were working there.

"The techs aren't sure yet, but it doesn't look as if the wires were cut. We'll know more in a little while."

"I don't care what they say. This place is dangerous." Alistair didn't wait to hear any more. He shoved his way through the crowd, and Gene Terry followed. Even when Bernie the bodyguard appeared out of nowhere and ushered them away, I could still hear Alistair's high-pitched bitching.

Gingerly, I touched the hankie to my lip. There was less blood than before. "Were you telling the twuth? Was it an accident?"

"You mean Alistair? And the lights?"

"And Vinnie. It's awfully coincidental."

Maybe, but if Quinn saw the connection, he didn't have time to tell me about it. His cell phone rang.

He talked for a minute, and when he snapped his phone shut, I snapped myself out of my thoughts and fell into step behind him. "I have to go," he said.

"You're going to let me wide along, aren't you? I mean, I can come with you, wight?"

"Not to the scene of a murder/suicide." The crowd of uniformed cops in front of him parted and Quinn didn't waste any time. He strode toward the revolving doors that led outside.

"But—" I scrambled to catch up. "But what about me? How am I going to get back to the cem-etewy?"

He paused for a fraction of a second before he pushed through the doors. A smile crinkled one corner of his mouth. "You can always take the bus."

I had the perfect comeback. Honest. But two things happened before I had a chance to deliver it. Number one, Quinn headed out the door and was gone. And number two . . . well, that might have had something to do with the voice I heard behind me. The one that stopped me cold.

"The angel of death circles overhead like a dove."

It sounded like something Damon would say. Or at least something he might have written in a song. But this wasn't Damon's voice. I turned just in time to see a thin woman with long, stringy hair shuffle past. I recognized her at once. She was the one who'd been cleaning Damon's exhibit the first time I visited the Rock Hall. And she'd been in Vinnie's class, too. Just like she had been that night, she was wearing beat-up jeans and a shirt decorated with beads and sequins. It was all topped off with a dirty denim jacket.

Now—as then—she had a coffee cup in her hands. It had *City Roast* printed on the side of it. The cup was empty, and she twisted it in bony fingers, breaking off tiny bits of Styrofoam and scattering them like a trail of breadcrumbs.

Or clues.

Remembering something I'd seen in Vinnie's apartment and, come to think of it, at Damon's grave, too, I perked right up. City Roast wasn't one of the big chains in the area. As a matter of fact, as far as I knew, their coffee was sold at only one place in the city, the West Side Market, an open-air extravaganza sort of shopping place not too far away.

Before she had a chance to get by me, I intercepted the woman. "Hey!" I tried for a friendly smile, but it hurt too much, so I gave her a wave before I pointed to what was left of her cup. "That's my favorite coffee, too. Vinnie liked City Woast. I know because he had some of the cups in his apartment. Were you a fwiend of his?"

She frowned. "He forgot to stop. He promised he'd come for me and he passed right by."

Something told me we weren't talking about Vinnie. Or even about coffee. I didn't have the luxury of wimping out, so I gulped down the heebie-jeebies. "You mean the angel of death? What, you guys had an appointment or something?"

"He's coming for me." The woman's eyes were so pale, they were nearly colorless. "He said he would, and he'd never lie. He won't disappoint me. Not again."

I was getting nowhere fast. I decided on another tack. "Alistair's glad the angel of death didn't stop for him."

"Alistair's my cat. He's a sweet little thing." Her brows dipped low over her eyes. "He doesn't like the dog next door. No, he doesn't. But my Alistair doesn't have to worry about the angel. I won't let him go outside so the dog can't eat him."

"That's weally smart." Since I couldn't smile, I nodded. "But I was talking about this Alistair. Alistair Cromwell. He almost got smashed by a light. And Vinnie . . ." Again, I pictured the coffee cups strewn around the penthouse. "When was the last time you saw Vinnie?"

"Vinnie's aura is all wrong. He's not a cat."

"No, he's not." It hadn't occurred to me until that moment that there might be anyone who hadn't heard what happened to Vinnie. It was obvious this woman was one bottle short of a six-pack. If I broke it to her, how would she take the news of Vinnie's death?

Or maybe I didn't need to tell her. If she knew Vinnie well enough to visit and leave her signature coffee cups behind, did she know him well enough to know what had happened to him?

Well enough to kill him?

I considered the possibility while I carefully

formed my question. "You know Vinnie is dead, wight? He died this morning."

"He died too young." A single tear slid down the woman's cheek. "He thought sandwiches were mother's milk. And all the sunshine was killing poison. He's circling now." She looked up and beyond the glass walls that soared overhead. When she smiled, I saw she had a couple of missing teeth. "He'll be back. He's coming for me. My lover." She was still smiling and mumbling when she shambled away.

"All wighty, then." Watching her go, I shivered and hugged my arms around myself.

"She bothering you?" Gene Terry was back from wherever—minus Alistair and Bernie— and when he saw me watching the woman as she got on the escalator, and headed toward the downstairs exhibits, he came to stand beside me. "Belinda's harmless."

"You know her? I thought she was on the staff here. You know, maintenance."

He laughed. "Belinda's not a cleaning woman. She's—"

"As cwazy as a loon."

"Yeah, she is that." Gene shook his head. "The psychedelic movement was kinder to some than others."

"So all that stuff about the angel of death and sandwiches . . . ?"

From where we stood, we could still see Crazy Belinda. She got off the escalator, and I wasn't surprised when she headed in the direction of Damon's exhibit. Gene was watching her, too. "Believe it or not," he said, "she was beautiful once. We were wild about her."

"We? As in the band?"

Gene nodded. "She spent a lot of time hanging with the guys. Then she just sort of dropped out of sight. When we arrived in Cleveland for this gig, she showed up out of nowhere. Acted like nothing had changed. Like we could just pick up where we left off so many years ago."

"And the guys in the band . . ." Yeah, I was being nosy. But remember, I was talking murder. Even if Gene didn't know that's what I was talking about. "Were they happy to see her?"

"What do you think?"

"I think she's got some cwazy fixation with death. And with Mind at Large. It's cweepy." I was sounding cwazy and cweepy, too, and I vowed to choose my words more carefully.

Gene dismissed the whole thing with a wave of one hand. "Belinda, she's just talking nonsense. Even before she destroyed her brain cells, she was a space cadet. She's harmless."

"And very cwee . . . Stwange . . . odd."

"There seems to be a lot of that going around."

I couldn't see Belinda anymore, so I turned toward Gene and found him looking at the stage and the light that had crashed down on it so hard, it left a crater the size of a Volkswagen Beetle. His expression clouded. "I can't believe we almost lost two of the guys today. Brings the whole thing back like it was yesterday. You know, about Damon."

"But Damon wasn't murdered."

"No, no he wasn't." Gene shook himself. "I was

just thinking, that's all. We've been through so much together, me and the band, yet when the guys need me most . . ." He shivered. "I was in Pittsburgh the night Damon died, checking out the venue for our next concert date. I spent a lot of years in therapy coming to grips with the fact that even if I'd been with him, there probably wasn't anything I could have done to save him. And this morning . . ." Gene sighed. "There I was, sitting on my duff back at my hotel, drinking espresso and eating eggs Benedict while somebody was slicing up Vinnie."

Since there had actually been more stabbing than slicing, Gene's comparison wasn't exactly accurate. I didn't bother to correct him. Mostly because I figured slicing or stabbing, it didn't much matter. Dead was dead.

"And then this happens to Alistair." Gene interrupted my thoughts just as they were about to latch on to the memory of Vinnie on the floor with that knife sticking out of his chest. For this, I was grateful. "It's strange, don't you think?"

"Exactly what I was twying to tell Quinn." Don't ask me why I bothered to look outside. Of course, Quinn was long gone.

"You don't think it was a coincidence." Gene studied me carefully. "Funny, you don't look like a cop."

I would have laughed if my mouth didn't hurt. "I'm no cop."

"But Officer Harrison said you sometimes work together."

"Did he?" I was surprised (and strangely gratified) to hear Quinn would ever admit it. "I'm a kind of consultant."

"You mean like a private detective."

"Sort of. But not weally." I felt it necessary to add this last bit, just so Gene didn't get it into his head that he wanted something investigated. I had enough on my plate. "I weally work as a tour guide. At Garden View Cemetewy."

Gene's eyes lit. "Where Damon is buried. Is that how you met Belinda?"

"I met her downstairs. She was cleaning Damon's exhibit."

Gene chuckled. "Thank goodness the folks who run this place are tolerant! Belinda's obsessed. Damon and the guys . . . well, she thought of them as family." The gleam in his eyes diminished, and he looked at me carefully. "How did you get involved in all this?"

I was all set to give him the same story I'd concocted for Vinnie. The one about how I was a big fan. But something told me Gene wouldn't believe it. For one thing, I was too young and obviously too with-it to be of the Mind at Large mindset. For another, I didn't want to risk having another old guy try to seduce me because he thought I was an easy target. Been there, done that, thank you very much.

With not one original idea in my brain, I fell back on an old ploy, one that had worked well for me when I was investigating Gus Scarpetti's murder.

"I feel silly admitting this," I said, and I made sure I gave Gene a tiny (the only kind I could manage) smile along with the explanation. He might be old, but he was a man, and I had yet to meet one who couldn't be schmoozed by a little feminine charm. "I got intewested in Damon Curtis because, like I said, I work at the cemetew . . . at Garden View. I'm hoping . . ." Here I looked away, then sighed. With any luck, he'd believe he was the first one who'd heard my secret. "I'd like to wite a book someday. About Damon. I've started my wesearch. That's why I went to talk to Vinnie."

Over the years, I'd bet Gene had heard this same story from a thousand people (though probably not with the preponderance of Ws). Big points for him, he didn't tell me I was wasting my time. In fact, he looked downright interested. "What have you found out?" he asked.

"About Damon?" I wasn't expecting this, and I scrambled. "Oh, you know, this and that. Vinnie was vewy helpful. He told me all about how Damon used to wite his songs." Since Gene didn't know which he my *his* referred to, this was technically true. I remembered the story I gave the Lakewood cops and decided a little corroboration wouldn't hurt. "He loaned me a couple things, too. You know, CDs and such."

"I'll tell you what . . ." Gene reached into his pocket, pulled out a business card, and handed it to me along with a pen. "You write down your name and address and I'll see what I have around that might help with your research. You'll hear from Zack." He looked across the hall to where a tall, skinny kid with long hair and bad skin was talking to a TV reporter. "He's our PR guy. Don't expect anything too soon. Between dealing with what happened to Vinnie today and getting ready for the big concert, we're going to be pretty busy."

I scribbled down the information and handed the card back to Gene. "You'll still do the concert?"

"The show must go on!" He tried for cheery, but I could tell he was hurting. "Vinnie wouldn't want us to cancel."

"And Belinda?"

When I saw that Gene was confused, I caught him up on my thought process. "I'm just wondering, that's all. If there's any weason, you know, that Belinda would think the show must go on. Or any weason she might want the concert to be canceled."

"You don't think—" Belinda was long gone but Gene automatically looked toward the escalator. "Nah!" He dismissed my suspicions with a snort and a shake of his head. "She's crazy, all right, but she's not dangerous. You don't think she and Vinnie—"

"I know she might have been there."

"At Vinnie's place? Did you tell Officer Harrison?"

"I didn't have a chance. Quinn doesn't hear anything Quinn doesn't want to hear."

"Then do me a favor, okay?" Gene put a gentle hand on my arm. "Let's keep this under our hats. There's no use pulling a mentally ill woman into the limelight if we don't have to. And you know . . ." He bent nearer. "That's exactly what you'd be doing if word of this gets out. You think every reporter in the country isn't just itching for a lead? They'd go chasing after Belinda in a minute if they knew she'd been over to Vinnie's place." He looked me in the eye. "And you, too, you know."

I'd never been one to shy away from the spotlight, but I knew exactly what he was saying. The Lakewood police had already decided that I was a high-priced call girl. My poor mom, hiding out in Florida because of what happened with my dad, didn't need another family scandal. If this made it's way into the press, she'd never be able to show her face in town again.

I nodded, silently agreeing to Gene's plan, but that didn't mean I was willing to completely relinquish responsibility. "But what if she's guilty?" I asked him.

"Belinda? Guilty?" Gene laughed, and when the PR guy waved him over, he patted my arm and took off in that direction. "Believe me when I tell you this, honey, because I know it for a fact. The only thing Belinda was ever guilty of was partying too hard."

Chapter 11

Over the next twenty-four hours, the chill in my lips spread through the rest of my body. It was uncomfortable to say the least. Especially when every time I shivered, I thought about kissing Damon.

Or maybe thinking about kissing Damon was what made me shiver in the first place.

Either way, the icy cold was a constant reminder that I was a dope. Thinking I could kiss a ghost and come away unharmed was bad enough. Recognizing that I was falling in love with that ghost . . .

I dashed the thought away and tried to look on the bright side. As so often happens in Cleveland in the fall, the temperature dipped considerably that night, so when I arrived at work the next day bundled in wool pants, a turtleneck, and a sweater, nobody questioned it.

I tucked my hands up into the sleeves of my sweater, but it was hard to type that way, and I had a monthly report to prepare on the tours I'd given. I was getting nowhere fast.

Which was pretty much the same place I was getting in my investigation.

Call it coincidence or karma or maybe it was just an accident. No sooner did the thought pop into my head than Damon showed up in the chair across from my desk.

"You okay?" he asked.

"Sure." When I smiled, my mouth hurt. "The swelling's down and my lips aren't bleeding anymore."

"But you're freezing."

"That's the downside of the Gift." I was too uncomfortable looking at Damon so soon after thinking about what he was doing to my self-composure (not to mention my common sense), so I typed a quick description of the tour I'd conducted for the fourth graders. Not to worry, I wouldn't dream of causing Ella apoplexy, so I left out the part about how six of them refused to get off the bus because they didn't want to step on dead people. I didn't mention the kid who we thought was lost and was found wedged between two headstones he shouldn't have been climbing on in the first place, either, or the four others who decided they were hot, took off their shoes, and went wading in the pond behind the chapel.

When I was done, I hit enter a couple of times, signaling that the paragraph—and with any luck, the conversation—was finished. "I'll be fine by tomorrow."

"You'll be warm by tomorrow." Leave it to a poet to pick up on the subtle difference. Damon was wearing jeans and a T-shirt that was torn at the neck and had a picture of Lyndon Johnson on it. His hands flat against his thighs, he leaned forward. "What are we going to do, Pepper?"

Damon wasn't talking about the investigation, but I did so not want to go where I knew he was headed. Acting dumb was better than taking the chance of being caught by the magic of his voice. Or the simmering sensuality that lit his dark eyes when he looked at me. That road led nowhere. Except to Popsicle Land.

And I was already cold enough.

"We need to find out if and how everything that's happening now has anything to do with your death. That seems like the key to me. I don't know if Quinn believed me or not," I said. "I mean about how Vinnie's death and the attack on Alistair might be related. He's hard to read."

I left it at that and hoped Damon would, too. We'd had our little heart-to-heart about Quinn back at the Rock Hall, and I didn't need to rehash it all. I skillfully deflected the conversation back where it belonged. "There's got to be a connection. It's all just too coincidental." Careful with the tips of my nails (I didn't want to chip my toffee-colored polish), I drummed my fingers against my desk and tried to make sense of it all.

Thirty seconds of that kind of thinking, and I was more confused than ever.

I slapped my hand against the desk. "Maybe I should just ask Vinnie," I said.

I was kidding.

Until I thought about it for a moment.

"Hey!" I jumped to my feet. "I'm the one with the Gift. Maybe I should just talk to Vinnie!"

Damon nodded. "That's a great idea. Go ahead. Do it. Contact him."

Now that I was on the spot, so to speak, I fumbled around for the right way to approach things, and believe it or not, I was actually embarrassed when I wasn't sure where to start.

"I've never tried to do this before," I told Damon, making excuses because excuses were better than admitting that, Gift or not, I didn't know what the hell I was doing. "I mean, I've never tried to contact a ghost on my own. Not until I knew the ghost, anyway. I'm not sure what to say to Vinnie."

"Just talk." Damon got to his feet, and we stood facing each other, the desk between us. "Maybe just say hello."

"All right." I scraped my palms against the legs of my wool pants. "Vinnie! It's me, Pepper." I sounded as unsure of myself as I felt, so I put a little more oomph in my words. "Hey, Vinnie! Come on, I need to talk to you."

Nothing.

I tried a different approach. "Pepper to Vinnie, Pepper to Vinnie. Come in, Vinnie."

More nothing.

Damon said, "Let me try," and went through the same routine.

He got the same results.

Disgusted, I glanced around my smaller than small office and headed for the door. "Maybe we just don't have the right vibes in here. We might have better luck out in the cemetery where there are more dead people."

Anxious to prove the theory, I hurried outside.

Like I mentioned, it had gotten considerably cooler, and though the sun was shining, I wasn't surprised that there weren't many visitors in the cemetery. A snappy breeze blew in from the north, rattling the trees that surrounded the office. I didn't want to attract any attention, so I crossed the parking lot and zipped down a road lined with oak trees. At a place where that road split off, left and right, I gauged my distance from the office (and from anyone who might look out the window), took the street on the left, and ducked into the closest section. There was a 1940s bandleader buried nearby, and a couple of times the summer before, I'd led visitors to his grave. I knew that not far away, there was an empty bit of land surrounded on all sides by monuments taller than me. I skirted the statue of a weeping woman and stepped onto the patch of grass. I was completely alone, except for Damon, of course, and with all the privacy I needed, I raised my voice.

"Hey, Vinnie. Are you around here somewhere?"

I didn't get an answer to my question, and as crazy as it seems, I felt I needed to justify my lack of results. "You know, Vinnie's body is being shipped back to California," I told Damon. "I read it in the paper this morning. Vinnie was front-page news. They said once the coroner is done with him, he's going to L.A. to be cremated. His first, second, and third wives are already fighting over the ashes. Maybe since his body isn't around here anywhere, his spirit isn't, either?"

"I don't know, I'm not exactly sure how it all works. I'll give it a try again." Damon closed his eyes and stood as still and as quiet as the angel on the monument nearby. He looked like an angel, too—a fallen one—and because that was something I didn't want to think about when I was supposed to be concentrating on contacting Vinnie's spirit, I closed my eyes, too.

I didn't open them again until a couple of minutes later when I heard Damon sigh. "I can't feel him anywhere near," he admitted.

"Great." It wasn't, and I knew it. I stomped out of my hiding place. There was a flat gravestone nearby, and I sat down on it. "Talking to Vinnie is exactly what we need to do. He might be able to tell us who killed him, and that might tell us something about the attack on Alistair, too. I wonder if we could do a séance or something."

I didn't know squat about how to conduct a séance, so before Damon could take me up on it, it was a good thing I saw movement out of the corner of my eye. For once, I was happy to see the ghostbusters.

They were prowling around an ornate mausoleum with pink and gray granite columns and an intricate iron door, and since they didn't look especially excited, I figured they weren't getting much in the way of readings. Hoping to keep it that way—at least for now—I told Damon to take a powder and hurried over before the busters decided to climb into the SUV parked nearby and head to another part of Garden View.

"Hey, what's up?" I waved and called to them.

I wasn't surprised to see Dan with the group and carrying a Geiger counter. I was surprised to see him looking like the Dan of old. Gone were the ignite-my-fantasies jeans and the black leather jacket that creaked and crinkled every time Dan moved. He was dressed much as he had been back in the days when I thought he was nothing more than a brainiac doing research at a nearby hospital, in brown polyester pants, a blue sweater, and gray windbreaker. He'd fallen in with the geek crowd, and he was apparently proud of it.

I figured Brian, the leader of the hunters, would be most susceptible to my suggestion, so while the others were busy taking temperature readings, snapping pictures, and playing with their tape recorders, I talked to him.

"I need your help," I said.

He didn't seem surprised. Then again, I suppose it goes along with the territory. When you're a ghost hunter, nothing much surprises you. "You want to conduct a hunt?" he asked.

"Something like that. I want to get in touch with Vinnie Pal."

This was my carrot on a stick, and it wasn't hard to see why. If the ghost hunters were dead set (pun intended) on finding Damon's ghost, then finding evidence of Vinnie's would be part of the package and bring them even more prestige in the eyes of other ghost-hunting dorks.

Brian's eyes lit, and he waved the rest of the hunters over. When they gathered, Dan somehow managed to end up right next to me. Did he know more than the rest of them about ghosts? I wasn't sure, but as the Magic Eight Ball would say, all signs seemed to point that way.

"What's the best way to find someone who recently died?" I asked him.

It was clear that as leader of the group, Brian felt it was his responsibility to be their spokesperson, too. Before Dan could answer, he jumped right in.

"That can be tricky," Brian said, and when he did, he sounded like he was repeating something he'd read in a book. "Sometimes the recently deceased aren't available for a while."

This was not news I wanted to hear and I wasn't willing to settle for it. Something told me Dan wouldn't be quite so wed to the party line. I turned his way so that there was no mistaking the fact that he was the one I was addressing.

"We could try, anyway, couldn't we?" I asked Dan.

He peered at me from behind his wire-rimmed glasses. "Trying implies that you believe in ghosts."

"And if I say I do, then can we try?"

He didn't take my admission (such as it was) as an outright surrender. But he didn't argue, either. "Brian's right," Dan said, "it can be a challenge. But . . ." He strung me along just for the hell of it. "We might have some success. If we had access to the place the person died."

I thought of Vinnie's penthouse condo. And the doorman who knew me on sight. I couldn't say I was certain that I'd be able to get past him, especially with a bunch of ghost hunters in tow, but I did know it was worth a try.

We set a time—eleven o'clock—and a place to meet—the service entrance of the condo building. After that, I hurried into the office, told Ella I needed to take an early lunch, and headed to the store. I needed a tape recorder, batteries, and a digital camera.

I was going on a ghost hunt.

* * *

As it turned out, it didn't matter if I knew the doorman, or not. He wasn't on duty that night. In fact, nobody was. To people in real cities, like New York or Chicago, this would probably seem a little odd. But we were talking Lakewood, Ohio, here, home of a private boys' prep school, dozens of mom-and-pop stores, and hundreds of the kinds of bars where everyone really does know your name. We were just over the western border from Cleveland, but apparently osmosis doesn't apply to crime. People feel safe in the suburbs, and high-priced or not, the lobby wasn't staffed at night.

This was good news, yes? It meant that when the ghost hunters and I trooped into the elevator, nobody challenged us.

But of course, there's the whole cloud-and-silver-lining thing. No questions asked; that was the silver lining. We discovered the cloud upstairs when we realized the door to Vinnie's condo was locked. Of course.

"I thought you said you could get us in here."

Apparently geeks with their hearts set on ghost hunting can get a little testy. Brian's words were sharp. They were aimed right at me.

I defended myself. "I did get us in. Into the building. Last time I was here, the door was open."

"But the cops never would have left it that way, would they?" Brian said this like I was solely responsible for the oversight. Since I wasn't, I didn't take it to heart. But I wasn't going to take it lying down, either.

"You're the one who wants to find Damon's ghost," I reminded him. "You know this is a perfect opportunity. If you contact Vinnie Pal, you might be able to get him to tell you how to find Damon." I looked around at the other busters, too, just so they didn't think they were going to get off the hook easily. "What do you usually do when you go somewhere to look for ghosts and you can't get in?"

"We leave. It's the legal way to handle things."

"It's legal when you have a key." Dan pushed his way to the front of the group. In fact, he didn't have a key, but surprise, surprise, he did have a set of lock picks. He sized up the lock, rummaged through the picks, and got to work.

Call me paranoid, but as he worked, I noticed Dan had thought of something none of the rest of us had. He was wearing surgical gloves, and even with them on, his fingers were quick and nimble. He never hesitated or fumbled, and realizing what it meant, my stomach went cold at the same time my curiosity turned white-hot. This wasn't his first time.

When the lock snapped open, Dan stepped back to allow the other ghostbusters into the condo. I waited until they were all inside. "Want to tell me how you learned to pick locks?" I asked Dan.

Unlike the other ghost hunters who were in the darkened living room spreading out the equipment they'd be sharing, Dan had brought a backpack of his own. He slipped it off his shoulder, put the lock picks away, and took out some gizmo that reminded me of a . . . well . . . a gizmo.

When he made a move toward the condo, I stopped him, one hand on his arm. "First it was karate, now it's lock picking. What else do you know how to do?"

He looked down to where my fingers were bunched around the sleeve of his windbreaker. When he looked back up at me, his eyes reflected the mellow light from the lamps over the paintings in the hallway. "You'd be surprised."

"Yeah, I bet I would. Just like I was surprised when I realized you were following me last summer. Just like I'm surprised to find you hanging around with these guys. You told me you were a research scientist. You said you were conducting a study. About my propensity for hallucinatory imaging. Remember? You said my behavior was aberrant."

Dan shrugged. "You're the one who wants to talk to Vinnie Pal's ghost. That sounds pretty aberrant to me."

"And you're the one who seems to think you can make it possible for me to talk to his ghost. Maybe I'm not the only one with aberrant behavior issues."

"Have you checked them out?" Dan glanced into the condo, and when he looked at the ghost hunters, he smiled. When he looked back at me, though, he was as serious as a heart attack. "The thing that interests me, Pepper," he said, "is that you never questioned if it was possible. You said you wanted to contact Vinnie's spirit and you asked for my help doing it. But you never doubted it could be done. That tells me a lot. A lot about you. How many ghosts have you had contact with?"

I wasn't expecting a point-blank question, so I wasn't ready with an answer.

Dan read through my hesitation. "I thought so," he said. "We need to talk. But not here. Not now."

One hand on the small of my back, he ushered me into the condo. I noticed that someone had straightened up. The cutout of the naked lady was still there (bathed in moonlight, as luck would have it). So were the beer cans. But the City Roast coffee cups were gone.

Before I could think what this might mean, we were met by the ghost hunters, who, even in the dark, didn't miss a trick.

"Is that an electromagnetic field detector?" His eyes on the gizmo in Dan's hands, John rushed forward. "That's way cool. We haven't saved up enough for one of those yet."

Dan offered his. "Take this one," he said. "I'm going to do a little work with my digital voice recorder." He grabbed my hand. "Pepper's coming with me."

Okay, so I admit it, spending a couple of hours in a dark penthouse apartment with Dan hanging on to me wasn't all bad. I never even had a chance to take out my new camera or my tape recorder, and I didn't care. What was disappointing, though (to me and certainly to the ghostbusters) was that when it was all over, we had nothing to show for our hunt.

A couple of hours later, we were gathered in one of those bars I mentioned earlier. Everyone there really did know Brian's name. Maybe the fact that he was a regular had something to do with how many ghosts he'd claimed to have seen on other hunts.

"Nothing," he said, scrolling through the last of the pictures on Angela's digital camera. "We got no EVP, no temperature readings that were interesting, and no photos, either. Let's call it a night."

John, Theo, Angela, and Stan didn't argue. They gathered up their equipment, drank the last of the pitcher of beer Dan had ordered and paid for, and then they were gone.

Dan had been sitting four seats away from me at the bar. He slid down and took the seat beside mine. "Disappointed?"

"More like bored." I yawned. "How many times were they going to go through those tapes they recorded tonight? There wasn't anything on them but the sounds of them shuffling their own feet."

Dan didn't seem to hold it against the ghostbusters. "You never know," he said. "Part of the process of finding paranormal evidence is following scientific procedure."

"Do you really believe that?"

"Yes, I really believe that's the way things should work." A smile crinkled one corner of Dan's mouth. "No, I don't believe they actually do work that way. Not always, anyway. Case in point: You don't follow scientific procedure. And you've still made contact."

It was late and I was tired. As if that wasn't enough of an excuse to avoid the subject, there was the whole bit about Dan, who he really was and what he really wanted. Sure, he'd saved my life once upon a time, and honest, I was grateful, but frankly, the fact that he'd been able to do it—skillfully and efficiently—left me with more questions. Until I had answers, I wasn't ready to talk. Not about my Gift or the goings-on on the Other Side.

There was an inch of lite beer left in my glass. I

swirled it around. "You're convinced you know a lot about me. You want to tell me how?"

"I showed you the photo of you and those two ghosts. And if it was anybody else standing with two white, misty shapes, I would have dismissed it as an interesting but insignificant photo. But then I thought about your brain scans. Your occipital lobe is different from other peoples', Pepper. You've got more activity there, and to me that means you're far more attuned to the paranormal. Deny it if you like, but in that photo, I can see it in your eyes. You're aware of the ectoplasm streams in the room with you. You're talking to them."

I remembered the picture. And the brain scans, too, come to think of it. I knew he was right. I took a sip of beer, put my glass on the bar, lifted it, and took another sip.

"You don't trust me, do you?"

Dan put into words what I'd been thinking.

"How can I?" I asked him. "You haven't exactly been Honest Abe. I'm not even sure who you really are."

"That's fair." His own beer was gone, and he rolled the empty glass between his palms. "I can tell you this; there's a lot more going on in the field of paranormal research than you can even imagine. We're making real breakthroughs every day. You could be the key to it all, Pepper. I'd like to see you on our team."

"*Our* team?" It was beginning to sound like a *Mission: Impossible* movie, and I didn't like it one bit. "Something tells me you're not talking about Brian and the boys."

"And Angela, don't forget." Dan's smile was fleeting. "I can't tell you more."

"And in exchange for *I can't tell you more*, you expect me to spill my guts." I slid off the bar stool. "I won't bother saying goodbye. I guess I'll see you around whether I want to or not."

"Pepper!" I'd already turned away when Dan's hand clamped down on my arm.

I was surprised at both the force and the power of his grip, and just as I turned to tell him to keep his hands to himself, Dan backed off.

"I'm sorry," he said, but he wasn't talking about the way he grabbed me. I knew that right away. "I expect you to trust me, but I haven't given you any reason you should." He reached into his backpack and took out the tiny digital recorder I'd seen him use back at the condo. He pressed it into my hands. "Here. Maybe I can prove to you that I'm worthy of your trust. No strings attached. Take this and see if it helps." He took a cocktail napkin from the bar and the pen the bartender had left nearby when she wrote out our bill, scribbled a number on it, and gave me that, too.

"That's my cell. You make the next move, Pepper. Until you do—until you're ready—I swear you won't see me around. I'm going to leave the ghost-hunting group and I'm going to stop following you. Maybe then you'll believe I'm worthy of your trust."

And without another word, Dan walked out of the bar.

It was getting close to closing time. I knew I should get moving, but I didn't want to wait until I got home to see why Dan thought the tape he'd recorded was interesting.

Eager to find out, I slipped into the nearest booth and turned on the recorder.

"Is there anyone here?"

That was Dan's voice. Like I'd seen the other ghost hunters do, he asked a question, then waited a long, long time to give the spirits a chance to answer.

This time, there was no answer.

"Can you tell me your name?"

Dan's voice again and again, a long pause with no answer. In fact, the only thing I heard was me mumbling in the background, but then, we were in Vinnie's magic room, and it gave me the creeps. I was anxious to get out of there.

"Vinnie, are you here with us?"

Listening to the tape was like reliving the whole ghost hunt. And the ghost hunt was as exciting as watching paint dry.

The bartender made the last call.

I moved my finger to flick the recorder off.

That's when I heard a voice.

"Yes. Here."

The hair on the back of my neck stood up. Even though it was a rough whisper and the words were drawn out and labored, the voice was unmistakably Vinnie's.

I swallowed hard and waited for Dan's next question.

"Vinnie, if you're here, can you give us a sign? Tell us something, something about what happened to you here."

Another pause. I held my breath.

"It hurt."

A shiver skittered across my shoulders.

"Do you have anything to say?" Of course, Dan didn't know he was getting any of these answers. He couldn't have known, not until we were done with the hunt and he was down at the other end of the bar listening to his own recording while the rest of the ghost hunters messed with their equipment and their big-ol'-nothing results. "Do you have a message for us?"

"Careful. Danger. The group . . ." Vinnie's voice faded. I bent closer to the speaker, but the only thing I heard clearly was me mumbling a curse. It must have been when I slammed my knee into the wall as I was stumbling around in the dark. I couldn't hear Vinnie again until my grumbling subsided. "One," he said. The single word was as drawn-out and anguished as a howl. "One more will die."

Chapter 12

The next day, I had to lead a tour at the chapel. Believe it or not, I usually don't mind that assignment. The chapel at Garden View is one of the few buildings in the country completely designed and built by Tiffany. Yeah, that lamp and window guy, and how he's more important than the guy with the jewelry store, I can't say, but a lot of people are impressed when they hear his name.

I like the chapel. In the summer, it's shady and cool. Any time of the year when the sun is shining, the place is awash in the colors of the huge stained glass window that dominates one wall.

Unfortunately, this was not one of those days. Heavy clouds hung just above the treetops. They were the exact color of the steel gray pants I'd paired with a white cashmere sweater that was gorgeous (and looked great on me), but wasn't nearly warm enough to keep out the chill. While I waited for the senior citizens to totter off the bus, the damp air seeped through me, chilling me to the bone. I was inside on the heels of the last little old lady.

The chapel is small but impressive, and when

folks are in there, they're usually so blown away by the mosaics on the walls, the inlay floor, and that spectacular window, they just walk around with their mouths open. That means they don't ask a lot of questions, and for a tour guide, that's always a big plus.

Especially when the tour guide has more important things to deal with.

I'm not a total idiot; I knew I had to satisfy them before I got down to my own business. I gave a quick spiel about the building, its design, and its highlights, and waited until the thirty-four members of the Bay Village Senior League were at the openmouthed stage. That's when I ducked into the back of the chapel where Damon was waiting for me.

"It's a job for the police," I said. Since I'd already told him the same thing earlier in the day and back at my office, he knew what I was talking about. My comment shouldn't have come as a surprise.

So he shouldn't have rolled his eyes. "And the police are going to believe you when you say you have a tape recording of a ghost who's telling you the guys in the band are in danger?"

This was farther than we'd gotten in our conversation back at the office because just as we'd started, Ella had come in to talk about the day's tours and the Christmas events she was planning. I hadn't had time to prove to Damon that I'd already thought through all of this. Now with the opportunity, I raised my chin, pulled back my shoulders, and gave him an I'm-on-top-it look. "I'll play the recording for them."

"They'll think it's a hoax."

He had a point.

I muttered, but I didn't have time to respond. At least not until I took care of the granny who was giving me one of those embarrassed half waves from across the chapel. I knew what it meant; she needed to find a ladies' room. After I got her headed in the right direction, I got back to worrying about what I was going to do about the message from Vinnie.

I was already chewing my lower lip when I realized I was biting off a fresh coat of Frosty Caramel Apple. "Okay, so I can't tell the police," I said. I made sure I kept my voice down after I'd zipped back to where Damon waited. "But it's not my job to handle this, either. I'm supposed to be helping you get to the Other Side. I'm not supposed to be solving crimes that haven't even been committed yet."

"That's the whole point!" Of course, the weather didn't matter to Damon, but just looking at him in jeans and that LBJ T-shirt made me shudder. "You've got to help the guys, Pepper. You're the only one who can."

I hated being responsible. For anything. I sighed my surrender. "I suppose I could warn them."

"That's not good enough. You have to protect them."

As I may have mentioned, Damon was a pretty laid-back guy. I'd never seen him angry or agitated. Until then. His cheeks dusky and his eyes on fire, he stalked to the far end of the chapel, right through a group of gawking geezers who immediately shivered and commented about the dip in the temperature. He got as far as the window, and I expected him to turn back. Instead he went right through it. A second later, he popped back up at my side.

Gift or no Gift, I'll never get used to the comings and goings of ghosts. I just about jumped out of my skin.

"There's a lot you don't know," Damon said.

I crossed my arms over my chest. The stance helped contain my heart (which was about to pound its way past my ribs), plus, when I stepped back with my weight against one foot, I looked a little more intimidating. "Tell me."

He hesitated. "The guys and me . . . well, you can't possibly understand." I could just about see Damon's anger dissolve. The look in his eyes had been riveting and fiery; now it wasn't focused on anything. Not on me or on the old people just a few feet away. He was seeing the past, I knew it as sure as I knew my own name, and his voice was soft and slow, like a man's in a dream.

"When a band comes together and everybody meshes and clicks, it's magical! That's what happened with Mind at Large. We all had the same artistic vision and the same drive and the same goals—kick-ass music and rock stardom." The tiny smile that touched the corners of Damon's mouth was nothing short of rapturous. "We set the world on fire. It was everything I ever dreamed of, and it blew my mind! But then . . ." Damon blinked back to reality.

"It isn't the money, you know. Sure, that's what people say. It's easy, and it explains everything. One day you don't have a dime and the next, you're rolling hundred-dollar bills and using them to light your joints. But hey, I got used to that quick enough. It was the drugs that messed with our minds. And the women . . . well . . . I already told you that part. I was a greedy son of a bitch. I wanted every single one of them. Between that and acting like an asshole because I figured I was a star and I had every right . . ." His shoulders rose and fell. "After a while, me and the guys, we were at each other's throats all the time. I couldn't take it. And I refused to admit any of it was my fault. I'd had enough. It was messing with my mind and my songs and it was getting me down. I knew what I had to do. I decided to leave the band. I was heading out on my own for a solo career."

In all the reading I'd done about Mind at Large and with all the people I'd talked to, no one had ever mentioned that Damon quit.

And no wonder.

It took me only a second to see the light.

"You told them, right? The band members. You told them you were quitting the night you died."

He nodded. "Everybody was there. Except Gene, of course."

I remembered what the agent had told me back at the Rock Hall. "He was in Pittsburgh. Did he know?"

Damon nodded. "I told him before he left. I figured I owed it to Gene. He'd been with us from the start. I didn't want him to read it in the papers. The way it was, I didn't have to worry, huh? I guess the news never made any of the papers."

And no wonder. "None of the books I've read about the group mentions you were leaving," I told Damon. "And none of the Web sites devoted to the group say anything about it, either. That's because you died that night. And if the band talked about you leaving right before you died . . . well, that drug overdose of yours sure was going to look suspicious. Nobody wanted any fingers pointed at them."

"I suppose you're right." Damon was thoughtful. "See, without me, Mind at Large was nothing. I know it sounds bigheaded, but it's the absolute truth. I knew it, and they knew it. Once I told them I was leaving, they knew their careers were sunk. Except—"

I put two and two together. For once, it actually equaled four.

"Except that once you were dead, it didn't matter that you weren't with the band anymore. Your death made the band a legend. And once Vinnie figured out how to channel you, the songs he stole put it back at the top of the charts. Damon, that means every one of the Mind at Large members had a motive to kill you."

"It does, but don't you get it?" Damon's enthusiasm for my theory did not equal my own. "Vinnie Pal and Al and Mighty Mike and Pete, they had every right to be angry. We were brothers. We were compadres. And I made the mistake of actually believing what people said about me. They said I was the sexy, bad-boy genius of rock, and, son of a bitch, but I was going to do everything I could to prove it was true! I stole the guys' chicks. I hogged the spotlight. It was my face as big as life on the cover of our albums, and most times, people referred to us as Damon Curtis's band. Then I got pissed, and I was all set to pull the rug out from under all their lives."

Damon looked me in the eye. "You're right, Pepper. Any one of them could have killed me, but I know these guys, and I know not one of them has the heart. Now, if what Vinnie says is true, they're all in danger. We can't let that happen, don't you see? It's taken me nearly forty years to figure it out, but I finally have. I owe them."

There are a lot of pluses to being a private detective, and someday when I think of what they are, I'll be sure to write them down.

Most days, my Gift and the job responsibilities that result from it are pretty much a big ol' pain in the ass.

The day Damon and I talked in the chapel was a perfect example. After hearing what he had to say about the band, how he felt responsible for their safety, and how I was the only one who could possibly help, I knew what I had to do. And I knew it was going to be a big ol' pain in the ass.

All the same, I slipped out of the office and into full investigation mode.

It would have been a whole lot more tolerable if the weather wasn't so cold and drippy. I sat in the car, huddled in my raincoat with the heat running full blast, and flicked the windshield wipers to their slow cycle. Every twenty seconds or so, they stroked the layer of mist off my window and I had a clear view of Damon's grave.

Swipe.

There was nothing to see out there but gray and gloom and the fog that collected in pockets along the hillside. I blew on my hands and waited, feeling more isolated by the moment as the rain coated the windows and I lost touch with the outside world.

Swipe.

Like I said, there were pluses to being a detective. This was one of them, the reassurance that my instincts were right on. Because this time when the window cleared, I saw Crazy Belinda walking toward Damon's grave.

I was tempted to hop right out of the car to intercept her, but I bided my time, eager to see what she was going to do. A coffee cup clutched in one hand, Belinda paused in front of the marker with Damon's name on it, and I could see that she was talking to someone. Not to Damon. At least not so that he'd hear. I hadn't seen him around since I left the chapel earlier that day.

When she was done, Belinda reached into the shopping bag she was carrying and pulled out a rag. She wiped down the headstone, removed each of the objects on the flat stone behind the marker, cleaned them, and set them back in place. The rain wasn't driving, but it was steady enough. She didn't even try to relight the candles in their colored-glass cups. Instead she took a wilted bouquet of flowers away and replaced it with a bunch of orange and gold mums that she'd brought along with her.

She was done, and it was time for me to spring into action. It was my job to make sure Belinda didn't get away before I had a chance to talk to her.

Gritting my teeth against the raw weather, I hopped out of the car.

"Hey! Imagine running into you here!" When Belinda turned at the sound of my voice, I waved.

She was wearing a blue plastic rain slicker, and though it had a hood, she hadn't pulled it up. Her hair hung around her shoulders, dripping. Belinda's toes stuck out of the worn sandals that were brushed by her long, tie-dyed skirt. Her eyes were glassy, and when she looked at me, I could tell she wasn't sure who I was.

I didn't want to spook her, so I closed in slowly. "We met at the Rock Hall, remember? I was talking to Gene Terry, the manager of Mind at Large. You know him, don't you? You know the guys in the band, too."

As if a fairy godmother had flitted by and done the bibbidi-bobbidi-boo routine, Belinda was transformed. Her face lit. Her eyes twinkled. "I'm with the band!" she said. "Don't need a backstage pass. I'm with the band."

"Yeah, that's right. You're always with the band. That's why I knew you could help me."

Belinda's expectant expression melted. "Can't help you find the angel. He promised he'd be here and he hasn't come." As if she was giving him another chance, she looked up at the leaden sky, and when the angel of death didn't appear (thank goodness!), her shoulders drooped. "Can't find Alistair, either," she said. "Bad, bad Alistair. He went out for the mail and he hasn't come back."

I was clearly fighting an uphill battle, but I remembered my promise to Damon. I told him I'd do everything I could to keep the band safe. So far, talking to Belinda was the only thing I could think of. "Alistair the drummer?" I asked her. "Or Alistair your cat?"

When Belinda shook her head, raindrops flew

around her. "Went out for the mail. He hasn't come back. And he took Damon along." She leaned in close and put a finger to her lips. "Don't tell anyone. He was in the living room. You know, the night he died."

"Damon was in your living room? The night he died?" I did my best to make sense of this piece of information. "But I though he died right before a concert."

"You're so funny!" With one grubby finger, Belinda poked me in the ribs. I promised myself my raincoat would go to the dry cleaner's first thing the next morning. "June 5, 1969," she said. "That's the night."

I thought of everything I'd read about Mind at Large. "But that's not the night Damon died," I said, even though I knew this was one person I didn't need to remind. Any fan obsessed enough to come out to Damon's grave in the rain would surely know he hadn't died until two years later. "And it wasn't the night he told the band he was heading out on a solo career, either, because that was the same night he died and that wasn't until seventy-one. So what happened in June of sixty-nine? Their first gold record?"

Belinda rolled her eyes, and the sound that escaped her wasn't exactly a laugh. She washed it away with a sip of coffee. "Everyone knows," she said.

Everyone, apparently, but me. "I don't know," I said. "Tell me."

Belinda's eyes were on her coffee cup, but it was clear her mind was a million miles away. Or more precisely, nearly forty years in the past. "They let me backstage," she said, and she smiled. "They said I was cute. That's when I met him. Damon. Damon, Damon, Damon." Her eyes lost their focus, and still mumbling, Belinda shuffled away.

A smarter person would have just let her go. But let's face it, there was something about her insisting that Damon had been in her apartment the night he died that was as fascinating as an auto accident. I couldn't turn away. Even if I wanted to, I wouldn't have been able to stop myself from following her.

Curious to know where she was headed and what she would do when she got there, I trudged behind Belinda through the rain, up the hill, and into the old, ornate part of the cemetery, and by that time, I was breathing hard and wishing I'd been smart enough to follow her in my car. Like I thought she'd walk all the way here? I told myself it wasn't possible but hey, like I said, there was that whole *crazy* thing to consider. When we got to the main gate and Belinda stopped to look both ways before she crossed the street, I was huffing and puffing, and—not incidentally since the rain started to come down harder than ever—soaked to the skin.

Did I let this stop me?

I'd like to say that in true detective fashion, I refused to give up on my investigation.

I reminded myself of that fact when Belinda paused in front of an old red brick apartment building within spitting distance of Garden View's main gates. She was just about to go inside (and I was all set to slip in right after her) when a movement in the overgrown rhododendrons to one side of the front door caught my eye. I saw a flash of gray and a peek of a little black nose.

I may have been soaked to the bone and as chilly as a frozen margarita, but I wasn't dumb, and I was willing to try just about anything to get Belinda to keep talking. I darted forward, stuck my hand into the bush, and came out holding a cat.

"Hey, look!" Holding up the wet critter so she could see it, I closed in on her and hoped that I wasn't barking up the wrong tree. (I guess that's a mixed metaphor, but since by this time it really was raining cats and dogs, I figured it counted.) "Is it Alistair? Did I find him?"

Lucky for me, it was the right feline. I knew this because Belinda tried to look stern when she said, "You bad, bad boy!" It might have worked if she wasn't smiling at the same time.

While she made a move to unlock the door, I kept a firm hold on the cat. "Go on ahead," I told her. "I'll bring him up."

Belinda didn't argue. A couple of minutes later, we were inside her apartment.

While she clucked and cooed and grabbed Alistair out of my arms to rub him down with a tattered towel and get him something to eat, I took the opportunity to look over the place. It was, to put it charitably, pretty basic. The living room contained nothing but a worn couch and a table across from it that was filled with pictures.

Rude or not, I didn't care. I reached for the closest gold-colored metal frame. It contained a faded color photograph of Damon. In it, he was standing with his back to the ocean where sunlight glittered like diamonds on the water. He was smiling.

Next to that photo was another one, this of Damon along with his bandmates and Gene Terry, as bald then as he was now. There was another photo of Damon to the right and another next to that one. Interspersed with the pictures was an incense holder filled with ashes and five colored glass cups. Each contained a burning candle. On the wall above the table there were a dozen more photos of Damon. They had been painstakingly hung in a perfect circle. It might not have struck me as odd that the center of the circle was empty—except for the rectangular-shaped patch of lighter colored paint there. And the empty picture hook.

When Belinda came into the room with Alistair in her arms, I was ready for her. "Something's missing," I said.

"Alistair was missing." She smiled down at the cat, who had lost no time and was sleeping soundly. "I told him not to get the mail, but he didn't listen. He isn't allowed outside. There are dogs, you know, and dogs eat cats."

"Then it's a good thing we found him." I tapped the empty spot on the wall. "But something's missing here, too."

Her eyebrows dipped. They needed a good plucking and an expert's hand when it came to shaping. "Damon was here," she said. "He left with Alistair."

There are those who say I am not the brightest bulb in the box (well, actually, Joel was the only one who'd ever really come out and said it). I was about to prove him wrong. Believe it or not, what Belinda said actually made sense.

"You mean that Alistair disappeared the same day the picture of Damon went missing?"

She nodded. "Alistair went outside. He shouldn't be able to reach the door handle."

I couldn't argue with that. So Belinda didn't get wind of what I was looking for (and maybe panic), I strolled over to the door that led into the hallway. The wood was raw near the lock, as if it had been scraped. As if the door had been forced open.

As casually as I could, I turned back to her. "Belinda, on the day Alistair went outside and took Damon with him, was anything else missing?"

As if she didn't understand, she narrowed her eyes.

I tried to explain without frightening her. "You know, a TV or a stereo. Maybe some jewelry or—"

Belinda's rough laugh cut me short. "Don't have any of those things. Don't need them. I won't be here long. Only until the angel spreads his wings and—"

"Yeah, yeah, I get that part." I did, and honestly, I wasn't in the mood to hear all about it again. "So nothing else was touched? Nothing else was taken?"

"Only Alistair." She cuddled the cat. "He's back. He promises he'll never do it again."

I nodded as a way of telling her that if the cat swore he was going to be good, I wasn't one to argue, and pointed to the empty spot on the wall. I had a feeling that by that time, Belinda had forgotten all about it.

"What was in this picture?" I asked her. "You know, the picture that disappeared the day Alistair went out for the mail? In the picture, what was Damon doing?"

This question was tougher, and considering it, Belinda sucked on her lower lip and stared at the empty spot on the wall. "It was the night he died," she said.

At this point, I should have been frustrated but actually, I wasn't. See, I was too busy realizing that when it came to my investigation, I was finally getting somewhere. Because I knew more now than I had a little while earlier.

Number one, I knew that Alistair the cat hadn't really gone out for the mail. (Okay, I actually knew that before, but I was sure of it now.) What I thought was that when the door was jimmied open, the cat escaped.

As to why that door was forced open in the first place . . .

I looked from the scratch marks near the door lock to the empty spot on the wall.

A picture of Damon. The night he died. And call me crazy, but something told me it must have shown more than that.

Whatever was in that picture, it must have been something important. Because somebody was willing to risk breaking into Belinda's apartment to steal it.

Chapter 13

It took me a couple of days, but I finally came up with a plan of sorts. While I waited to put it into action, I sat in my office, alone and grumbling, trying to make sense of everything I'd found out while I tapped my fingers against my keyboard. Maybe the constant *tap, tap, tap* would jump-start my brain.

That's when Ella poked her head in the door. "I heard you typing. You're not too busy for company, are you?"

Since my monitor wasn't on, she should have seen I wasn't. I waved her inside, and while she bustled over to my guest chair, I flicked on the computer monitor, just so she didn't ask any questions.

"You're so much better at computers than I am," Ella said. Her cheeks were rosy, just like the sweater she was wearing with a black skirt that brushed her ankles. "All those bytes and bits and such . . ." She made a face. "It makes me crazy. My girls are terrific with computers, of course. Kids have no fear and they learn things so quickly. But I can't ask them for help. Not with this."

When it came to her daughters, Ella was as protective as a lioness with her cubs. I couldn't help but be curious. What was she up to that she didn't want the girls to know? Internet compatibility profiles? Internet dating? Internet sex?

I shuddered at the thought and carefully phrased my question. "Is there something you need help finding? I can show you how."

"Oh, no. I'd rather have you do it for me." Ella chuckled. She was wearing a dozen strands of black, sparkling beads, and they shimmered when she shook. "I want to surprise the girls. We're all going to the Mind at Large concert."

I guess I looked surprised because Ella smiled. "I'm not such an old fogy that I'm not still rockin' and rollin'."

"Yeah, I can see you wanting to go, but the girls—"

"Oh, don't worry about them. They're hip. They're down. They're into the groove. We've been talking at home, you see, about the sixties. I think they'll get a real kick out of seeing one of the bands that defined the era. Of course, now that Vinnie Pal is dead . . ." She shook her head. "What a shame! I'm glad they didn't cancel the concert. They said Vinnie would have wanted the show to go on. Even without him. I want to order tickets now. Before they're all gone. You know how it is, Pepper, once a rock musician dies—especially mysteriously—the legend grows."

It was so much like what Damon and I had discussed back at the chapel earlier in the week, it was uncanny. Maybe it wouldn't hurt to get the opinion of someone who'd lived through the Flower

Power generation and come out the other side *without* frying her brain.

"Is that what happened after Damon Curtis died?" I asked Ella. "Was the group more popular than ever after that?"

"Well, for a while, yes, of course. Not that most of the fans cared much about the rest of the band. Really, all Alistair and Vinnie and the rest of them ever were was Damon's backup band. But that Damon, now he was another story! He was the one all the girls went to see. What a face! And that voice! Dreamy with a capital D. After he died, the group scattered for a while. I hear that at one time, Mighty Mike was working at a golf course. And Alistair went back home to London and opened a pub. Of course, they had plenty of money. Their old music—the stuff they recorded when Damon was alive—that became more popular than ever. But the stuff they recorded right after his death . . ." A devotee to the last, Ella shivered.

"Then Vinnie wrote the music for that Disney animated movie. You remember, the one about the aliens in New Jersey. Or was it the one about the stray cats that take over the boarding school? Either way, Vinnie wrote the music and he brought the band back together to record it. After that, they were bound to be famous. All the lite rock stations started playing their songs."

I cringed on Damon's behalf. "You know an awful lot about these guys," I said. "You don't look like the type who was ever into the psychedelic scene."

Ella winked. "You never know by looking, kid. I've had an adventure or two in my day."

"And now you want your girls to see what it was all about." I could relate. My first trip to a spa was with my mom. I logged onto the Internet to search for tickets, and Ella came around from the other side of the desk and watched over my shoulder.

"Just get us four seats, anywhere you can. It probably won't be near the front or anything. That would be asking too much."

"I dunno . . ." I moved the cursor around the screen, clicking at the appropriate spots and checking out ticket availability against the seating chart on another page. "Looks like you can get a ticket just about anywhere."

"Really?" Ella peered at the screen. "How cool is that? Let's go . . . here." She pointed a finger at the seating chart, and I noted the section number, went back to the ticket page, and added four tickets to the shopping cart.

"There's always room for one more," she said, handing me her credit card. "You sure you don't want to come with us?"

I was sure. At least about the concert. See, what Ella didn't know was that I already had plans to see Mind at Large up close and personal. The next day, they were scheduled to record the single they were releasing to promote their concert. Clever me, I'd managed to get myself invited to the session.

How?

It wasn't hard, really. Not once I called their agent, Gene Terry, reintroduced myself, and reminded him about the book I was supposed to be writing. Oh yeah, I reminded him about something else, too. Like that I was the one with Vinnie when he died and that I had a message for the band—from Vinnie.

Anybody who lives in Cleveland and most people who've ever visited know about the Flats. It's the area along both the east and west banks of the Cuyahoga River, literally the flat land in the center of a city. From what I remember from Ohio history class (and believe me when I say that's not much), it's where the first pioneers settled, and a few decades ago, it was home to dozens of industries.

Cleveland's days as a powerhouse of manufacturing are over, but the Flats still hangs on. I remember when I was back in high school and it was the place to party. It was hopping, night to morning, with nightclubs and bars. A bunch of muggings and a couple of murders put an end to that, and though there are still a few clubs around and a number of developers who are trying to revive the area, most of the party action has moved up the hill to the Warehouse District.

These days, a lot of the Flats is deserted, and the businesses that remain are mostly small manufacturers, lake shippers, and warehouses. The roads that wind under massive bridges and over railroad tracks are pocked with potholes.

I maneuvered my Mustang around one the size of the bathroom back at my apartment and checked the address I'd written on a piece of paper against the numbers on the nearest boarded-up building. It just so happened to be the biggest, the most dilapidated, and the spookiest-looking place on the block. It was also exactly the place I was looking for—the home of Ajaz Recording Studios.

I parked the car and tiptoed my way across a parking lot dotted with murky puddles, empty beer cans, and bits of paper that scuttled along on a stiff breeze off nearby Lake Erie.

Once inside, I found myself in a long, dark hallway that opened into a gargantuan and very empty warehouse. There were more puddles (I didn't want to think of what), scritchy and scratchy noises (I didn't want to know what made them), and an AJAZ sign above a doorway that was all the way on the other side of the building.

My heels clicked against the concrete, and the sound echoed up the high walls and off the broken glass of what was left of the windows that faced the river. To my left on the second, third, and fourth stories of the building was a walkway that overlooked the warehouse floor. Beyond it and through the gloom, I could see what must once have been offices.

The door into the studio was secured, and I got buzzed in. Fortunately, the Ajaz offices were lighter, brighter, and far cleaner than what I'd seen outside. The purple-haired receptionist with multiple eyebrow piercings explained that Ajaz's shabby exterior was a great way to keep burglary to a minimum and showed me into a control room with a panel so chock-full of dials and lights and buttons, it looked like the bridge on the Starship Enterprise. I smiled briefly at Bernie, the Mind at Large bodyguard. He was somehow managing to munch donuts, even though there was a cute girl in a short, short denim skirt and a top that showed off her belly button ring on his lap. I nodded to the roadies who were standing around looking bored.

Crazy Belinda was there, too, sipping City Roast coffee while she rocked back and forth mumbling something about death and destruction. I was careful not to make eye contact. Yeah, I had plenty I still needed to talk to her about (like what, specifically, was in that missing photograph), but I would handle that sometime when there was nobody else around.

The moment I walked in, I had planned to introduce myself to the two techies sitting behind the control panel and apologize if I was interrupting them while they worked, but it turned out, I didn't have to bother.

Like everyone else in the room, the two sound technicians weren't working. They were watching the melee on the other side of the glass wall that separated the control room from the sound studio, where Mind at Large, troubadours to the Make Love, Not War generation, were going at one another like cats and dogs.

"What the bloody hell!" Alistair threw down his sticks, got up from his seat behind the drums, and kicked a hand-tooled leather cowboy boot straight through the bass drum that had *Mind at Large* painted on it in psychedelic purple lettering. Even the resulting noise wasn't enough to drown his voice. "Are you ruddy amateurs?" he screamed. "Have you forgotten how to make a friggin' recording? You know to use an eight-beat count-off instead of four. The last two beats are silent, Mike. Did you forget to bring your fuckin' brain with you when you crawled out of your bottle this morning?"

Mighty Mike's eyes were streaked with red and when he threw down his guitar, his hands shook. Since there was a bottle of Southern Comfort open beside him, I didn't think the trembling had anything to do with how angry he was. The way he jumped out of his chair did, though. Just like the way he got in Alistair's face.

"Here we go again." One of the guys at the control panel groaned and flicked a couple of switches, turning off the sound between the studio and the control room. From where we stood on the other side of the glass, we were witnesses to the silent ego war. We could see the bandmates battling, their mouths opening and closing, their fingers pointing and their expressions ranging from livid (the ever-pleasant Alistair) to downright I'm-so-frickin'-mad-I'm-gonna-kill-you (Mike, but that might have had something to do with the fact that when Pete rushed forward to put in his two cents, he kicked over Mike's bottle of booze). Thank goodness, we couldn't hear a thing. We really didn't need to. Lip-reading skills are not required to recognize the f-bomb.

Technician Number One had apparently seen enough. He laid his head on the table in front of him. The other techie sat back and made himself comfortable. He reached for a pack of cigarettes.

"They've done this before, huh?" Since nobody else seemed to be paying attention to what was happening in the studio, I directed my question to Techie Number Two. It wasn't as polite as the introduction I'd been planning, but it was the best way I could think to remind him I was still there and waiting. "How long is this going to take?"

He grabbed a chair and pushed it in my direction. "You might as well have a seat, honey. If it's anything like the five or six other fights they've already had today, we could be here until the wee hours."

I reached for the chair, but before I had a chance to sit, Ben, who'd been tossing his opinions into the melee from the fringes, caught sight of me. His eyes lit, not so much with interest as with curiosity. Ben reached around Pete (who was so mad he was hopping up and down) to hit a button on the microphone that allowed him to talk to the control room. "Hey, is this the chick?" he asked.

Techie Number Two looked up at me.

"I'm the chick," I said.

"Hey, assholes!" We were back to hearing everything that was going on in the studio, and Ben's voice rose above the babble of voices. "The chick is here."

Mighty Mike had his back to me. Hanging on to a microphone for balance, he pivoted to get a good look. Pete kicked over a music stand and stomped to the other side of the studio, but not before he glared at me. Alistair shot a death-ray look at both of them, and then, just for good measure, sent one just as nasty my way.

I swallowed hard. "Your agent said I could talk to you." Though I probably didn't have to, I automatically raised my voice so they could hear me. "All of you."

Nobody threw a hissy fit. In my book, that was as good as an engraved invitation. Before anybody could change their minds, I headed where the technician pointed.

I've never been accused of being sensitive (well, except to cheap wool sweaters and pierced earrings that aren't silver or at least 14-karat gold), but even I could feel the bad blood there in that studio. It was as heavy in the air as the smell of the cigarette Ben was puffing on. I stopped just inside the door, checking out the cramped quarters and gauging the best place to stand and keep out of the way of the toxic vibes.

Was it next to Mighty Mike, who was rummaging through a cooler in search of a new bottle of Southern Comfort? Or Pete, so short and skinny, he looked like a starving refugee from some dusty country? (Which, come to think of it, might have been the reason he was eyeing me up like something he'd ordered in from the deli.)

It wasn't anywhere near Alistair, that was for sure. I'd seen Alistair in action back at the Rock Hall, and I wasn't taking the chance of getting in his way, especially not when his face was so red, it looked as if his head was going to shoot off like a bottle rocket.

I opted for Ben, partly because I thought maybe his animosity for his bandmates didn't run as deep as theirs. After all, he was the newest member of Mind at Large. *Newest* being a relative word, of course. I knew from my research that he'd once belonged to a band called Frame Forward; he'd joined Mind at Large as lead singer after Damon's death. Besides the benefit of history (or in this case, the lack thereof), there was a tattoo of a crucifix on Ben's left arm. I figured with tempers running high, a religious guy might be my safest bet.

Until I saw that the crucifix was topped with a crown of thorns and that it dripped blood and had fire and brimstone shooting out from the sides of it.

And that Ben's right arm was tattooed with the face of a leering red Satan and the words *Praise the Lord*.

I wondered which arm applied to his current stage of spiritual development. I wasn't sure which scared me more.

No matter. I had a job to do, and just so there was no mistaking that I wasn't going to be intimidated into not doing it, I employed my slightly-pissed-and-not-going-to-take-it-anymore tour guide voice, the one I used with the senior citizens who were convinced they could chatter with one another and wander off when I was trying my damnedest to educate them. It was loud enough to command attention, friendly without being too sweet. Let's face it, coming out of a five-foot-eleven redhead, it was also bound to make an impression.

"I talked to Gene Terry yesterday," I said. I waited while the grumbling and the curses faded to a dull roar. "He told me I could stop in and see you."

I had used both common sense and fashion sense that morning. Remembering Vinnie's lecherous looks, I'd chosen a black pantsuit and a yellow shirt with a high neckline and long sleeves.

It didn't stop the guys from leering.

"Come on in, pretty lady." Mike's anger was forgotten in a moment. He bowed and ushered me closer with a gesture that sent a tsunami of alcohol fumes my way. "Gene told us you were coming. He didn't tell us you were a hot little number."

Pete was skinny enough to slip between Mike and the equipment so he could get nearer to me. Up close, he looked more emaciated than ever. He was as pale as one of those fish that live so far below the surface they never see the light, and his face was a map of wrinkles and lines. I'd seen dead people who looked more alive. I knew a couple of them personally. I guess that's why when Pete looked me up and down and licked his lips, it gave me the willies.

"Don't listen to this old man," Pete purred. "I'm the only one here who can get you backstage passes to the concert."

"Bullshit." Ben finished one cigarette and lit another. "This chicky don't need no stinkin' backstage pass. She's gonna be too busy to go backstage." He wiggled his eyebrows. "In the tour bus with me."

"Actually, I already bought my ticket for the concert." Yeah, yeah, so I lied. Like it was some big deal? "I was surprised to see there are so many seats left."

"You should have seen sales before Vinnie did us the favor of getting himself offed." When Alistair tried to remove the broken drum from his drum set and it wouldn't budge, he gave it another kick. He glared at the drum before he glared at his bandmates. "Of course, what the bloody hell did we expect? Who'd want to come see a bunch of old, has-been musicians?"

"Plenty of people." Pete played bass, and the way I remembered it, he didn't sing much. No wonder. His voice was high-pitched and nasal.

"We're still on top of the world. Nobody can touch us."

"Nobody would want to touch you." Mike thought this was pretty funny. He laughed and choked and pounded his chest.

"Yeah, well, things are going to change." Pete made a grab for a sheaf of music that was on a nearby table, and I had a feeling he'd been through this tirade with his bandmates before. They turned away. I was a new audience, and he took full advantage. He waved the music under my nose. "Now that Vinnie's out of the picture, maybe Gene will listen when I tell him I've got some good songs in me, too. We can record my songs instead of Vinnie's and then—"

"Then the whole world will know what a loser you are!" Mike laughed.

When I saw Pete's top lip curl, I knew I had to take charge.

"Hey! Listen up!" Pete was near the glass window that looked into the control room. Alistair was directly opposite him, over near his drums. Mike was standing across from me, and Ben was facing him from the other side of the studio. I marched into the middle of the pack. Maybe I had a death wish, but at least for as long as they kept their mouths shut, I also had the floor.

"I know you must be busy," I said. "I'm sure it takes a long time to record a song. I don't want to hold you up."

"Oh, baby, I could hold you up," Mike purred. "Over my head, while I—"

"That's why I'm going to say what I have to say and get out of your way." I cut him off before he could elaborate on the fantasy. "As Gene may have mentioned to you, I have a message for you. All of you." I looked around the circle. "It's from Vinnie."

"Yeah, we heard." Mike cracked open the new bottle of liquor, took a swig, and offered the bottle to me. When I declined, he drank my share. "I didn't think Vinnie still had it in him to catch the eye of a babe as fine as you. So, he was banging you before he got killed, huh?"

"No." My protest was swift and vehement. "I took Vinnie's class at the Rock Hall. That's how I knew him."

"So if Vinnie had something to tell us while he was teaching that class at the Rock Hall, why didn't he just call?" Ben asked and added, "Oh yeah, we all thought Vinnie was a jerk. Nobody would have wanted to talk to him, anyway."

"He didn't give me the message at the Rock Hall."

"You're the girl who was with him when he died." Pete thought he had it all sorted out. He pulled himself up to his full height. It might have been effective if he was bigger than a Munchkin. "So Vinnie said something to you before he died, right? Like one of those deathbed speeches. Don't tell me, let me guess. He was sorry we spent our time recording his shitty songs instead of my good ones."

"He didn't give me a message before he died."

"Yeah, right." Pete dismissed me with a good-riddance wave of one hand. "Like he gave it to you after he died!"

"Well, see . . ." I looked from Alistair to Mike, and from Pete to Ben. "He did."

Not too long before this, if I heard someone confess to talking to the dead, I would have been speechless. Sure, I would have thought that person was a little crazy. Or a lot crazy. But for all its faults (and considering that my dad would be spending the next ten years as a guest of the federal government, I admit that these faults are many), my family raised me right. Early on, I learned to be tolerant and polite. Unless it was for something vitally important (like a sale at Saks or—come to think of it—a murder investigation), I knew better than to make a scene.

Of course, Alistair, Ben, Pete, and Mike hadn't been brought up in the Martin family. In fact, my guess was that they'd probably been raised by wolves. Or maybe it was hyenas. That would explain why they all started to laugh.

I gritted my teeth in a grin-and-bear-it way and realized that I'd learned a couple of things that day. Number one: I did not ever want to spend time with ancient rock and rollers again. Number two: I don't like the smell of Southern Comfort. Number three: It's humiliating to make an important announcement and have it met with complete and total disbelief.

I guess that's what really pissed me off.

I ditched the tour guide voice for something sure to attract a little more attention. "Laugh if you want. You know it's possible. At one time, you were all involved with black magic."

"Big deal." Ben wheezed and fingered the tattoo of Lucifer on his arm. "You don't think we actually believed any of that garbage, do you?"

"Vinnie did."

Mike thought about taking another drink and changed his mind. He hung on to the neck of the bottle. "It's true," he said. "But how do you know it? Is that what he told you when he was dying? About the spells he used to cast? Shit, leave it to Vinnie to spend his last minutes on earth still talking that trash. We only went along with him and the whole magic scene because sometimes his freakin' magic bullshit included orgies. Did he tell you that, too?"

"He told me—"

"Wait a minute!" Squeaky voice or not, Pete knew how to make himself heard. His words cut across mine like a knife. "What's this really all about? Are you a cop?"

Like I may have mentioned before, guys aren't always good about picking up on the obvious. I was much too well-dressed to be a cop (well, except for Quinn, who was much too well-dressed to be a cop, too, even though he was a cop). "I just sort of ended up in the wrong place at the wrong time as far as Vinnie was concerned," I told the band right before I remembered that old saying about being in for a penny and in for a pound. I wasn't sure what money had to do with how much something weighed, but I knew all about taking chances. And about how if I didn't, I might not get the opportunity again.

"Actually," I said, glancing around at the bandmates, "it's not just Vinnie I'm here about. What I'd really like to figure out is what really happened to Damon and how it's keeping him stuck here on earth."

Amazingly, the mention of an almost forty-year-old

death was exactly what was needed to bring Mind at Large together. I could practically see a wall go up. The band on one side. Me on the other. Oh yeah, they were wary all right, and realizing it, my Spider-senses tingled.

As if he knew it, Mike looked me up and down. I had a feeling that for the first time, he was really seeing me. "You one of Damon's bastards?" he asked. "You don't look like him."

"And duh, I'm not anywhere near old enough!"

"Then why do you care?" The question came from Alistair. Since it was the first completely civil thing I'd ever heard him say, I paid attention.

I was tempted to come up with some story to make them happy, but I opted for the truth, instead. For one thing, if I expected them to take Vinnie's warning to heart, the least I could do in return was be honest. For another, there was already too much hot air in the room. I didn't want to add to it.

"I care," I said, "because I happen to know that Damon isn't resting in peace. And because I think his death and Vinnie's murder might be connected."

"Except Damon wasn't murdered." This, from Ben.

"Yeah, that's the story, and who am I to dispute it?" I didn't want Ben to think I was singling him out, so I looked from man to man. "But you all know Damon had too much to look forward to. He wouldn't kill himself. He was heading out on his own."

"That's what Vinnie told you!" Mike's expression just about screamed, *Aha!* "Ain't nobody else knows that but us, so it has to be. Is that what you came here to do? Accuse us of something? Blackmail us?"

I threw my hands in the air. "What did I come here to do? Honestly, I don't know. It sure isn't because I want anything from you. Any of you. I'm just trying to make sense of it all. If Vinnie didn't tell me—"

I was tired of trying to explain and getting nowhere fast. I dug in my purse and pulled out Dan's digital tape recorder. Before I turned it on, I looked over my shoulder and into the control room. Techie Number One and Techie Number Two didn't look so bored anymore. Bernie had a donut in one hand, but he wasn't eating it. The roadies had gathered around just on the other side of the glass wall, their heads bent, anxious to hear more.

I remembered how Ben had communicated with the control room earlier. "Can you make it so they can't hear us?" I asked him, and when he hit all the right buttons—I knew because the expectant look on the technicians' faces dissolved—I turned on the recorder.

"Careful. Danger. The group . . ." Vinnie's familiar voice scratched out the words. The guys bent closer to hear. "One. One more will die."

I flicked off the recorder. "Anybody need to hear that again?"

Since nobody did, I slipped the recorder back in my purse.

Suddenly sober as a judge, Mike shifted from foot to foot. "What are you going to do?" he asked.

"What am *I* going to do?" I parroted the question and thought through my options. Sad but true, I had only one. "I'm going to investigate Vinnie's murder. There's got to be a connection, and it's got to lead back to you guys. And maybe to Damon, too. So . . ." I glanced around the circle. In an effort to hear the recording better, the bandmates had all moved closer, and one by one, I looked them in the eye. "Let's start by coming clean. Did one of you have something to do with Damon's death?"

"That's bull." Alistair snapped out of the shock of hearing his dead bandmate's voice. He scratched a hand through his straw-colored hair. "None of us had a reason."

"You all had reasons." I shouldn't have had to point this out, but since nobody seemed willing to cop to it, I had no choice. "He was going to destroy your careers."

"But he didn't, did he?" Ben's grin was anything but pleasant. "He might have thought that walking out would ruin Mind at Large, but the band only got better."

"Like you'd know." Pete snorted. "You weren't part of us then. You never would have been. If Damon lived." Pete's eyes lit, and he pointed a finger. "Frame Forward was trash, man. You were going nowhere. Until you joined us. You had the most to gain."

"Yeah, just like you"—Ben emphasized this with a stab of one finger every bit as accusatory as Pete's—"had a reason to kill Vinnie. So we'd start recording your songs for a change." Ben puffed out a breath of annoyance. "You all had as much at stake as I did. None of you were anything without

Damon. Which means every single one of you must have been mad as hell when he said he was leaving. You were dead in the water, man. You would have stayed that way if I didn't step in."

"Bollocks!" A vein bulged in the side of Alistair's neck. "You were the one who wanted to be our lead singer. You wanted it bad. Bad enough to kill Damon?"

"Bad enough to kill you to shut up your stupid mouth." Ben kicked aside the nearest chair and went after Alistair.

And in one pristine moment of clarity, I realized that Vinnie's message from Beyond was spot on. These guys were in danger.

What Vinnie had failed to mention was that they were going to kill each other.

Truth be told, I figured the sooner, the better.

I didn't bother to say goodbye. I grabbed my purse and headed out the door. When it closed behind me, it shut out the sounds of the new argument breaking out.

But only for a moment. Before I got even as far as the control room, the door banged open and the guys stomped out.

"Had it with these assholes," Ben called into the control room. "I'm outta here."

"Can't stand them anymore," Alistair yelled. He pushed past Pete and nearly ran me down to get by me.

"We'll be back tomorrow," Mike called, and Pete added, "Maybe."

And all I could think was that no matter what they were paying the guys back in the control room, it wasn't enough.

I stepped out of Ajaz offices and back into the creepy warehouse, and though I wasn't alone, I didn't feel any more comfortable than I had when I walked in the place. Now instead of having to worry about mysterious noises and puddles of ooze, I had to wonder who was going to punch who before we made it as far as the door.

The way I remember it, we were almost there when the first shots rang out.

Chapter 14

The second I heard that first ear-cracking shot and the crazy, ping-ponging echo that bounced from wall to wall and caromed off the ceiling, my emotions took over.

And who could blame me? I had a history with this sort of thing. A hit man once tracked me down at the cemetery and tried to shoot me.

Experiences like that are hard to forget.

Just like then, I choked on my fear. My stomach flipped. My heart pumped high-test adrenaline. Every bone in my body turned to mush. Fortunately, I'd learned a thing or two from my experiences with the local mob. Duck and cover was one of them.

I went down like a rock, and grit scraped my cheek. Too late, I realized I'd dropped right into a puddle of I-don't-know-what. I didn't have the luxury of switching my position. Another shot splatted into the floor not ten feet from where I was huddled with my arms over my head, and about a million tiny chips of cement rained down on top of me.

I heard Ben gasp and feared the worse—until he grumbled something about crushing a new pack of smokes. Pete whimpered, and though I hadn't realized she was behind us as we left the studio, Crazy Belinda was nearby, too. Proof positive that she was as weird as they came because instead of fearing for her life like any normal person, she was chanting. Hard to say exactly what it was all about, but I swear I heard something about welcoming the angel of death. Go figure.

Alistair was on my right, swearing like a son of a gun. I heard nothing at all from Mike, and thinking about what it might mean, a sour taste filled my mouth. I didn't dare look to see if my fears were justified. There was nothing I could do to help Mike or anyone else. All I could do was stay rolled in a ball with my head covered. Oh yeah, and cringe when the wet whatever seeped through my pant leg and soaked my skin.

Another shot slammed into a pile of wooden pallets stacked near the wall on my right. It was still reverberating when the door to the studio banged open.

"Somebody's shooting!" I recognized the voice of one of the techies. He wasn't dumb enough to come out into the open. He ducked back inside. "Quick, call 911!"

Maybe that's what scared the shooter off. Suddenly the vast warehouse was as silent as a Garden View tomb. I hoped that was where the similarities ended.

The next second, full-scale bedlam broke out. I dared to look up just as Bernie came huffing and puffing through the studio door, a donut in one hand and a gun in the other. He tossed the donut on the ground and scanned the warehouse, and I guess he didn't see anything because he looked up at the walkways that ringed each floor. Even I knew a bad guy could hide for days in the offices up there and never be found.

Hot on Bernie's heels were the techies and the soundmen; Zack, the PR person; and even the receptionist with the purple hair. When it came to moral support, believe me, it was nice to see them all. It was not so nice when they all started jabbering at once. Their voices mixed with the sounds of gunfire still echoing in my ears, and like Jägermeister and Red Bull, they packed a punch right between my eyes.

"Holy shit!"

"Everybody okay?"

"Anybody hurt?"

"I'm calling Gene. Right now. He needs to get over here ASAP."

Their shouts bounced through my brain and made my head buzz. Maybe that's why when I pushed myself up on my elbows, I heard an odd, chirping sound. Or maybe I didn't. The acoustics in the old warehouse left a whole lot to be desired—and the wailing of a police siren outside didn't help.

I sat up, shaking my head. The puddle was bigger than I thought. My butt was soaked. Rather than think about it, I thanked my lucky stars for being alive and took inventory. It looked like everyone else had come through unscathed, too.

Alistair, Ben, Pete, and Mike were all breathing hard and handling the pressure with their usual aplomb. Alistair was swearing up a storm. Pete was in tears. Mike screamed to one of the flunkies for his Southern Comfort, and Ben simply sat in the middle of the warehouse floor, fighting to get a cigarette out of the pack that had been crushed when he hit the floor. Belinda, of course, was still chanting.

I don't know how long we all sat there trying to make sense of what had just happened. I only know that's how Quinn found us all when he arrived.

Just my luck. Was he the only damned cop in Cleveland?

"Somebody want to tell me what happened here?"

Quinn should have known better. *Everybody* wanted to tell him, and they all wanted to do it at once.

I may have mentioned that Quinn isn't the most patient guy in the world. He listened, for maybe like half a second, then he held up his hands, a sure signal that the circus had to stop. Now.

Their voices trailed off, and one by one, Quinn took a look at the Mind at Large band members. He knew Alistair from the incident at the Rock Hall, so when he got to the drummer, he stopped and pointed. "You," he said. "What happened?"

"Are you stupid? Do you think we always sit around on our butts in the middle of a friggin' warehouse? Somebody took a friggin' shot at us, that's what happened."

"Not a shot. Shots. Lots of shots." Mike felt obligated to set the record straight. One of the gofers showed up with a bottle, and after a few glugs, Mike's voice was quieter and his hands didn't shake nearly as much. He pointed up to the walkway that bordered each floor of the warehouse. "The shots came from somewhere up there."

"Or not." Ben got to his feet. He was breathing

hard, and there was blood on his shirt near where his sleeve was torn and his arm was scraped. He had half a mashed cigarette in his hand, and he snapped his fingers, waited for a roadie to light it, and took a long drag. "I hunt, so I know a thing or two about guns," he said, releasing the smoke with a sigh. "The shots . . ." He turned and pointed toward the door where an army of cops was getting ready to fan out to search the building. "They came from over there."

"And I nearly got killed." Pete sniffled and wiped his nose with this sleeve.

"Oh yeah. Like you're the only ruddy one." Alistair's glasses hung crooked on his face, and he ripped them off, tossed them on the floor, and ground them under his heel. "Why don't you stop feeling sorry for yourself, Petey, and—"

"And feel sorry for you?" Pete might have been small, but he was wiry, and let's face it, emotions were running high. He jumped to his feet and rounded on Alistair. "Why don't you just admit it, Al, you're scared shitless. Just like the rest of us."

"Just like you." Alistair's sneer was monumental. "Like all of you."

Ready to rip Alistair's head off, Mike shoved the bottle of Southern Comfort back to the guy who'd gotten it for him. "Why you rotten mother—"

Quinn didn't say a word. He didn't have to. He stepped between Alistair and Mike to stop them, and with one laser-sharp look, advised Pete and Ben not to get involved.

Alistair grumbled, and just for good measure, crunched his glasses one more time.

Mike ripped the bottle out of the hands of the kid who was holding it. He took a long drink.

Pete snuffled and demanded a cold cloth for his forehead, and when one of the roadies went to get it, Ben stepped forward.

"Maybe you should ask her." I'd like to think the animosity in Ben's voice and the suspicion in his eyes were the result of residual shock. I mean, it's not every day a person nearly gets his head blown off. It's kind of hard to feel charitable, though, when the person tossing the accusations has his eyes right on you.

Startled, I sat up a little straighter.

"We were fine until she came around." Ben pointed at me with his cigarette. "She's the one who told us we were in danger. Don't you think it's a little funny that no sooner does she tell us that we're all going to die than somebody starts taking potshots at us?"

Quinn swiveled to get a better look at me. A muscle jumped in his jaw. "I don't know. What do you think, Pepper? Do you think it's funny? As funny as me finding you here with these guys?"

"I think it's plenty coincidental. But this . . ." My fingers were sticky. I dared a look at my hand. It was covered with nameless grime and coated with goo. I wiped it against the leg of my pants and struggled to my feet. Quinn didn't offer me a hand up. I started to dust off the seat of my pants, but when my hand met wet fabric, I thought better of it. "This is definitely not my definition of funny. Looks like I was right." I glanced from bandmate to bandmate, firmly ignoring Crazy Belinda, who was on her knees, rocking back and forth. "Somebody's out to get you guys."

Quinn's gaze was penetrating. "And you deduced this how, Sherlock?"

"She spoke to him. Does all the time." The louder Crazy Belinda talked, the faster she rocked. "He told her. He told her somebody's going to die."

I think when it came to Belinda, Quinn pretty much got the picture. He nodded in a way that told the nearest uniformed cop to get her out of there pronto and looked my way. "And the him in question is . . . ?"

"Vinnie, of course." One of the omnipresent gofers handed Alistair a bottle of water and a couple of pills. He popped them, washed them down, and shoved the water back at the man. Fortified, he slid a glance from Quinn to me. "This little bird here communicates with the dead."

Sometimes when I'm bored, or when I'm feeling especially down-and-out and wishing Quinn and I could get together, I imagine breaking this news to him myself. On good days, I picture me dropping the bombshell and him nodding thoughtfully. Then he tells me to sit down, gets me a glass of wine, and confesses (his hands on mine and looking deep into my eyes) that though he'd never been able to pin it down, he'd always known I was different. It was why I fascinated him so. He says he wants me to tell him all about my Gift. But not until he's done kissing me.

On bad days (and truth be told, most of them are bad) I pictured me dropping the bombshell—and Quinn laughing his ass off.

All of this explains why I had to give him credit when Alistair did the bombshell dropping and all Quinn did was eye me carefully.

"So . . ." One corner of Quinn's mouth thinned. It wasn't exactly a smile, but it was close enough. I curled my hands at my sides. I couldn't vouch for my temper, not if he laughed. "Vinnie told you the band was in trouble. Vinnie Pallucci. After he was already dead."

"Something like that." Yes, I'm touchy about my Gift. Who wouldn't be? That would account for my voice being caustic. That, and the fact that Quinn had that same look in his eyes he'd had when he instructed the patrolman to cart Belinda away.

I sighed my frustration. "I went on a ghost hunt, all right? I wasn't sure anything would happen, but the ghost hunters . . . well, they contacted Vinnie's spirit." Yes, I left out the part about Dan entirely. This was not the time. "If you need proof . . ."

I fished the digital recorder out of my purse, and found it soaked with slime. I'm not a techno-junkie, but I knew what was what when it came to equipment casualty. I shoved the recorder back where it came from. "What difference does it make, anyway? Even if I played the recording for you, you wouldn't believe it."

"Maybe it makes plenty of difference." Quinn looked me up and down. "Maybe it explains—"

"What the fuck is going on around here?"

Gene Terry had arrived, and even though he was being detained over at the main door, his voice echoed like thunder through the warehouse. I turned just in time to see him stomp one sneaker-clad foot against the wet concrete. His cheeks were as red as the flashing lights on the police cruiser outside the door. His eyes bulged.

Quinn didn't give the situation a chance to get any more out of control than it already was. He motioned the cop to let Gene in. The moment the agent was near enough, he dropped the briefcase he was carrying and raced from bandmate to bandmate. "Are you guys all right? Nobody's hurt? Nobody's bleeding?"

"My damned glasses are broken again." Alistair's expression was sour.

"We nearly died, Gene." Pete started up with the waterworks again.

"And damn, but I am bleeding!" Mike looked down at the scrape on his arm and then over at the paramedics who were shuffling around near the door. "Somebody want to come over here and take care of this?"

"And she . . ." Ben pivoted to include me in the conversation. "She knew all about it. Before it happened. She told us, Gene. She told us she talked to Vinnie. He's the one—"

"Is that so?" The agent whirled around, and I guess I couldn't blame him for being mad. His meal ticket had nearly been blown to smithereens. That would tend to make a guy a little testy. "Who the hell do you think you are?" he demanded. "First you're with Vinnie when he dies, then you're at the Rock Hall when Al has a light fall on him. Now you're here when somebody's shooting? Don't you think that's a little suspicious?"

I set him straight with a sneer. "I wasn't at the Rock Hall when the light fell. I was there after the light fell. And yes, I was with Vinnie when he died.

And I was here for the shooting. But that's the whole point, don't you see? That's what I came to warn you about."

"I allowed you access to the band because you told me you were writing a book. If you think you can disrupt—"

"Pepper? Disruptive?" Surprise, surprise, Quinn really did have people skills after all. As smoothly as if he'd been corralling angry agents all his life, he closed in on Terry, put a hand on his arm, and took him aside. "Don't worry about her. She's harmless. A little crazy, but harmless. For now, we've got a lot of ground to cover and a lot of questions to ask. We'll talk about Ms. Martin's wild imagination another time. Let's start at the beginning. Who knew Mind at Large would be recording here today?"

They talked as they walked away, and I knew I wasn't missing anything because I already knew Gene Terry's answer. Who knew? Everybody! I'd seen the recording session mentioned online and in the morning's *Plain Dealer*.

Left to my own devices and with the cops who were swarming the place too busy to worry about me, I decided to do a little sleuthing. There was no use trying to talk to the band again. They were each too engrossed with their own troubles to worry about mine. There was no use looking around the warehouse, either. The cops would find whatever evidence the shooter might have left behind, and besides, I wasn't about to go exploring the place on my own. I had my standards as well as my common sense. Even if I don't always show it.

I kicked around the warehouse, eavesdropping

on the roadies (who said nothing of interest), the cops (who said nothing useful) and even Crazy Belinda (who had one of the uniformed cops cornered near the door and was telling him how disappointed she was because once the shooter vanished, she missed this chance to join her true love in the arms of death).

I was just about to give up and ask somebody if I could leave when I realized I was standing near Gene Terry's briefcase.

He wasn't a suspect, but I was bored.

And who knew what kind of secrets a guy like him carried around?

I used my foot to nudge the briefcase closer. It was one of those big, old-fashioned ones, the kind with two zippered compartments, one on either side of a middle section that just snaps closed, and it wasn't snapped. That's practically an invitation to look inside, right?

I bent to take a closer look. Imagine my surprise when I did—and saw a gun.

I thought I was playing it cool, but I guess Quinn must have seen me jump. When I looked around to find him, he was looking my way.

He excused himself from Gene Terry. "Now what?" he asked.

"I know who did it."

"You do." It was nice of him to buy into my theory so quickly. Or was that a note of skepticism I heard in his voice? He crossed his arms over his chest. "Want to let me in on the news?"

Gene Terry was watching us. I put a hand over my mouth.

"It was him," I mumbled.

"It was . . ." Quinn bent closer. "Who?"

"Him." I turned my back on Gene, the better to disguise the fact that we were talking about him. "There's a gun. In his briefcase."

If Quinn was half the classy guy I imagined him to be, he would have been a little more gracious. This definitely would not have involved calling Gene Terry over.

"What are you doing?" I hissed. But it was already too late.

"Miss Martin says you have a gun," Quinn informed the agent.

Gene gave me a dirty look. "Miss Martin needs to mind her own business."

Since the dirty look wasn't aimed at him, Quinn wasn't intimidated. "Do you have a gun?"

"You're damned right." Terry scooped the briefcase off the floor and opened it so Quinn could see. "It's a Glock 9 mm, and yes, it's licensed. We get a lot of crazy fans."

I was not paranoid. This criticism was aimed at me. Just in case I missed the significance, though, Gene went right on.

"This particular crazy fan . . ." He was shorter than me, but he moved in close and raised his chin so I didn't miss his glare. ". . . better stay clear from now on. No more wild accusations. No more contact with the band. I'm hiring extra security. That ought to take care of any threats. And it better mean I never see you anywhere near Mind at Large again. If I do, I'll be in court faster than you can say *restraining order.*"

"Aren't you going to arrest him?" I asked Quinn practically before Gene had walked away.

"For . . . ?"

"He's got a gun."

"He does."

"And somebody was just shooting at us."

"But not him."

"And you know this, how?"

"Pepper . . ." Quinn put both hands on my shoulders and turned me toward where the crime scene techs were hard at work. "See those bullets they're digging out of the concrete? They came from a rifle," he said. He patted me on the back before he walked away. "If you're going to play detective, get your facts right."

"Get my facts right." Watching Quinn head into the recording studio to talk to the witnesses there, I grumbled the words. It didn't help my mood to realize that he was right. I couldn't have been getting my facts right because if I was, this whole case would be making more sense. More than none, anyway.

A chill raced up my spine, but believe me, it had nothing to do with how I was feeling. Which was hopeless and defeated.

My clothes were soaked. My hair was a mess. I hated to think what kind of shape my makeup was in. The good news was that I'd been to the mall the weekend before and the new outfit I bought was still in the shopping bag that was still in my backseat. I could head back to Garden View, get cleaned up, and get back to work.

My real work.

There were only so many times I could use the excuse of the County Archives to account for my absences.

Chapter 15

How many ways could I say I was glad when that day was over?

I didn't even try, I was just glad it was. Dirty clothes in the shopping bag and me feeling as if I'd been wrung out and hung up to dry (or more accurately, like I'd been witness to more catfighting than on the women's mud wrestling circuit, been shot at, been chewed out by a pissed-off talent agent, and been humiliated by a man I would love to love), I drove home in a daze. I parked my car and for a couple of minutes, I just sat there, appreciating the quiet and the being alive.

The downtime gave me a chance to think and thinking . . . well, it actually improved my mood. Because it didn't take me long to realize there was an upside, even to a day like that. For one thing, in an effort to forget everything I'd been through (see above), I'd forced myself to keep busy when I got back to Garden View, and I'd actually gotten some honest-to-gosh work done. This was a plus because Ella not only noticed, but announced to everyone within earshot that I was living proof that the work ethic was very much alive. As the dearly departed don would remind me if he was on this side and not the Other, this was what was known as a bargaining chip. Or at least it would be if Ella remembered her high praise and cut me some slack the next time I disappeared because I was doing something I shouldn't have been doing on Garden View time.

The best part of it all was that once I'd gotten cleaned up, freshened my makeup, and changed out of my grimy clothes and into skinny black pants, a black cardigan, and a tawny-colored tank top that brought out the auburn highlights in my hair, I looked fabulous.

Good thing, too.

I wouldn't have wanted to look like hell when I finally hauled myself out of the car, rounded the corner of my apartment building, and nearly ran smack into Joel.

Goodbye, good mood. Hello, annoyance.

I set down the shopping bag. It was heavy because the dirty clothes in it were wet, and I didn't want to clutch it in two hands and look as if I was trying to disappear behind it. Besides, I figured it wouldn't hurt for Joel to see the Nordstrom name on the side of the bag. Maybe then he'd remember that nobody knew fashion like Pepper Martin knew fashion. Not even Simone Burnside, girl attorney.

"Pepper!" For a guy who was hanging around outside my door, he looked awfully surprised to see me. "I didn't think you'd be home this soon."

"So you were going to, what, camp out here until I showed?"

"That's not what I meant." Just like the last time

I saw him, Joel looked like a million bucks in a suit that didn't come off the rack, a shirt that I bet had his initials embroidered inside the collar, and a tie that was the exact same color as the tank I was wearing.

We matched.

I shuddered, and found comfort in the thought that I looked good on a shoestring. No way Joel could claim the same resourcefulness. He had the Panhorst millions to play with.

Naturally, thinking about Joel's family made me think about Grandma, and thinking about her made me think about her ring. It didn't take a detective—to the living or to the dead—to figure out what Joel wanted.

I cut to the chase. "No. I told you—"

"You didn't sell the ring to a jeweler, Pepper." Joel was pretty quick on the uptake. Or maybe he was just itching for a fight. "Sure, that's what you told me the last time we talked, but really, you should know me well enough to give me a little more credit. Your story is a total fabrication. How do I know? You forgot, that diamond is registered, and according to the registry, there's no record of a transaction."

"Oh, aren't you the clever one!" This was a good way of covering and better than the *Damn, you figured it out* that threatened to leave my lips. My smile was as sleek as the move I used to scoop up the shopping bag from the sidewalk. With the backside of one hand, I nudged Joel aside and moved toward the door. "Thanks for stopping," I said, my voice as breezy as the look I gave him. "Tell Simone I said hello."

"That's what this is all about, isn't it? It's all about Simone. She's more successful than you. She's richer. She's prettier."

I couldn't deny the *richer* or the *more successful* part. But *prettier* was a low blow.

Especially since it wasn't true.

I'd already walked past Joel, and I looked at him over my shoulder. "I bet she stinks in bed." I didn't wait for Joel to confirm or deny. Who was I kidding? He wasn't about to besmirch Simone's reputation. Not in front of me. As much as I hated to admit it, this was actually admirable.

But that didn't mean I had to put up with it. Or with Joel. Not for a moment longer.

I dug into my purse for my keys, and once I found them, I clutched them in one hand and turned long enough to raise my chin and give him a super-size glare. "I've been reading up on restraining orders," I said, even though technically what I'd been doing was being threatened to have one issued against me. "I know enough of the law to know that you can't bother me anymore."

"And I know that you can't refuse me. Not when it comes to the ring. It's mine, Pepper." Joel's eyes shot fire. "I want it back. Right now. And don't try to bullshit me about—"

"Selling it to a jeweler? You're right." I wondered if my smile looked as sheepish as I intended, and I guess maybe it did, because Joel's chest puffed up. My words were as sure and precise as if he had written them out for me and I was reading the confession. "There is no record of the sale of the diamond to a jeweler because I didn't sell it to a jeweler."

I stuck my key in the apartment building door. "I pawned it," I said, turning the key and pushing the door open. "Got a hot two hundred fifty bucks for it, too."

"Two-fifty." Joel's jaw dropped. His skin was ashen. It was an image I hoped to carry with me for the rest of my life. I stepped inside and closed the door behind me.

There was a window in it, and just to make sure he didn't miss my parting shot, I tapped on it.

"Gotcha!" I said, and before he recovered, I raced up the stairs.

My keys were still in my hand and so when I got to my apartment door, I was all set to unlock it. Except I didn't need to. Unlock it, that is.

My door was already open.

I had been feeling pretty full of myself. After all, I'd had the last word in the last conversation with the last ex-fiancé I hoped to ever have. But one look at the splintered wood of my doorjamb and the way the door hung from one hinge as if it had been kicked, and it was hasta la vista time for my self-confidence. An icy claw of fear gripped my insides. My knees quaked. I really didn't need to push the door open, I knew what I'd see, but holding on to the doorknob helped keep me from falling to the floor in a heap. Besides—and here I swallowed hard and gave myself a stern talking to—there was an off chance that I was being overly imaginative, paranoid, or both.

Or not.

Just as I suspected, my apartment was trashed.

I looked at the couch that had been turned over and the chair that was lying on its side in the living room. From where I was standing, I could see into my bedroom, and I realized that all the drawers had been yanked out of my dresser. There were clothes everywhere and magazines ripped and tossed all around. Even my kitchen cupboards had been torn apart. There was a trail of dishes between the kitchen and the bathroom, and silverware mixed in with the scattered pages of the morning's paper.

In one horrified glance, I took it all in.

And a funny thing happened.

The ice in my veins melted. Then again, maybe that wasn't so funny because it was replaced by a surge of anger so powerful, I couldn't have controlled it if I tried.

And I didn't try.

In far less time than it took me to get upstairs, I was back outside again. I was just in time, too. Joel and his black Audi were about to pull out of a parking place. He was looking away from me, waiting for traffic to clear. I guess that's why he was at a disadvantage when I jumped in front of his car and pounded on the hood.

Except for Quinn, who pretty much was off the scale, Joel could be as cool as any guy I'd ever met. But not when he was surprised. And boy, was he surprised! His eyes popped open. They were as round as marbles. His mouth dropped. It was not an attractive expression.

He hit the right button, and the driver's side window glided down. "What the hell—?"

"Don't you what the hell me, Joel Panhorst." I marched to the side of the car, and three cheers for me, I must have looked hopped up enough to intimidate even Joel. The window had been all the way down. He closed it partway and leaned back and farther away, but not until he double-checked to make sure the doors were locked.

"How dare you?" My voice shook. So did my legs. I grasped the car door. "Who the hell do you think you are? How could you?"

Joel was a lot of things, but dumb wasn't one of them. If he was, I never would have fallen in love with him. That was why I did so not appreciate it when he tried to act confused. "How could I . . ." As if it would help clarify the situation, he shook his head. "What are you talking about, Pepper?"

I choked on my anger. And my words. My hands were curled into fists, and I forced myself to relax. I flexed my fingers. And fisted them again. "No wonder you looked so surprised to see me," I said. "You thought you could slink away before I got back."

"Why would I want to avoid you when I came here to talk to you in the first place?" His mouth pulled into a thin line, and this time when he shook his head, it wasn't as if he was trying to clear it. It was more like he was feeling sorry for me. "Maybe what people are saying is true. Maybe you are—"

"What?" He didn't know I could move that fast. I didn't know I could get my head through a car window that wasn't open all the way. Eye-to-eye, we glowered at each other. "What are our old friends saying about me, Joel? That I'm a washed-up, down-and-out cemetery tour guide? Or are they just saying I'm crazy?"

He snorted. "They don't need to say it. It's obviously true. If you can't afford professional help—"

"I don't need professional help. Except maybe from the cops. Maybe when they show up, you can explain to them how you kicked in my door and trashed my apartment looking for that damned ring."

As if I'd tossed a handful of ice cubes down his back, Joel sat up straight. He shivered. "Are you accusing me? You think I'd do something like that?"

"Oh, come on!" I live in a neighborhood that is traditionally Italian, and I don't think it's going out on a limb to say that many Italians are emotional and passionate. No doubt my neighbors, many of them longtime residents, had seen their share of operatic arguments before. That didn't keep some of them from opening their windows and sticking out their heads. Or others from stopping on the sidewalk across the street so that they didn't miss a word.

I welcomed the audience. Witnesses are a good thing.

My neck was cramped, so I wasn't giving ground when I pulled back from the car and stood up straight. Just so Joel knew it, I kept a grip on his door. "Enough games, Joel," I said. "Asking for the ring is tacky enough. Trying to steal it crosses the line."

"You're right. It does."

Was I delusional? Did I just hear the great Joel Panhorst admit that he was wrong and I was right?

The very thought cheered me right up. Until Joel opened his mouth again.

"That's why I didn't do it," he said, and he eased the gearshift into drive.

It took a moment for the message to sink in. "What do you mean you didn't do it? Joel, this is important so you'd better not be bullshitting me. Are you telling me—"

"I'm telling you that you're right, you'd better call the cops. Because I might have thought about it, Pepper, but you know me better than that. Unlike certain of your relatives, I wouldn't take the chance of breaking the law, hurting my reputation, and destroying my family. I didn't break into your apartment, and you know what that means, don't you?" I was so stunned, I'd let go of the door handle, and Joel moved into traffic. When he sped away, his voice wafted back to me.

"If I didn't do it, that means someone else did."

The first thing I did when I got back upstairs was call the cops.

The second thing? I looked for the ring, of course.

In a day that had been filled with bad news, this was the one bright spot. The ring was exactly where I left it—in the toe of my slipper.

"Now you're glad you listened to me, aren't you?"

I didn't need to turn around to know Grandma Panhorst had joined me.

"You bet." I stuffed the ring back into my slipper and turned toward my bed. It was heaped with the clothes that had been ripped out of my closet, but of course that didn't stop Grandma. She was seated on top of the pile, her legs crossed and one foot—and the pink, fuzzy slipper on it—swinging. "Thanks for the advice. About the ring in the slipper, I mean. If it wasn't for you—"

"Any time, kid." Grandma waved away my thanks with the hand that held a cigarette. "Wouldn't want somebody to make off with my ring."

There didn't seem to be any point in being careful, so I scooped up some of the clothes on the bed and tossed them on the floor on top of the pile of necklaces and earrings that had been emptied out of my jewelry box. "Was it Joel?" I asked Grandma. "He said it wasn't, but I don't trust him as far as I could throw him."

"That makes two of us." Grandma finished her cigarette and flicked it away. "But as for this mess . . ." She brushed her hands together. "Sorry, honey. I can't help you. I didn't see a thing."

"I thought you said you stayed with the ring."

"I do. I mean, usually. But not when my program is on. Oprah. Don't you just love her!"

"Then maybe it wasn't Joel. But maybe it was." I can't say why this cheered me. Thinking that Joel had pawed through my clothing was less nauseating—at least a little—than thinking that a stranger had done it. Unfortunately, as much as I would have liked to go on believing that Joel was guilty, I remembered what he'd said right before he pulled away.

"Who else but Joel would have the nerve to try and prove his innocence by insulting my family!" The upshot seemed clear and the nausea factor ratcheted up. I shivered. "Maybe it was some stranger. That gives me the creeps."

"You and me both. He could have swiped the ring."

"And since it's a family heirloom . . ."

I hadn't meant to make this sound like a bad thing, but apparently the anger I was feeling seeped into my voice.. Then again, who could blame me? My apartment had just been burglarized. It was only fair that Grandma cut me some slack. Instead, she clicked her tongue.

I knew she was offended, and rightly so. I apologized automatically. "I know. It's not something I should take lightly. I mean, the whole thing about Paris and the Nazis and—"

Grandma's shriek of laughter stopped me cold. "Who would be stupid enough to vacation in a country that's about to be conquered?" she asked.

My head came up. I looked at her hard. "You mean—"

"Horse hockey," she said. "Every word of it. You'd think someone would have figured it out by now. Then again, my son was always a trusting soul. A little stupid, but trusting. And my grandson . . . well, I didn't want to be the one to break it to you, but I guess by now you have it figured out. Joel was never the brightest bulb in the box. Truth is, kid, I've never set foot in Paris. Not in my life. And not since. What really happened is that me and Arnold, we ran off to Atlantic City together. My father would have had Arnie's head if he knew we were in a hotel making whoopee, so we concocted the story about getting married in Paris. Back in the eighties when they started registering diamonds, we told the jeweler the same story we'd been telling our family all along. It kind of took on a life of its own, you know? Thank goodness they didn't have diamond registration back when Arnie bought that ring off a guy we met on the boardwalk. I bet it was hot."

I'd bet it was, too. As a way of thanking Grandma for letting me in on the secret, I grinned. "I'm glad it didn't get stolen again this time," I told her. This cheered me up, and I would have stayed that way if another thought didn't hit. Curious to know if I really saw what I thought I saw when I walked into the room, I jumped up and kicked aside the clothes I'd just shoveled off my bed. I knelt on the floor to take a closer look at my spilled jewelry. "My gold chain is still here," I told Grandma, and just to prove it, I held it up for her to see. "And the birthstone ring my parents bought me that Christmas we spent in the Bahamas."

I didn't hear or see Grandma move, but when I looked up again, she was on the floor, too, kneeling directly across from me. She raised her eyebrows. "Expensive?" she asked.

"Expensive enough." I did a little more excavating. My own grandmother had once given me her gold watch. It was thick and heavy and old-fashioned-looking and I never wore it, but call me sentimental, I'd never get rid of it. Just thinking it might be gone soured my stomach.

Not to fear. The watch was there, too.

"Funny, don't you think," I said, but I wasn't laughing. "Somebody took all the trouble to break in here, but nothing of any value is missing. So why bother?"

Grandma pursed her lips. "You're talking like a detective."

"Am I?" Thinking, I tapped my top lip with my index finger. "Maybe it's time I starting acting like one, too."

Grandma shivered with anticipation. "Oh, are we going to investigate?"

"I'm going to investigate. I know this has got to have something to do with Damon and Vinnie and Mind at Large. Trouble is I can't get close to the band anymore."

"So what are we going to do?"

It was a legitimate question—well, except for the *we* part, but I ignored that for now because I needed someone to talk to and I didn't want Grandma to get offended and vanish. The least I owed her for her advice about the slipper and the truth about the ring was a clear and concise answer. The kind she'd expect from a real detective. Maybe that's why she looked at me in wonder when instead of saying anything at all, I hopped to my feet, the spark of inspiration in my eyes.

"I can't get close the band," I said. "But I can still get close to the next best thing."

In a flash, Grandma was on her feet, too. She angled her head and squinted at me, just like she used to do back when she was alive and we talked about something that really interested her and she couldn't wait to hear more. "And all this, it means what?"

I was sure I'd hit on the perfect solution, and I was so full of myself, I was already two steps ahead of her. I checked the time on the clock radio that was lying on the floor, upside down next to my nightstand. It was too late to do anything that evening and besides, I needed to wait for the cops and fill out a report about the burglary that wasn't. But first thing the next morning . . .

I was already putting my clock upright and setting the alarm for the ungodly hour of six when I remembered that I hadn't answered Grandma.

I hit the volume button on the radio so it would go off nice and loud and I couldn't sleep through it and glanced at her over my shoulder. "The answer is simple," I told her. "Coffee."

No one should get up that early. Especially on a Saturday.

No one should have to go out when it's still dark, either, but I knew I had no choice. Not if I was going to catch Belinda before she headed out for a day of coffee and Damon-worship. It was that or miss a chance at—maybe—getting my investigation off dead center.

Because I figured there was no way I was going to run into anyone I knew (or at least anyone I knew who I cared cared about how I looked), I slipped on jeans and a black sweater and sneakers, pulled my hair into a ponytail, and left my apartment before I could convince myself that I might be wasting my time.

As it turned out, I was. When I got to her apartment, Belinda was already gone.

Time for Plan B.

Next thing I knew, I was the first one in line at the City Roast coffee stand at the West Side Market.

The market is a historic landmark in Cleveland, but truth be told, it is not my kind of place. There's a covered walkway outside lined with stands brimming with fruits and vegetables. Attached to that is a massive building where I stood. In it, vendors sell everything from meat to baked goods, cheese and nuts, and ethnic specialties. Oh, I'd heard all the rah-rah from people like Ella who shopped there religiously: The prices were impossible to beat, the food was the freshest in town, the merchants were friendly and helpful and they knew their customers and their customers' preferences. But for a girl who's used to shopping at stores where the food is neatly packaged, the aisles are wide and roomy, and music plays from the overhead sound system, the whole place is a little overwhelming. It's big and it's noisy. It's what people call colorful when they're being politically correct and what they really mean is that on any given day, you're just as likely to see suburban shoppers in their minks inside the market as you are the homeless right outside its doors. Of course, it's an up-close-and-personal experience with food in its least-processed stages, too. As I stood there waiting for my latte (skim milk, no whipped cream), a butcher walked by carrying the carcass of a skinned pig.

Need I say more?

Lucky for me, I wasn't even halfway through my latte when I saw that my instincts were right on. I wasn't wasting my time, after all. This *was* the first stop Belinda made each morning.

"Good to see you again!" Before she could say a word, I whipped out a five and plunked it on the counter to pay for whatever she was going to order. "You remember me, right? I'm Pepper. We were at your apartment and—"

"You were with us," she said. "When Death tried to collect our souls." Like a bobble-head doll that had been given a good jostling, she nodded, and hoping to establish some kind of rapport, I nodded, too. I don't think she heard me groan; I was hoping that first thing in the morning, Belinda would be a little less crazy.

Rather than show my disappointment, I smiled. "That's right. But I also found Alistair. Remember? And I was at the recording studio. And remember what I said there? I told the guys that I talked to Vinnie. He asked for my help. But there's nothing I can do. Gene Terry won't let me talk to the band anymore."

"I'm with the band!"

It wasn't the first time she'd told me as much, and just like last time, I had a hard time pretending I cared. "I know that," I said, hoping to divert her from memory lane. All I really wanted to talk about was the missing photo of Damon. "You knew all the guys in the band, but you liked Damon the best."

"Liked him?" Belinda's face scrunched with confusion. "That's not true. I didn't like Damon. I loved him. And he loved me, too."

Maybe the early hour was messing with my mind. There was no way I heard her correctly. "Are you telling me that you and Damon, you—"

"Screwed our brains out, every chance we got!" Belinda's laugh was loud enough to turn heads. It was exactly the effect her words had on my stomach. I backed up and gave her a careful look, but like I said, she was so lost in the past, I don't think she remembered I was there. "We fell in love. We're still in love. He's my—"

"Angel of death." This part of the puzzle clunked into place. Realizing it, I sucked in a breath. "That's why you're always hanging around Damon's grave. It's why the band lets you stick with them. You and Damon—"

"We're soul mates." Belinda's eyes were as dreamy as her words. "Till death do us part. Only it didn't. That's why I stayed when Damon passed ahead of me into the arms of Death. To take care of him. To watch over him in his grave. He's waiting for me." Her expression was transcendent. "When my time comes, he'll welcome me with open arms. My demon lover. My beautiful devil. My joy. My love. My all."

Still mumbling and grinning, Belinda took her coffee off the counter with one hand and scooped up my change with the other. Right before she walked away.

And me? I was too stunned to do much of anything but watch her go.

Which is exactly why I didn't realize Damon had popped up beside me.

For once I didn't jump. I was knocked for a loop by all I'd just heard. And maybe busy feeling a little envious, too.

"You and that?" Okay, it wasn't a polite question. But who could blame me? Naturally, I figured Damon had pretty good taste. He liked me, didn't he? So that nobody could see me talking to myself, I ducked behind the table where the sugar packets and the cup covers were stacked. "She's just talking crazy, right? I mean, she's an obsessed fan, sure, but she can't be serious. You and Belinda?"

"Me and . . ." When I poked my head around the corner, Damon looked where I was looking. Belinda had put her coffee cup down on top of a trash can so she could scratch her stomach. "Who is she?" he asked.

I breathed a sigh of relief. "She says she's the love of your life. But I gotta tell you, I didn't believe her from the start. I mean, really, look at her."

Damon did. His thoughtful expression melted into recognition. "Did she say we met in Los Angeles?"

My stomach swooped. "You're not telling me it's true?"

He acted like it was no big deal. "Come on, Pepper, I told you. Chicks were my thing, and I guarantee you, that chick, she was just as crazy, but she was way better-looking back then."

"Then it is true? You and Belinda, you were—" I couldn't bring myself to say it, all that stuff about soul mates and until-death-do-us part. "You told me you loved women. You never said there was one special person in your life."

He'd been watching Belinda, and Damon turned my way. "Special? I wouldn't say that. She was good for a few laughs, sure, and a couple nights of really good sex, but after that . . . well, I guess I lost interest. She must have hooked up with one of the other guys. She was always around. But I swear, we never spent another night together."

"So why does she think that once she dies, you're going to be waiting to welcome her with open arms?" Did I sound like a crazy, jealous lover? I consoled myself with the fact that I couldn't have. I might be crazy, but I'd never be Damon's lover. Not like Belinda had been. The thought ripped through me, and damn it, tears filled my eyes. "She says you two were soul mates," I told Damon. "That's why she stays here in Cleveland. To take care of your grave. She says you're going to love her for all eternity."

"Well, then I'm sorry." Damon looked into my eyes when he spoke. "I'm sorry for you, Pepper, because I can see that it hurts you to think I kept a secret from you. Believe me, that's the last thing I want to do. I'm sorry for her, too." He glanced back toward the trash can, but Belinda had moved on. "I never promised her a thing. Once she walked out the door, I didn't even remember her name. And she's devoted forty years of her life to me." He rippled like a reflection on a pond. "She's wasted all the time she's been given here on earth. Because of me." His voice was muffled, but there was no mistaking the regret in it. "It's sad. And pathetic." Little by little, the color drained out of Damon until he looked like an old black-and-white photograph. He faded. "I never meant for it to happen. To me, it was a one-night stand. To her—"

"It's been her whole life." I finished the sentence for him, and it's a good thing. When I looked to where he'd been standing, Damon was gone.

And it was just as well.

Because epiphany moments, as important as they are, aren't necessarily meant to be shared.

And this was one I wanted to keep to myself.

I thought about Joel and Grandma Panhorst's

ring. I thought about how all these months, I'd been struggling to pretend life could be like it had been before my dad ended up in prison and my world fell apart. I thought about Damon and the fact that as crazy as it sounded—as crazy as it was—I'd fallen in love with him.

And I realized that me and Belinda, we had a whole lot in common.

We were both hanging on to the past.

And if I wasn't careful, it was going to destroy my future. Just like it had hers.

Chapter 16

What all this led to, of course, was a weekend of examining my life. This is a good thing, or so I'm told, and can lead to all sorts of wonderful revelations. Unfortunately in my case, all it left me with was the unshakable and depressing realization that my life was in desperate need of resuscitation.

Oh yeah, and me feeling sorry for myself.

I wallowed in my misery and proved it by finishing off an entire pint of chocolate ice cream (Harmony's latest check had yet to arrive, and I couldn't afford Ben & Jerry's and had to settle for the cheap stuff), a bag of Oreos, and every single cannoli I bought from Corbo's, the really good Italian bakery down the street from my apartment. And no, I won't say how many that was.

By the time Monday rolled around, the carbs had worked their magic, and I knew what I had to do—in addition to eating nothing but salad for an entire week.

I had to stop it with the self-pity.

I had to quit being jealous of a woman who was old and crazy and of the forty-year-old affair she'd had with a man who was as off-limits as any guy

I'd ever met, and for the best of reasons, too, since he was dead.

I had to reclaim my life. Get over it. Get on with it. Get real.

With that in mind, I went through the motions of my job, and at five o'clock, I put away the research I was using to write an article for the next Garden View newsletter on Christmas traditions at the cemetery. Then I did a couple of things. Number one, I pulled out both the business card where Quinn had written his home phone number and the cocktail napkin on which Dan had scrawled his cell number. Number two, I spent a long time thinking about calling them. Both of them. If I was in search of a life, there didn't seem a better way to prove it than by establishing a relationship with a guy who was actually breathing.

Number three . . .

Well, number three was that I took a good, hard look at those phone numbers, I thought about Quinn and Dan a little more, and I decided to do nothing.

Yes, I know, such wishy-washy behavior is the true sign of a wimp. But look at things from my vantage point: I couldn't talk to either Dan or Quinn. Not without sounding as desperate as I felt. And I wasn't about to let either one of them know that.

All was not lost, however. With the messy personal stuff taken care of (sort of), I could concentrate on my professional life.

And I wasn't talking about that article on Christmas traditions.

I pulled out a legal pad and made a list. It was an

obsessive/compulsive sort of thing to do, and I am anything but. Still, as I had learned from working my other cases, lists help me order my thoughts. Right about then, that was exactly what I needed. More order, less oh-poor-me.

I divided the page into three columns and wrote "Damon" to the left and "Vinnie" in the middle. On the far right I scrawled "Mind at Large." After that, things got dicey. I took a deep breath, told my brain it was time to get in gear, and in the appropriate places, I filled in the few facts I knew for certain.

"His death was an accident but maybe not an accident," I wrote beneath Damon's name and spoke out loud while I did. "He could have been murdered, which might explain why he's tied to this plane and can't leave. Photograph missing. Maybe it's important? Or maybe it's not missing?"

I considered the possibility and dismissed it instantly. Belinda was a lot of things, but as the shrine to Damon in her apartment proved, careless wasn't one of them. No way had she misplaced the photo. She valued it too much.

And so did someone else.

"Someone knows something," I said, and since I wasn't sure where this factoid belonged, I wrote it across all three columns. "Otherwise, they wouldn't have broken into Belinda's apartment."

And what about the burglary at my place?

It wasn't the first time I wondered if the two incidents were related, but this time, like all the other times, I shook my head. What did Belinda and I have in common? In a word, absolutely nothing (and yes, I know that technically that's two words).

Or did we?

There was Damon, of course, but heck, I hadn't told anybody that I talked to him on a regular basis. And certainly, though everybody knew Belinda was still in love with him, nobody could possibly suspect how I felt. If they did, I'd get carted away by guys in white lab coats.

Other than that, Belinda and I both hung out at Garden View a lot (for totally different reasons), we both lived nearby, we'd both been at the Rock Hall at the same time on two occasions and at the recording studio together on another day.

What any of this meant or why it was important, I didn't know. And none of it changed the fact that both Damon and Vinnie were dead and I didn't have a clue as to why. Or that, if Vinnie's information was to be trusted, another Mind at Large band member was sure to follow in their ghostly footsteps. This last bit I took personally. After all, I'd been with the band when someone shot at them. I could have ended up dead, too, and I was so not ready for that.

For another fifteen minutes or so, I went on thinking and writing and muttering. Don't get me wrong, though I say I was ordering my thoughts and making notes about my case the way any real private investigator would, I am not completely delusional (except of course on humid days when I try to convince myself that for once, my hair was not going to frizz). Even I didn't miss the number of *coulds* and *maybes* and question marks in my list.

Sad but true, when push came to shove, the only fact I knew for sure was this: I didn't know squat.

Groaning, I tossed my pen down on the legal pad and plunked back in my chair. Maybe (yes, another *maybe*) I just needed a break. Maybe some downtime would restart my brain. At this point in my investigation, my thoughts should have been flowing. Instead they plonked through my head in heavy boots and made a noise like—

Like the sound of the footsteps I heard outside my office door.

My head came up, and I leaned toward the door and listened closely, trying out my deductive skills and congratulating myself when I came up with three very good reasons why I shouldn't be afraid:

1. I was the only one in the office. I knew that for sure because both Jim, our administrator, and Ella, who was always the last one out the door, had already stuck their heads in to say good night.
2. Ghosts didn't make noise when they walked around, so it couldn't have been a visitor from the Other Side.
3. It was too early for a burglary.

I know this doesn't exactly sound logical, but think about it and it actually makes sense. What burglar in his right mind would risk coming into an office when all the lights are on and there are still cars—okay, one car—in the parking lot?

The upshot was clear. I was imagining things. Since imagining was what I was trying not to do, and sticking to the cold, hard facts was, I got back to work.

"Damon, Vinnie, Mind at Large." One by one, I

tapped my pen against the words written on the pad. "If someone still cares enough to steal the photo of Damon, then that someone might be the same someone who had something to do with his death. Maybe."

My brain hurt. I tossed down the pen so I could run my hands through my hair.

Which is when I heard a sound in the hallway again.

I've watched enough bad movies to know the last thing I should have done was get up and go to the door. But I was working without a script and was so eager to find answers, I was willing to take a chance.

"Hello!" I opened my door and stuck my head into the hallway. There was no one around. No one I could see, anyway. "Is that you, Jim? Ella?"

No one answered, and suddenly getting in my car, locking the doors, and heading for home sounded like a really good plan. With that in mind, I ducked back into my office long enough to get my purse and take out my keys. I fisted my keychain in one hand and poked the keys out from between my fingers. With my other hand, I grabbed a paperweight off my desk. It was a promotional item Ella had insisted on gifting me with after a recent cemetery conference, a Lucite half circle, flat on the bottom and rounded on top with the picture of a simpering angel statue inside it. Lucky for me, though the paperweight wasn't big, it was plenty heavy. Weighing it in one hand, I headed for the door. I edged down the hallway, rounded the corner into the lobby area—

And ran right into Crazy Belinda.

"Holy shit! Don't do that to me." I clutched the paperweight to my heart and fought to catch my breath. It wasn't until after I finally managed not to keel over that I realized Belinda didn't look any calmer than I felt. There were bright spots of color in her cheeks, and her eyes were aflame. She was breathing hard. She craned her neck to look over my shoulder.

"What's going on?" I asked her.

"Couldn't find you. Didn't know which office. Have to hide." Belinda ran her tongue over her lips. "It isn't the angel. I would wait for the angel. You know I would. I would be so happy. But angels come on shiny clouds. They don't follow in the dark."

"Somebody's following you?" I looked over my shoulder, too. There was no sign of anyone in the office, and from what I could see through a nearby window, nobody out in the parking lot. "You're sure? This is for real?"

Even though I knew I was justified, I felt guilty for even asking. Then again, that might have been because one look at Belinda, and I was reminded of everything I'd heard about her. Once upon a long time ago, she was beautiful. These days, she was nothing but a shell of her old self. Yeah, that was pretty much enough to make me feel guilty. But wait (as they say on those commercials), there was more.

For one thing, I'd spent the entire weekend being jealous of the old Belinda, a woman who no longer existed, one Damon didn't even remember. For another . . . well, that was really the deal breaker. Because no matter what I thought of Belinda, who she was now, who she used to be, or what she'd ever meant to Damon, nothing could change the fact that there was stark terror in her eyes.

No one has ever accused me of being warm and fuzzy (well, except for Joel, and only once, but that was when I was in the first throes of wedding-induced madness and looking at cake tops—could I be blamed for thinking hearts and flowers?). Be that as it may, I am not that insensitive.

I set down the paperweight. "Come on," I said, checking the window one more time. The coast was clear. "I'll drive you home. Then you won't have to worry about anyone following you."

Belinda's knees locked. "But he'll find me and he'll get you, too."

This was not the calming reassurance I needed.

A drumbeat of fear started up inside my chest. "Nobody's going to get me. Or you," I told her. I figured talking tough might make both of us feel better. "My car is right outside. We don't have far to go. So if he's following you—"

My own words brought me up short.

"He who?" I asked because asking meant I was back in logical mode, and that was better than giving in to the panic that shivered through Belinda's voice and threatened to infect me. "Did you see the man? Do you know who he is? What he wants?"

"He's the wolfman. He eats the hearts of innocents."

This piece of information would have sent any normal person screaming into the night. But truth be told, I guess I'm not all that normal. Hearing this actually made me feel better. Belinda talking about werewolves was like Belinda talking about the angel of death, and I was much better dealing with an overactive imagination and a fried brain than I was with real threats.

I breathed a sigh of relief. "Let's get going."

She held back, but I was persistent, younger, stronger, and a whole lot taller. When I got tired of sweet-talking and grabbed her arm, she came along with me. A few short minutes later, we were in my car. It was dark and the security light over the office door threw odd shadows, but there was no mistaking the relief that swept across Belinda's expression when I finally locked the doors.

Her eyes glistening, she sank back into the passenger seat and didn't say a word. At least not until we were halfway to the side gate the employees used to leave by when they worked late and the main gates were already closed. There was a fork in the road directly ahead of us. Beyond that and across a swathe of grass was one of the older sections of the cemetery. When my headlights raked the tombstones, Belinda sat bolt upright and pointed toward the windshield with one trembling finger. "He's there! He's waiting! Hurry, Pepper, hurry! He's following me."

My heart jumped, and I don't think I can be blamed for stepping on the accelerator. I took the fork in the road on two wheels.

Fortunately, since it was already dark and there are no streetlights in Garden View to illuminate the roads that twist and turn, common sense conquered my knee-jerk fear. Whoever Belinda thought she saw among the tombstones, no way he could keep up. I let up on the gas.

"You have to tell me what's going on, Belinda.

Why you think someone's following you. Is anything else missing from your apartment?"

She shook her head.

"Did you see anyone hanging around, maybe outside your place?"

Another shake.

"Then where?"

"He found me. At Damon's grave." She fingered the collar of her denim jacket. "He walked on kitty cat feet. His hands squeezed my throat."

"He snuck up behind you?" Was the attack real or a product of Belinda's warped imagination? It didn't much matter. Just thinking about a dark cemetery and a surprise attack made me shiver. "Did he say what he wanted? Or why he chose you? Did he say anything about Mind at Large?"

She shook her head again, right before she looked over her shoulder and out the back window. When she did, her mouth fell open and her eyes bulged. One look in my rearview mirror and I saw why.

There was a car on the road behind us, and it was closing in fast. Its headlights were off.

No matter. I didn't need them to see the truth. Belinda *was* being followed. And now, whoever was after her was right behind us.

"Hang on," I shouted to Belinda.

I stepped on the gas and thanked my lucky stars that I'd had six months to learn my way around Garden View. In the dark, one road looked like another, and it was easy to miss turns. I found the road I was looking for. The side gate was less than five hundred feet away. We were almost there when the car behind us gunned its engine and closed the gap. Talk about tailgating! The next thing I knew, my car bucked as the car behind us slammed into my bumper.

"Hey!" I looked at the dark sedan in my rear-view mirror and shook my fist. Like whoever was driving that car would see. Or care.

Another bump. My neck snapped. My seat belt tightened around me like a python.

The car behind us backed off and snuck up on my left side, and I had no choice but to move, too, or risk a crumpled bumper or worse. Luckily, the timing was just right. We were at the spot where a road intersected the one we were on. I turned right. I knew exactly where we were: The chapel was up ahead and to my left. If we stayed on this road, we'd eventually come to the main gate. Yeah, it was locked. But there was a busy street just to the other side of the iron gate, and there were always plenty of cars around, and on a night as mild as this, there would be walkers and joggers, too. That meant plenty of witnesses, and maybe enough of a deterrent to make our attacker back off. If we could just keep far enough ahead . . .

I drove faster. The other car fell back. I stepped on the accelerator even harder, and I'd just convinced myself that I actually had a chance of outrunning the dark sedan when it came around from the other side. Instead of being forced to my right, I was forced to my left. I held my place as long as I could, but my left tires were already on the grass. I couldn't slow down. I couldn't move over. Before long, the Mustang was off the road completely and the chapel was getting closer by the second.

The way I saw things, I might have been able to handle this situation a little more lucidly if Belinda wasn't wailing like a banshee. Her screams pierced the air and scrambled my thought processes. Instead of worrying about the way the steering wheel vibrated beneath my hands or the way the car bumped and thumped across the grass and made my head rock and my spine feel as if it was about to snap, I wondered what I'd say when Ella showed up at Garden View the next morning and found my Mustang sticking out of the Tiffany window.

Of course, I was assuming I'd be alive to say anything at all.

The bad news: Thoughts of my impending death froze my insides. But there was a flipside, too. Somehow, thinking about dying made me realize there was no way in hell I was going to let that happen. Even though Belinda's screams deafened me, my brain jump-started. Instinct took over, and my instincts told me that I had one choice.

As hard as I could, I yanked the steering wheel to the left.

There was a rolling hill behind the chapel. I knew that. Still, I have to admit I was surprised when we went airborne. The Mustang drifted for one second, two, three, and I actually might have enjoyed the sensation of floating through the air if not for the fact that by that time, Belinda's screams had morphed into shrieks. I braced myself, yelled to her to hang on (though to what, I can't say) and waited for the landing.

It was rough enough to make my teeth rattle. They were still knocking together when the first of the water started to seep in under the door.

"We're in the pond." Yes, had Belinda been thinking more clearly, she would have been justified in replying with *No, duh*. But she was frozen with fear, and I knew I had to act, and fast. My fingers trembling, I undid my seat belt. Then I leaned over and unhooked hers, too. "We've got to get out of here, Belinda. Before the car sinks. Can you swim?"

Belinda swallowed hard. "Goldfish swim in boats of sugar," she said. "Turnips float and ice cream cones—"

"Just shut up." I gave her a shake, partly to get her moving. Mostly to keep her quiet. "Because of the pressure of the water, I don't know if I'll be able to open the door. Even then . . ." I gulped down my fear. "You've seen those shows on TV where they show you how to survive a disaster, right? If we can't open the doors, we're going to have to kick out the windshield." This was not the fate I had envisioned for my lizard T-strap pumps, and rather than resign myself to it, I decided on a bold move. "I'm going to try the door now," I told Belinda. "Maybe if I push really, really hard." I braced my shoulder against the door. "Ready? One, two, three . . ."

I didn't expect the door to open so easily. That would explain why I used so much force and why, when I used that much force, it popped open, and I tumbled right out of the car and into the pond. It wasn't hard to see why. The water wasn't any more than a couple of feet deep.

My butt in mud and water to my chin, I groaned and looked at the Mustang. It was submerged to its bumpers. "You can come out, Belinda," I said. "You won't drown. The water isn't deep enough."

Instead of opening the passenger door, she scooted across the front seat. On her stomach, she peered out the door at me. "But he'll find us. He's following."

It wasn't like I'd forgotten about the dark sedan or its driver, but let's face it, I'd been a little preoccupied. Now I automatically looked up the hill toward the chapel. There was no sign of the dark sedan, but from a distance, I heard voices. My stomach bunched, and I was about to pull Belinda out of the car and make a run for it through the knee-high water when the owner of one of the voices came into sight at the top of the hill.

"You okay down there?" Brian the ghostbuster called, and when I waved to signal that I was, he turned and gave the high sign to the rest of his crew and crab-stepped his way down the hill and to the edge of the pond.

"We've got ropes," he called. "Back in the truck. Stay put and we'll pull you out."

"No need," I told him. Of course, that was before I attempted to stand. The mud sucked at my feet, and I lost both my shoes.

"Damn!" I bent to try and find my shoes, lost my balance, and tipped. I went down like a rock.

When I spit out a mouthful of foul water and finally pulled myself to my feet, mud and water sluiced off me. My car was a mess and would need to be towed. My clothes were ruined, and somewhere in the dark, someone who wanted Belinda dead was no doubt watching and maybe planning another attempt on her life.

And shit, that wasn't even the worst of it.

Even as I stood there watching the ghostbusters come to our rescue, I could practically feel my hair getting frizzy.

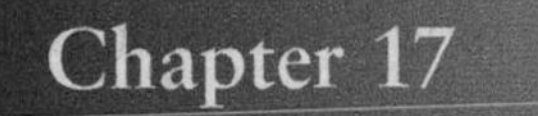

Chapter 17

As often happens in Cleveland, the Halloween weather was mild. It's just a cruel tease, of course. Anybody who's been around these parts long enough knows that though this one day might be pleasant, the next few months of cold temperatures and snow were sure to be hell. No worries. Clevelanders are a tough bunch, and when it comes to weather, we've learned to take what we can get and be grateful for it.

Since my car was still stuck in the muddy pond and the towing company I'd called to pull it out couldn't fit me in until that afternoon, I walked to work. It took longer than I expected to get up the hill from Little Italy, and by the time I did, the cemetery was already hopping. Mild temperatures and sunny skies equal lots of visitors, and on that particular holiday, they had more on their minds than simply saying hello to loved ones. Brian and his bunch (I couldn't help but notice that Dan wasn't with them) were working near one of the mausoleums, and just as I walked by, a group of teenagers with tape recorders went into the huge building where President James A. Garfield is laid to rest.

It was sure to be a busy day, and who could blame me for not being in the mood. It wasn't even nine o'clock and I was already exhausted. My body ached from head to toe. Part of my general yuckiness was because of the jolt I'd taken the night before when the Mustang landed hard in the pond. But most of it, I knew, was from the shoes I shouldn't have worn for a walk this long and the heavy overnight bag I was carrying. I moved the bag from my left hand to my right to give my left arm a rest.

Besides, it had taken me hours to get home the night before, what with explaining my voyage into the pond to the police, my insurance agent, and Ella (who I felt obliged to call even though I would rather have put it off). True to form, Ella was more worried than critical. That only made me feel worse about almost destroying a building that was on the list of national landmarks.

"I heard what happened last night."

It says something about my fatigue that I didn't jump when Damon popped up next to me. We were just passing through a section where tall headstones hid us from the nearby road, and I felt free to talk.

"By now, I'll bet everyone's heard." I had no doubt that Pepper Martin and her driving skills (or lack thereof) were the main topic of conversation at the office. If he'd been hanging around over there, that would explain how Damon had already caught wind of the story.

Careful to watch where I was going, since in addition to the standing stones, there were plenty of close-to-the-ground grave markers in that section and I didn't want to trip, I looked at him out of the corner of my eye. "Did you see anything?"

"You mean who was driving that other car? Sorry." Damon twitched his shoulders. "I was over at the Rock Hall watching the roadies set up the band's equipment for tonight's concert. If I was here, maybe I could have helped."

"Or not." No sooner were the words past my lips than I felt lousy for saying them. I stopped and turned to Damon. "You know I didn't mean it that way," I told him. "I just meant—"

"That ghosts can't do shit when it comes to intervening in the things of this world. I know." He stopped, too, and scooped a lock of hair out of his eyes. I noticed he didn't use his left hand, and it was no wonder why. It was so faded, I could barely see it. So was his left wrist, his arm, his shoulder, and seeing it—and realizing he'd never been so faded before—I gulped down the knot of panic in my throat.

"I hate it that I can't help you," Damon said.

I tried for a smile, but it was mushy around the edges. "I hate it that I can't help *you*. You're disappearing."

His smile was more genuine. "I disappeared a long time ago. It took you to make me real again."

I looked at the ground and kicked at a tuft of grass. "I wish."

"Hey, little girl." Damon reached out, and I think he was about to chuck me under the chin with one finger. At the last second, he pulled his hand back to his side. "Have I told you how grateful I am for everything you're doing?"

"Which is pretty much nothing." My gaze still on the ground, I sighed.

"Have I told you how nice it is that after all these years, I have someone to talk to?"

Caught by the mesmerizing warmth of his voice, I looked up. It would have taken a stronger woman than me not to smile in response to the fire in his eyes.

"Have I told you . . ." Damon leaned nearer. Not to worry, we'd both learned our lesson when he kissed me at the Rock Hall. He settled for the next best thing; the look he gave me was as intimate as a kiss. And a whole lot less chilly. "You're special, Pepper."

My eyes filled with tears. I tried for flip, but my words were watery. "I don't think we have much of a future."

"But we do have a present." Damon backed away. I was glad. It was too easy to be caught in the tractor beam of his smile. Not to mention the smoldering look in those dark eyes. "I want to help you. You know, with your case."

There's nothing like the mention of an investigation to destroy a romantic moment. I backed away, too, automatically shaking my head. "There's nothing you can do."

"There is. I've been thinking about it. I can be your eyes and ears. You know, with the band."

The idea had merit, but . . .

"The concert's tonight," I reminded him. "They're leaving town tomorrow. At least that's what it says in the paper this morning. Once the guys are gone, there's nothing I can do. I can't follow all of them around to make sure they're safe."

"Which means we'll have to do something tonight."

I was one step ahead of him, and to prove it, I held up the overnight bag. "I've got a change of clothes in here and a jacket because I know once the sun goes down, it's going to get cold. I'm going to the concert tonight."

He nodded. "So am I."

"No way." I dismissed the idea instantly. "You didn't even go to the recording studio with me. It was too painful for you to watch the band play and know you couldn't be with them. A live concert would be worse. It's—"

"Our last chance."

He was talking about keeping Mind at Large safe, and for all I knew, he was right. Once they left town, I was going to lose any chance I ever had of protecting the band.

"But I haven't been protecting them, have I?"

When I spoke out loud, Damon looked at me in wonder, and I caught him up on my thought process.

"I was just thinking, I'm worried about the band leaving town and me not being able to protect them. But I haven't been protecting them. I can't, because Gene won't let me near them. And it hasn't made any difference at all. Since that day at the recording studio, nothing's happened. Not to any of them. There haven't been any more accidents or shootings or—"

"You're right. If there were, I would have heard

something about it at the Hall. Nothing's happened."

"Not nothing. Something's happened all right, just not to the band."

Like most simple solutions to complex problems, this one had been staring me in the face and I had been ignoring it. Now, it seemed so obvious, I would have slapped my forehead if I wasn't worried that I might muss my hair. It had taken a deep oil treatment the night before and a leave-in conditioner that morning to get rid of the frizz, and I wasn't taking any chances.

"Belinda . . . well, she's sort of part of the band, isn't she?" I asked Damon, warming to the theory even as I talked it out. "At least that's what she always says. She says she's with the band. Which means that when Vinnie talked about someone in the band being in danger, maybe he didn't mean someone in the band was in danger, you know?" Suddenly I wasn't so tired anymore. I whirled around and started for the office, eager to pull out the list I'd started the night before and read it over in light of this new theory.

Lucky for Damon, there were a couple of advantages to being dead. One of them was not having to scramble to keep up with me. When I picked up my pace, ducked around a tall headstone, and sidestepped around another, I found him waiting for me. He was leaning against the statue of a weeping woman, and he pushed off from it and stepped in front of me.

"I don't understand," he said.

"I don't, either." My nervous energy got the best of me, and I shuffled from foot to foot. "But it's the only thing that makes any sense. Belinda said somebody was following her last night, that somebody snuck up on her and tried to choke her. I didn't believe her until that car came after us. But think about it, Belinda's apartment was burglarized. Belinda was at the recording studio the day of the shooting. Belinda was in the car last night when we were forced off the road. She was at the Rock Hall, too, that day the light fell on Alistair, and sometime before he died, I know she was at Vinnie's apartment. I saw her coffee cups all over the place. I don't know, Damon . . ." I stepped around him and continued toward the office, eager to put my theory to the test. "I think we've been looking at this all wrong. I don't know why, but I think maybe Belinda is the killer's target."

"Or it's you."

I froze and turned, responding the way any rational person would. "No way!"

"Why not? It makes just as much sense as what you're saying. Belinda wasn't the only one who visited Vinnie at the condo. You were there, too. You were also at the Rock Hall the day the light fell."

"But not until after the light fell."

I guess Damon hoped I wouldn't notice the flaw in his logic because he went right on. "You were in the car with Belinda last night. You were at the recording studio. Your apartment was broken into, too. What if the killer isn't after Belinda? What if he's after you?"

If what Damon said was true (and it was hard to argue, which was why I kept my mouth shut), it was exactly what I had warned him would happen the day he first asked for my help. My cases always resulted in some whacked-out psycho trying to make sure I took up permanent residence at Garden View.

With that in mind, I knew I was completely justified bringing up the I-told-you-so element.

I didn't. For a couple of reasons. One was that admitting he might be right and there was a killer after me freaked me out too much. The second reason? There was so much concern in Damon's expression, so much pain, I knew he felt responsible.

"No way is anybody after me." I tried for glib, but even to my own ears, I came off sounding as uncertain as I felt. "What would they want?"

"What difference does it make? You're not going to that concert tonight."

"Don't be crazy. I have to go. It's my last chance to investigate."

"It's too dangerous."

"Nobody's going to try anything in front of ten thousand people."

"But they could."

"But they won't. And why bother?" I clung to what I saw as a logical argument because it was better than giving in to fear. "I sure don't know anything about you dying. Heck, I wasn't even born yet. And I don't know anything about Vinnie's death, either."

"But maybe the killer doesn't know that." When I didn't counter this straight off the bat, Damon figured he had me. "I'm going to the concert tonight," he said, his words ringing with authority. "You're staying home."

"But—"

"You're not going." I guess he thought maybe I'd understand it better if he spoke slowly and pronounced each word carefully.

I did, but it wasn't going to stop me. "But—"

"I'm not going to let anything happen to you, Pepper." It took every ounce of self-control Damon had to keep his voice to less than a dull roar. Just as quickly, it dropped to a whisper, and every syllable percolated with emotion. "I love you too much."

Affairs of the heart always trump logic. Especially since it was my heart we were talking about. I gulped down the sudden knot of emotion in my throat and got all set to reply even though, truth be told, I didn't have a clue what I was going to say. Turned out that it didn't matter. I never had a chance to answer. Before I could, Damon winked out.

Just like he had back when Vinnie was channeling him.

"Damon?" I called to him and turned to look around. Just as I turned back, he flickered back in the exact spot where I'd last seen him. I rushed closer. "What's going on?"

A stab of pain twisted Damon's face. His right hand curled into a fist. "I don't . . ." Static interrupted him. He shook his head. "I don't know."

"You're not—?"

He was gone again before I had a chance to finish the sentence.

For what was probably less than a minute but felt like forever, I stood there in the shadows of the tall headstones, wringing my hands and wondering what to do next. I had just decided that I didn't know when I heard a noise like the roar of wind, and Damon showed up out of nowhere. He was lying on the grass, panting and writhing in pain.

I knelt beside him. "You're not being channeled, are you?" I asked him.

He tried to respond, but it was clear from the start that it hurt too much. Because he couldn't talk, he simply looked at me, his eyes pleading for help, his mouth pulled into a grim line.

Then he screamed and disappeared completely.

Shaking and sobbing, I sat back on my heels. This time, it didn't take me any time at all to make up my mind about what I was going to do.

I was going to get to the bottom of things once and for all and find out how, even though Vinnie was dead, Damon could be channeled.

I was going to put an end to his suffering and stop him from fading any further.

I was going to that concert.

Even if there was a killer waiting there for me.

"I'm so glad you decided to come with us!" Watching her daughters find their way to their seats on the bleachers that had been set up in the wide plaza outside the Rock Hall, Ella hunkered into her winter jacket and beamed a smile at them, then turned the same expression on me. "I've always felt like you're one of the family. And the girls are thrilled to have you here. They really look up to you, Pepper. You're their role model."

I don't think she would have said that if Ella knew I wasn't there for blast from the sixties past, but to catch a killer.

"I appreciate the ride," I said, because I couldn't explain about my case and I really was thankful for her help. Once my car got dragged out of the mud, it had ended up in a garage so its underside could be checked for damage.

The girls had gone over to the right, and my seat was with theirs, but I had no intention of sitting down any time soon. There was time yet before the concert started, and I needed to find Belinda. I stepped to the left. "I'll meet you after the show, over by—"

"You're such a card!" Laughing, Ella wound her arm through mine. "You're not going to have to meet us. We'll be together. Weren't we lucky to be able to get one more seat in our row? It's perfect. At intermission, we'll grab some hot chocolate—my treat. I want to talk to you about a cemetery conference in Chicago. Don't get too excited." She patted my arm. "I'm not sure if I can fit it into my schedule but maybe, maybe you can go in my place. Then when the show is over, I promised the girls we could go into the gift shop and pick up a few Mind at Large CDs. I know they're going to love the band."

"And I am, too. I promise." I untangled my arm from hers. On our way over to the plaza, I'd noticed a long line of Porta Pottis set up across the street. I looked that way. "I need to go over there first," I said. As if. "I'll be right back."

Ella couldn't argue, and since she was shorter than me, she couldn't keep an eye on me when I started out across the street, then turned sharply to head in the opposite direction. I skirted the fringes of the crowd, then cut up the aisle farthest to the left to head closer to the stage.

I actually might have gotten all the way there if a guy in a yellow jacket that said *Events Staff* on it in big black letters didn't step into my path.

"Hi!" I sparkled.

He'd been well-trained. He was immune.

I looked past him and what I could see of the maze of backdrops, props, and sound equipment that lined the path backstage. "I'm with the band," I said.

"Right." He crossed his arms over his chest. "Nobody gets back there. Not even cute chicks."

"You think I'm cute?" It was a minor victory of sorts so I tried the sparkling routine again. "We could have a drink after the show."

"We could. But that's not going to get you backstage."

My lip curling, I backed off.

Lucky for me, just as I did, I caught sight of a flutter of color behind one of the amplifiers. I wasn't sure, but it looked enough like a gauzy purple skirt for me to take the chance.

"Belinda!" I raised my voice and called, and when she poked her head out and saw me, I waved. "I need to talk to you."

I think Security Guy was going to argue, but since Belinda was already backstage, there wasn't much he could say.

When he stepped aside, I grinned. "Told you," I said. "I'm with the band."

A second later, I stepped backstage and straight into pre-concert chaos. Roadies and technicians scampered all around me, their arms laden with guitars and microphones and what looked to be miles of heavy black cable. There were extra clothes hanging from a nearby rack, a change of denim shirt (Pete's usual attire), a couple of jackets in case one of the band members got cold, even an extra cowboy hat. I had no doubt it belonged to Alistair. Mighty Mike's bottle of Southern Comfort was out on a table, but there was no sign of Mike or any of the other Mind at Large members.

"Is everything okay?" I asked Belinda.

Much to my surprise, I actually got a straight answer. Sort of. "You mean, has he been back? Not since he tried to make the car swim. I'm not worried." Her stringy hair flapped around her shoulders when she shook her head. "Pepper helps me hide from the man with the kitty cat feet."

I was grateful for even this much clarity. "That's right," I said. "I helped you hide. And I'll keep you safe, Belinda, but to do that, I need your help. I need you to think very hard, about the picture of Damon that was in your living room. You remember, the one you took of him the night he died."

"I remember that night." Her bottom lip trembled. "I loved him. We're soul mates."

"Then you can do something to help him. You want to help Damon, don't you?"

"Help?" She tipped her head, studying me. "He's in trouble?"

"He is. Yes. Someone's trying to hurt him. You have to think, Belinda, you have to tell me what was in that picture. Besides Damon, of course."

Belinda closed her eyes. She chewed on her lower lip. And I held my breath. She'd had nearly forty years to memorize every inch of that photograph. She had to know—

"A ball. Like the sun." When she opened her

eyes, Belinda looked pleased with herself. "Shiny."

I won't repeat what I said in reply.

While I tried to think of a way to get through to her, I stood there grumbling under my breath. It might have been easier to see my way clear if I could think straight. But every time I tried to order my thoughts, an image of Damon formed in my head. I saw him the way he looked that morning at the cemetery.

Someone—or something—was tearing at Damon's spirit. He was in torment.

And I was the only one who could help.

My heartbeat racing, I scrambled for a plan. But before I could come up with one, a curious thing happened.

I heard a chirping sound.

"What was that?" I asked Belinda, but I was wasting my breath. She'd already lost interest in me. She was wandering around, mumbling to herself and getting in everyone's way.

I heard the chirping again.

It sounded awfully familiar.

My head bent, the better to listen and let the sound guide me, I wound my way through the maze of equipment and farther backstage and hey, who could blame me for feeling as if I was on the right track?

Because as strange as it seems, I actually recognized that sound.

It was one I'd heard back at the recording studio.

Right after someone tried to blow our heads off.

Chapter 18

I found myself all the way at the far end of the plaza, behind and under the stage in a makeshift sort of room. Just beyond the perimeter of tarp someone had the good sense to drape all around to block the wind, the ground sloped. When a stiff breeze blew the tarp, I could see the sharp drop into Lake Erie. There was a table in the room with the remnants of a couple of party trays on it. Bread, luncheon meat, pickles. Someone had spilled a two-liter bottle of Coke, and it pooled on the table and drizzled to the floor.

Even as I stood there looking around, I heard the chirping noise again. It was coming from a phone that had been left atop the piano directly across from where I stood. A phone that was also a walkie-talkie. That wasn't the only thing on the piano. There was a fat, black candle there, too, and a framed photograph of Damon. One I'd bet any money had been taken right off Belinda's wall.

I had already made a move toward the piano when I heard a voice from somewhere out in the maze of jury-rigged hallways.

"How the fuck am I supposed to answer the damned thing when I can't find it?"

When Gene Terry hurried into the little room, he found me with the picture of Damon in one hand and his cell phone in the other.

"What the hell are you doing here?" he asked.

I could have tried to come up with some bullshit story, but there really didn't seem to be much point. Instead, I held up the phone for him to see.

"I think that's actually my question. What the hell were you doing *there*? When the roadie called you to get over to the recording studio after the shooting, you were already there. I heard your phone."

He yanked the phone out of my hand and shoved it into the pocket of his suit coat. "Yeah, and I'm the only one in America with a walkie-talkie."

Was I discouraged by this little piece of logic? I was not. Because, see, there was still the photo of Damon to consider. Gene didn't give me a chance to mention it.

"Are you done?" he asked in a way that said if I wasn't before, I sure was now. "We've got a show to do and you have no business being back here."

There was no use arguing the point. Except for the whole bit about truth and justice, of course. I was still clinging to the photograph, and I turned it around so that Gene could see what I could see.

"A ball. Like the sun. Shiny," I said, pointing to the man just barely visible in the background of the picture. He was bald and his head . . . well, it looked like Belinda knew what she was talking about after all. His head looked like a shiny ball. "You were supposed to be in Pittsburgh that night."

"What the fuck are you talking about?" Gene ripped the photo out of my hands and tossed it on the table with the band's leftover dinner. "So I'm in some old picture of Damon. So what?"

"So maybe that overdose Damon took wasn't accidental. Otherwise, I don't think you would have lied about the trip to Pittsburgh. Damon was leaving the band and I'll bet you were plenty pissed. Your gravy train was about to hit the skids. It all makes so much sense, I'm amazed I didn't think of it sooner. Then again, Damon doesn't know you're a liar. He believes you were exactly where you said you were. If he suspected you weren't in Pittsburgh, he would have said something to me about it."

Just as I expected, the comment got a rise out of Gene. His eyes flew open, but I had to give credit where credit was due. He knew better than to lose his cool. He laughed. "What are you smoking, kid? No way you could have talked to Damon. He's been dead since before you were born."

"Dead, but not gone. And I've been talking to him. Don't say it can't be done," I added quickly when I saw Gene was going to tell me I was nuts. "You know it can. You were all involved in black magic. That's what Vinnie told me. Only I thought when he said *all*, he meant the band. But you're as much a part of Mind at Large as any of the band members. You were just as involved as they were. My guess is that you knew Vinnie was channeling Damon's songs, too. He said the thought of channeling terrified him. Maybe you're the one who pushed him into doing it?"

I didn't wait for Gene to answer my question. I didn't have to. I could tell by the way his eyes narrowed the slightest bit that I had hit upon the truth. Considering that I was alone with a killer, it was insane to be jazzed, but I couldn't help myself. The threads of this investigation had been dangling right in front of my eyes. I was finally able to gather them together—and maybe help Damon find some peace, too.

"You didn't give a damn how he got them, Vinnie's songs made you a fortune. But then he told you he wasn't going to channel anymore. I'll bet you were as mad as hell. Just like you were when Damon said he was quitting the band. That's why you killed Vinnie. And it's why you broke into my apartment. And Belinda's. Damn!"

I could have kicked myself. "You knew you had to have something personal of Damon's or you couldn't channel him. You knew Belinda had visited Vinnie's place. And you knew I was there, too. You thought one of us had Damon's things, the stuff Vinnie used for channeling. That's what you were looking for when you broke into my place. And here I thought it was my lousy ex. Don't go there!" I warned him when I thought he might ask. No way I was going to get into a conversation about Joel.

"News flash, Gene, you were wasting your time. I had all the stuff, all right. I destroyed every last bit of it."

"Then you're as brain dead as Belinda."

"Who's not so brain dead after all." For all I knew, this wasn't true, but it didn't hurt to let Gene think I had a backup plan. And a little corroboration when it came to my theory. "Sooner or later, Belinda's going to remember what—and who—is in that photo of Damon. That's why you knew you had to kill her. She's already starting to put it together." I let my gaze drift to Gene's bald head. "She's the one who told me about the shiny ball."

"The bitch!"

Yeah, I was trying to get a rise out of Gene and maybe get him to confess in the bargain. I didn't intend to send him over the edge. When he whirled toward the doorway with fire in his eyes, I knew he was hell-bent on finding Belinda. When he did, I knew there was nothing I could do to protect her.

"No!" I sprang forward and grabbed his arm, but as I might have mentioned, though Gene is short, he's got a powerful build. He shook me off like a gnat.

I wasn't going to let that stop me. I wrapped both my arms around one of his, and no way was I going to let go.

Of course, it's the whole action and reaction thing. I held on tight. Gene tried to shake me off. Pretty soon, we were dancing around the room in a crazy sort of rhythm, knocking into the dinner table, banging into the piano. In the best of all possible scenarios, someone would have heard the scuffle, but no sooner had we started than the stage above us shook, and a guitar riff designed to make the audience scream cut through the air like a knife through butter. The crowd went wild, and I knew after that, nobody was going to hear me.

I kicked Gene in the shins. He biffed me in the shoulder. Hard.

His phone was in his pocket and I knew if I could get it, it wouldn't matter if I held on to Gene or not. I could call 911 and have reinforcements here in a matter of minutes.

I loosened my hold on Gene.

Big mistake.

Because when I did, he grabbed one of the big metal party tray platters and smashed it over my head.

The last thing I remember is stars exploding behind my eyes.

Oh yeah, and hitting the floor like a rock.

* * *

Lizard scales and devil's wings.
Bloody, spoiled soul.
I'll leave you, love, in your heat, in your sweat.
Sated, gorged.
My black butterfly body,
Wet from the chrysalis.

I was dead and in rock and roll heaven.

Or was it hell?

I wasn't sure, I only knew the familiar lyrics pounded through my head along with the driving beat of Alistair's drums and the wail of Mighty Mike's guitar. For a guy who was mostly blind drunk, he sure could rock.

If all this sounds absurd and a little disjointed, it's no wonder. My head felt as if it was going to explode.

I groaned and opened my eyes. That one, crystal moment of clarity when I realized I wasn't dead should have cheered me right up. Except that was exactly when I also realized that I couldn't move my arms or my legs. There was heavy cabling wrapped around me. And Gene Terry was bent over me.

"Good, you're awake." Like I weighed nothing (and before there are any comments about my weight or my dress size, let me just set this straight: I am perfectly proportioned and a size six, but even I know I don't weigh nothing), he lifted me and threw me over his shoulder like a sack. When he carried me to the tarp wall, he barely staggered. "It'll be more fun thinking of you wide awake when this happens."

This? Happens?

I didn't like the sound of that, and I let him know it. I kicked and I squirmed, but with my arms pinned to my sides and my legs tied together, it was a futile effort at best.

Which didn't keep me from kicking and squirming more when he brushed aside the tarp and I got a bird's-eye view of the lake, some twenty feet below.

"Maybe this will teach you to keep your mouth shut," he said, and he tossed me into the air.

He was wrong.

I didn't keep my mouth shut. In fact, I screamed my head off.

Too bad Mind at Large was playing so loud nobody could hear me or the splash I made when I hit the water.

Water? Damn!

My hair was going to look like hell.

A funny thing happens when you know you're going to die. You get sort of comfortable with the idea and a kind of peacefulness settles over you.

For maybe about two seconds.

Then the panic kicks in and the struggling starts.

That's pretty much what I did, struggle and panic, not necessarily in that order.

I cursed myself for wasting my breath on screaming now that I needed every bit of air left in my lungs. I kicked my legs and twisted my body in an attempt to bob to the surface, but instead of rising, the weight of the cabling carried me down. Above me, the bright lights of the Rock Hall glimmered on the water like diamonds. The music from the concert was muffled and distorted. Too bad. I recognized one of Damon's old songs. It would have been nice if I could enjoy it since it was the last thing I'd ever hear.

My lungs burned. My throat tightened. I needed air, and I needed it badly.

I drifted farther down into the murky water.

And for the second time in just a couple of minutes, I figured I was already dead.

That would explain the splash I heard and the shadow I saw come between me and the sparkling lights on the surface. It was the only thing that made any sense when I saw a figure slip up next to me. It was dressed in white, and the brightness hurt my eyes. I closed them just as the figure grabbed me.

I don't know how long it took for us to break the surface of the water, I only knew that when we did, my hair was in my eyes and my lungs felt as if they were going to pop. I hauled in a breath and got a mouthful of water along with it, and whoever had ahold of me held on a little tighter when I choked and coughed and thrashed around. A short while later, I was lifted onto dry land.

"Ambulance is here!" I heard someone shout. "Give us room to work."

"I will. I just want to make sure . . ." A gentle hand swiped my wet hair out of my eyes, and the next thing I knew, Quinn Harrison was looking down at me. He was wearing a white dress shirt and was soaked to the skin.

"You—" I hoped he didn't hold it against me that I barfed up a stomach full of lake water, and I guess he didn't because when the paramedics put me on a stretcher, Quinn was still at my side. It hurt to talk, but I had to know. I gulped in a couple more precious breaths. "How—"

Somebody draped a blanket over his shoulders, and Quinn sank into the warmth and sighed. "Good thing my timing was right. I had just arrived to arrest Gene Terry when I saw him toss you in the lake."

"Arrest?" The paramedics hurried me over to a waiting ambulance, and my voice bumped along. "How did you—"

"He got careless. His fingerprints were at the warehouse."

Even in my weakened condition, I recognized his mistake. "He was there," I said, and when Quinn climbed into the ambulance with me and the paramedics slammed the doors, I was able to continue my argument. "Of course . . . fingerprints there . . . Gene was at warehouse. You . . . you saw him."

"He was at the warehouse, all right." When the ambulance siren split the air, Quinn bent closer.

He rested a hand on my forehead. "But not up on the third floor."

I refused to stay at the hospital overnight. I was fine, considering, and besides, I couldn't just lie around, not when I was still so worried about Damon. The last time I'd seen him, he'd been in terrible pain and now I knew why: Gene Terry was channeling him. Quinn had assured me that Gene was behind bars.

So where did that leave Damon?

In my weakened state, I figured that since I couldn't drive myself home (no car, after all, and there was the whole just-been-nearly-murdered thing), Quinn would play chauffeur. But of course, assuming all this meant I was underestimating Quinn. And I should have known better than to do that.

We weren't at the hospital for five minutes before he called Ella, and once he did, well, there was no way she was going to let anyone else take care of me.

She somehow managed to find a pair of jeans, a sweatshirt, and a pair of sneakers that were my size, and she insisted on driving me home. I was not so easily put off. I played the pity card and got her to take me to Garden View instead.

"You need to be home in bed, Pepper," she said as we cruised through the employee entrance. Ella's three daughters were in the backseat, and they were either so blown away by their Mind at Large experience (I was doubting this), or so shocked by all that had happened to me and how their evening had been cut short by an attempted murder and a visit to the ER, they were as quiet as mice. "I don't understand why you'd want to stop at the office."

"Not the office." When we came to a turn, I pointed her in the direction of the valley. "I need to go to Damon Curtis's grave."

She figured I was in shock. Or maybe that my late-night swim had done damage to my brain. "Damon isn't part of the group anymore, so if you're looking to pay him some sort of tribute—"

"I'm not."

"And you can always go in the morning."

"I can't."

"But—"

Lucky for me Ella is the compassionate type. She's also a little bit of a sucker. She couldn't argue with a woman who'd nearly been killed, and when I insisted that she park her car in a spot that would make it impossible for her to see Damon's grave, she didn't protest.

I'd been hit on the head, dumped in the lake, and nearly drowned, after all.

I deserved some concessions, no matter how crazy they seemed.

Safely on my own, I inched my way through the dark to Damon's grave. Fortunately, a couple of Belinda's candles flickered there. Their fluttering light made it possible for me to see Damon. He was lying on the flat stone behind his marker, gasping for breath. The entire left side of his body was so faded, I couldn't see it.

"Are you all right?" It was a stupid question, but if there was one thing I'd learned in the private eye business, it was that shock and worry often make people ask stupid questions. I hurried to his side. "You're in pain."

"No." When he saw me, he smiled. "Not anymore. I was. Gene's talent for channeling wasn't nearly as good as Vinnie's. When he did it, he did it wrong."

"And he caused you to disappear even more." The entire left side of Damon's body was gone, and realizing it, my throat clogged. It was as painful as when I was sinking in the lake and couldn't breathe. "What's going to happen now?" I asked him.

Damon sat up. "It's time for me to go."

I swallowed hard. It hurt. "You can't."

"Because you'll miss me?"

"Because I love you." Finally saying it made me feel better. I sat on the stone next to him, and for a couple of long minutes, I thought of everything that had happened and all it meant. "I guess that's exactly why I have to let you go, isn't it?" I asked him.

Damon's smile glittered at me through the darkness. "It never would have worked out between us," he said.

"It might have." I shrugged. "If you weren't dead."

"Yeah." His smile was sad. "But even that can't change what we had while we had it. It can't change the fact that you're brave and you're beautiful. Or that you'll take everything you learned from our relationship and be a better, stronger woman for it. Come on, little girl." His voice teased me into looking his way. When I did, I saw him flicker, not like he had when Vinnie or Gene was channeling him, but softly, like the light of a candle flame.

"Crave the possibilities," he said, and when he did, his voice was muffled and low, like it came from far, far away. "Laugh and run." He flickered and faded softly.

"Naked in verdant meadows." By this time, I couldn't see him at all. I only heard his voice. It was all around me, and it tangled around my heart. I knew it would stay there forever.

"Drunk with your power. Open to me. Give your body. Your soul. Your love. Your all."

Chapter 19

There's nothing like a broken heart to bring out the worst in a girl.

I ought to know. Given half the chance, I would have left Garden View that night and locked myself away in my apartment for as long as I could. I would have pigged out on chocolate and ice cream, wondering where Damon was and hoping—whatever his nirvana—he was happier there than I was here on earth, alone and miserable. Or maybe I would have passed on the endorphin-producing goodies altogether and simply given in to the blues, pulling my blankets over my head and spending my days thinking about how much I missed him.

No matter. I didn't have the luxury. And truth be told, it was all Damon's fault.

He was, after all, the one who'd taught me that life was meant to be lived to the fullest. If I didn't grab it by the tail and hang on for the ride, I'd end up like Belinda. And believe me, bad fashion choices aside, that was not a fate I envisioned for Pepper Martin.

I knew what I had to do. It was time to put the past behind me once and for all. Keeping the thought firmly in mind (along with the fact that though I'd shopped on a budget, I looked better than anybody I passed when I walked into the Intercontinental Hotel the next Saturday night), I gave my very best smile to the tuxedo-clad maître d' who stood between me and the door to the Founder's Ballroom.

Did I mention that I was wearing a little black dress cut up to here and down to there? I don't think he noticed my smile.

"There has to be some kind of mistake," I said with a sigh. "I've got to be on the guest list. These are my very best friends."

"Maybe, but there's no Martin here." He looked over the list again, and even though I knew he'd never find my name there, I wasn't discouraged. He might be trying to follow the rules, but he was wavering. I could hear it in his voice.

I leaned closer. "Maybe you could just check with someone? For me?"

Okay, I admit it, I batted my eyelashes. I don't usually resort to such blatant ploys, but there's that whole thing about desperate times calling for desperate measures.

I promised him I'd wait right there while he went to check, and as soon as his back was turned, I hurried into the ballroom.

I was just in time for the champagne toast.

"Ladies and gentlemen, this is a special evening, and I can't tell you all how happy we are to have you all here with us to celebrate."

This sounded vaguely familiar, and no wonder. Leave it to Joel to pull out the same speech for engagement party number two that he'd used at engagement party number one.

"Simone and I . . ."

Of course, this part was different. As I recall, at our party, he'd used my full name, Penelope. But that was because Joel was a pompous ass and he was trying to impress our guests.

"Simone and I are so happy you are with us. We'd like to—" Joel's words snapped in two. No big surprise since he caught sight of me heading for the front of the room. Not to worry, he's a real trouper when it comes to social situations and avoiding embarrassment at all costs. He tried his best, the poor darling.

"Simone and I, we'd like to—"

By this time, I was within spitting distance of the head table. I wasn't surprised when a murmur went through the room. After all, a lot of the people at *this* engagement party were at *that* engagement party.

Joel's face went pale, but he recovered in a moment, setting down his champagne flute, patting Simone on the shoulder, whispering in her ear.

Before he could move away from the table and head me off at the proverbial pass, I closed in on the happy couple.

"Hi!" Apparently my reputation preceded me. That would explain why my attempt at congeniality was met by Simone shooting out of her chair.

I was a foot taller than her, and since she was dolled up in cream-colored silk shantung and I was in black, I suspected we looked like a smackdown between Good and Evil. Before anyone could take the thought to its logical conclusion and call Security, I got down to business.

"I just wanted to stop in. You know, to wish you guys good luck."

Joel didn't look convinced. He wrapped a protective arm around Simone. "You're kidding me, right?"

"Not kidding." I reached into my purse. A collective gasp rose from the crowd. I guess they were surprised when, instead of an Uzi, I pulled out a wooden box decorated with a smiling, yellow sun. I handed the box to Joel.

"This is yours," I said.

I didn't wait for him to open the box, or even to say anything. My work there was done, and my head high and my shoulders steady, I walked out of that ballroom. I wasn't surprised to find Grandma Panhorst waiting for me near the door. She'd dressed for the occasion in the same turquoise gown she'd worn to my engagement party. Her hair was as stiff as Styrofoam, and tonight's choice of lipstick was a vivid shade of pink.

Grandma didn't care about the THIS IS A SMOKE-FREE ENVIRONMENT sign on the wall just behind her. She took a drag of her cigarette and let out a long stream of smoke. "Made up your mind, huh?"

"I made up my mind as soon as Joel walked out on me," I told her, and though I'd never put it into words before, I knew it was true. "I guess I just needed to tie up some loose ends."

She smiled and looked over to where Joel was just opening the box I'd given him. On tiptoe, Simone looked over his shoulder, and her mouth fell open.

"I'm going to stay with the ring," Grandma said. "I hope you don't mind."

"Not at all. Stop in sometime if you're looking for someone to talk to."

She gave me a wink. "I'll remember that, kid."

By this time, Joel was blubbering something about Paris and the Eiffel Tower, and Nazis.

"You think they'll ever figure it out?" I asked Grandma.

She grinned. "Doesn't matter, does it? That's the whole point. Where the ring came from, that doesn't make any difference. All that really matters is what it stands for. You think they'll be happy?"

Before I walked out the door, I glanced over my shoulder toward the front of the room. Joel was just slipping Grandma's diamond on Simone's finger.

"I hope so," I told Grandma. "I really do."

I couldn't have been inside the hotel for more than twenty minutes, but by the time I stepped outside, it was colder. Not wanting to ruin the fashion statement, I hadn't bothered with a coat. I slung my purse on my shoulder and chafed my hands over my bare arms.

I had one more thing to do before the night was over.

Before I had a chance, though, a rush of wind nearly knocked me off my feet. I braced a hand against a lamppost and closed my eyes to keep out the grit and dust that blew around me, and I didn't open them again until I felt something slap against my leg.

I bent to retrieve it. It was a postcard. No big deal, right? Except that it wasn't a picture of Cleveland, and let's face it, that's what I expected, a postcard someone had purchased and dropped.

This postcard showed an imposing array of granite pillars. It reminded me of some of the monuments I'd seen at Garden View.

I turned the card over and read the caption, "Graceland Cemetery," it said. "Chicago."

Weird, yes? But wait, things were about to get even stranger. Because that's not all it said. In the spot where folks usually write their wish-you-were-here messages was one single word, written in red ink.

"Help."

A shiver skittered over my shoulders, but hey, was I worried?

Not a chance!

For one thing, Chicago was far away, and I wasn't planning on going there anytime soon. And for another . . . well, I had better things to worry about.

I tucked the postcard in my purse and pulled out two pieces of paper. One was the card where Quinn had written his phone number. The other was the cocktail napkin Dan had given me the last time I saw him, the one with his number on it. While I was at it, I grabbed my cell phone, too.

It was time for me to get on with my life, to laugh and run. I was suddenly craving all the possibilities life had to offer, and I knew just where to start.

I made the phone call.

land, and let's face it, that's what I expected, a postcard someone had purchased and dropped.

This postcard showed an imposing array of granite pillars. It reminded me of some of the monuments I'd seen at Garden View.

I turned the card over and read the caption. "Graceland Cemetery," it said. "Chicago."

Weird, yes? But wait, things were about to get even stranger. Because that's not all it said. In the spot where folks usually write their wish-you-were-here messages was one single word, written in red ink.

Help.

A shiver skittered over my shoulders. But then, was I surprised?

Not a chance!

For one thing, Chicago was far away, and I was not planning on going there anytime soon. And for another... well, I had better things to worry about.

I tucked the postcard in my purse and pulled out two pieces of paper. One was the [illegible] on which Quinn had written his phone number. The other was the cocktail napkin Dan had given me the last time I saw him, the one with his number on it. While I was at it, I grabbed my cell phone, too.

It was time for me to get on with my life—to laugh and [illegible], and I was suddenly craving all the possibilities life had to offer, and I knew just where to start.

I made the phone call.